CAGES

A Novel

SYLVIA TORTI

SCHAFFNER PRESS

First Edition
Trade Paperback Original

Cover and Interior Design: Jordan Wannemacher

Library of Congress Cataloging-in-Publication Data
Names: Torti, Sylvia, 1968- author.
Title: Cages / Sylvia Torti.
Description: First edition. | Tucson, Arizona : Schaffner Press, Inc., [2017]
Identifiers: LCCN 2016051879 (print) | LCCN 2016059184 (ebook) | ISBN
    9781943156184 (softcover : acid-free paper) | ISBN 9781943156214
    (Mobipocket) | ISBN 9781943156207 (Epub) | ISBN 9781943156191 (Pdf) |
    ISBN 9781943156191 (Pdf) | ISBN 9781943156214 (Mobi)
Subjects: LCSH: Animal welfare--Moral and ethical aspects--Fiction. |
    Triangles (Interpersonal relations)--Fiction. | Self-actualization
    (Psychology)--Fiction. | Self-realization--Fiction. | Scientists--Fiction.
    | BISAC: FICTION / Literary. | FICTION / General.
Classification: LCC PS3620.O68 C34 2017 (print) | LCC PS3620.O68 (ebook) |
    DDC 813/.6--dc23
LC record available at https://lccn.loc.gov/2016051879

ISBN: 978-1-943-156-184 (Paperback)
ISBN: 978-1-943-156-214 (Mobipocket)
ISBN: 978-1-943-156-207 (Epub)
ISBN: 978-1-943-156-191 (Pdf)

Printed in the United States

CONTENTS

For Adrian

There you will understand unspoken words
Too subtle for the ears of mortal birds.

The Conference of the Birds

CAGES

AUDITORY FEEDBACK

When the wall of windows glazed with first light, the birds rustled, wings against wire, and stretched their scaly toes from wooden perches. The robin un-tucked his head, and with short shakes, ruffled his feathers. An aging Inca dove scratched at the newspaper lining his cage. A starling, in white-speckled winter plumage, probed the air before his yellow beak, remaining to one side of the cage, not quite sure of the hollow space at the center. Six canaries lined themselves up on a dowel. Side by side, they preened pale yellow feather after pale yellow feather.

There were Bengalese finches, Brewer's sparrows, cowbirds, yellow-headed blackbirds. Hundreds of zebra finches, housed four or five to a cage, hopped up and down, on and off perches. A male zebra finch landed in a food dish. As if surprised, he sat immobile for a moment before fluttering out once more, scattering seeds like shotgun pellets onto the floor. When he called, the others instantly erupted into a chorus of nasal *mee mees*, their small striped heads and orange cheek patches jerking right and left. Dissonant bursts, sounds understood only by them, perhaps meant to warn each other or appeal to drab females nearby.

On the floor a white picnic cooler served as a soundproof chamber. The white-crowned sparrow inside could not see the morning sun nor hear his fellow birds rustling, calling and hopping in the brightening laboratory. He knocked his beak against the plastic wall and let out a short whistle. The sound was followed by silence. He pecked at a seed. He flew up to his perch. He cocked his head to one side. Conscious of the limits to his auditory space, the fact that nothing could hear him, he sang again and listened to the whistle, buzz and trill of his own, five-note song.

From the hallway, David heard the muffled chirps of birds. He inserted a key and pulled on the heavy door. When he flipped on the lights, the birds responded with an urgent burst of sound. The laboratory turned from night to day. Silence into song. Each morning began exactly the same way. Birds beckoned him. Light and chorus marked his arrival.

He put down his briefcase, rolled up his sleeves and set to work, taking his time going from cage to cage, ensuring that each bird was okay. He stopped in front of the Inca dove, opened the cage and took hold of it. The dove, which had been hand-raised by Sarah, settled easily into his palm, its small black eyes staring back at him with unusual calmness. David rubbed his finger lightly on its breast and then set it free on the counter. The dove flew up, perched on a light fixture and let out an almost inaudible call, one that had always sounded to David like "no hope, no hope."

He glanced at his watch. He had an hour to clean before he was due to teach the first class of the semester. Pulling the water and food trays from the first row of birdcages, he filled the sink with soapy water and began to scrub.

Outside the window, the winter morning had brightened. Beyond his own reflection, he saw a flock of waxwings swoop up the hillside and land in a serviceberry bush. Seven, eight, maybe twelve plump birds, unmistakable in silhouette. Birds that settled into the valley during the winter months and then migrated north to breed in the spring, and odd for songbirds because male and female waxwings looked and sounded alike. Mirrors of one another. In most birds, the males sang and the females listened, deciding which male song sounded best. Singing was a sex-specific behavior traced to brain wiring, to physiology, to ecology and evolution. It made sense, except that in waxwings it wasn't that way. An exception that remained unstudied.

David filled the now clean containers with water and seed, slipped them back into the cages and pulled another set from the next row. With his upper right arm, he leaned in and brushed a curl of his long hair away from his eye. Over running water and background calls of hungry finches, he could hear Sarah's voice. *Fundamentally, you're shy. Not exactly insecure, but there's a curve to your chest, a shyness imprinted along your upper back.* He rolled his shoulders back, stood up straighter. *You blush easily. I think it's why you keep your hair long.*

He felt the low-grade pounding in his head, the pulse and thud of a persistent headache that had been with him for some months now. The comfort he'd once enjoyed at being known so well by Sarah had switched to irritation and uneasiness whenever he heard her voice in his head. Had she never considered the possibility that he was too busy to remember to make hair appointments? Couldn't there be a practical explanation, rather than an underlying emotional or psychological reason, for his longer hair? He finished the morning routine, collected his computer and hurried off to class, the sound of birdsong fading as the lab door swung shut behind him.

Though shy, David was a master teacher. In front of a class, he found it easy to cultivate a lively persona. He began the lecture by projecting images of a human baby and a bird chick. "These two might not look similar, but songbirds are very much like humans," he said. "They both develop learned vocal communication and they do it in a similar way. Like humans, baby birds first listen. Later, they babble. Finally, they learn to sing."

He played a recording of a bird learning to sing. "Listen and you will hear these sounds changing from a kind of babbling to a fully developed robin's song."

In the early years, David had managed remarkable success. He'd been the first to poke through a bird's skull and insert fine wires into single neurons, a technique that allowed him to survey a new landscape, mark the places on a brain that could, and did, acquire a type of language. When these antennae-crowned birds sang, the sounds and electrical impulses were recorded. Numbers were sifted through software programs, analyzed and written up into scientific publications. He was called a pioneer and received grant after grant. His technique, now used internationally, allowed scientists to listen in on the unconscious thoughts of birds, the neuronal firings that triggered song. Songs, although he would never say it out loud, that might be a proxy for love.

He moved the class through the basics of birdsong, explaining the difference between calls that all birds made instinctually, and songs which they learned after hearing the males of their own species singing. And birds, too, had dialects. A white-crowned sparrow in Washington State had a different accent than one in Colorado. He told them that like humans, an isolated bird with no hearing could never learn to sing. And, like humans, if a bird went deaf later in life, it would lose its song just as deaf humans lose their ability to speak.

"When you talk your brain is paying attention," he said, "comparing how you sound to a template for how you should sound in your head. If you lose the auditory feedback, you eventually lose your speech." He played recordings, showed slides, paced across the lecture stage, answered questions, and then the hour was over.

"What's the take-home message today?" He paused for emphasis. "To communicate with others, you must be able to hear yourself."

After class he passed by the main office to retrieve his mail. There was a memorandum about a recent theft at the institute, another about a group of animal rights activists in Oregon. More and more sophisticated security measures were becoming necessary. Everyone was supposed to keep their lab doors locked at all times. Of course, there would be increased fees charged to researcher grants to cover these extra costs. Terrific. More overhead would be taken from his dwindling grant. He dropped both flyers into the recycle bin and then flipped through the table of contents of the new *Neuroscience* magazine. Cell, cell, cell. Reductionists, all of them. Searching for the smallest denominator possible, they wanted to find "the" cancer gene, "the" secret to cell-cell communication, or the holy grail: "the" memory engram.

Almost every neuroscientist dreamed of unraveling memory, of finding out where memories were stored. Back in the 1920s, the behaviorist Karl Lashley had come up with the word "engram" to name the place where he thought he would find evidence of memories imprinted on nerve cells. As if memories could be exposed like a photographic image on film. But so far, no one had found the physical engravings.

David rolled the magazine into his fist, clear on the fact that cell or engram, his lab had produced nothing for many months. The rate of success he'd enjoyed the past decade had abruptly decelerated. Shrinking research funds had forced him to let the animal care technician go. He had no undergraduate or graduate students, and was waiting for the arrival of a new post-doctoral fellow. Whereas before, his lab bustled with post-docs, graduate students, undergraduates and animal care technicians, now he was alone with no new resources in sight. How had the "Decade of the Brain" passed so quickly?

Ten years earlier, he and other neuroscientists had successfully lobbied

Congress for funding, making the case that although the brain was composed of a hundred billion neurons, it could be and would be understood. Signal molecules had been retained throughout the millennia of evolution, they said. Electrical impulses and nerves connected all living beings. The brain was electricity. You flip the right switches, sections turned on. Flip other switches, and sections turn off. Everything that ails—Alzheimer's, Parkinson's, Huntington's Chorea—not to mention drug addiction, epilepsy, even problems with speech, hearing and perception, could be cured if they understood the brain.

They promised to cut open the skull and tease meaning from pink fatty tissue. Studying neurons, they assured Congress, would allow them to create navigational maps much like early explorers did for Africa, the Amazon and the Arctic, maps that would help people find their way inward, from behavior to nerve to gene, helping them grasp the most elemental understanding of themselves and the sentient world. If nerves were like yarn, they said, they could loosen the skein, untwist the knots, find the beginning.

Congressional support was bipartisan: the brain and its diseases had no political enemies. A bill was passed and the president signed the "Decade of the Brain" into existence. Neuroscientists, buoyed by their swollen budgets, worked overtime in an exhilarating combination of collaboration and competition. Europe responded to the American investment with its own brain focus and everyone benefited from the increased funds, arriving early to work and trying to stay later than their competitors.

David became famous in those first years for teasing apart and piecing back together how a bird sang. He and his students showed that they could follow a molecule of air as it entered the nostrils and traveled down the trachea into the air sacs tucked behind a bird's lungs. They figured out which nerves attached to which muscles, how the muscles expanded and compressed those air sacs like the bellows of an accordion, and how the sacs pushed breath out past the flaps of the syrinx to become waves that made sound. Their work was published in *Science* and *Nature* and every paper was celebrated with champagne, but unlike other laboratories, there were no cork dents in the ceiling, no uncontrolled frothing or spilling of cheap bubbling wine into plastic tumblers. In David's lab, glass flutes were poured to perfection, a dry tangy drink to be savored, not gulped, a reward for good solid work, clever experiments, nifty techniques, and determined scientists. And always, they toasted the small, resilient singing birds.

Lately there had been no such successes. In the past eighteen months there had been dead birds and dead ends while the expiration date on his remaining grant advanced. There was an Italian post-doc set to arrive in a month and David hoped he'd be worth the balance of the funds. He walked faster down the hallway. If he didn't have some sort of break through soon, he wasn't going to be doing any research at all.

Back in his laboratory, he heard ringing and passed quickly into his office. The throb in his head had not lessened. As he leaned for the phone, he glanced at the caller ID and saw a jumble of numbers span the screen. An international call. Possibly Sarah. Probably Sarah. He let go of the *Neuroscience* magazine and it sprang open on his desk. He reached for the phone and then stopped, his hand hovering above the receiver. In the laboratory, a zebra finch tooted and a starling whistled. The ringing continued two, three, four more times and then it stopped.

He opened the top drawer of his desk and took out a bottle of aspirin. He popped the top, shook out two pills and swallowed them hard without water. He sat down at his desk and stared at the large glass jar of armadillo fetuses that Sarah had given him as a present. Four white armadillos with ridges on their backs, eyes closed, suspended in fluid, connected by a single umbilical cord, never to become adults. *The babies we won't have.* Sarah. At every moment. Sarah. He closed his eyes. In twenty minutes the aspirin would be working, taking the edge off the pain. Thoughts and memories weren't as easily dulled.

I t's not as simple as that," Sarah was saying. They were in their graduate school apartment in Louisiana and she was leaning against the armrest on the couch with her left leg bent, the other sprawled over David's thigh. The evening was muggy and the rotating table fan did little to dry the perspiration beading on her tanned skin. Ed, their roommate and best friend, sat across from them on the wooden floor, back against the wall, his arms resting on his knees, a bottle of beer dangling from one hand. The room was mostly dark, only a pale fluorescence from the kitchen illuminated half of Ed's face.

"Who said it was simple?" David asked.

"You did. You said there's a signal, there's a receiver, but..."

"That's not the same thing as saying it's simple," Ed said. He set his beer down and pulled his long damp hair back into a tight ponytail at the nape of his neck and then took up his beer again.

David looked at Ed—bearded, rugged—and then back to Sarah. They'd been talking and drinking since dinner and now it was nearing midnight.

Tomorrow Ed would be leaving again for four months in the tropics and neither David nor Sarah was anxious for him to go.

"All I'm saying is that signal and receiver are only part of communication, and only a small part at that. It's more about collaboration."

Both men took sips of beer, waited for her to keep going. Each loved it when she was like this, slightly drunk, excited and argumentative.

"Collaboration?" Ed said.

"Yes. Collaboration. And context and perception. A signal, or the *perception* of a signal out of context is meaningless at best, confusing and problematic at worst."

David looked over at Ed. "I told you. Beware of a formidable woman."

Sarah kicked David in the thigh with her heel. "What's that supposed to mean?"

"Everything," Ed answered. And then, looking straight at Sarah, "And... that he's in love with you."

Sarah rolled her eyes. David held his beer bottle up to the light and realized it was empty. "Last round." He lifted her leg from his thigh, stood up to go into the kitchen. "Sarah?"

She shook her head no.

"Ed?"

"Of course."

From the kitchen David heard Ed say, "And you intimidate him a little."

"Don't be absurd," Sarah said.

Two days after Ed left Sarah came home late from the clinic and found David sitting on the couch surrounded by papers about birdsong. Immersed in a new research topic, he barely glanced up.

"Do I intimidate you?"

David looked up. She stood in the doorway, hands on her hips, thin arms jutting out at the elbows like a cormorant drying itself after a dive. "Terribly." He turned the page on the manuscript he was reading.

"Ed says I do."

"Ed's full of shit."

Sarah sat down next to him on the couch. David put his papers to the side.

"You're not serious are you?" he asked.

"Haven't you noticed that we talk more when Ed's around?"

"Of course. Three mouths versus two."

"No, I mean you and me. You talk more when he's here."

"That's ridiculous."

"I think we're more honest with each other, too, when he's around."

"We're always honest."

"Are you?"

"It's just," he hesitated and smiled, "let's just say I'm the opposite of a male bird. You sing. I listen."

David hadn't truly stuttered as a child, but as an adolescent he'd shown a lack of fluency when it came to putting emotions into words. His parents had assumed their son's muteness in the face of feelings had more to do with teenage lethargy than anything else. It wasn't until he met Sarah that he'd learned there was a name for his condition.

They lay in bed one night. "Alexithymia," she said.

"What the hell is that?"

"Difficulty identifying feelings and describing them to others, lack of fantasies, operative thinking while appearing to be super-adjusted to reality." She twisted a curl of his hair around her finger.

"So now people who are well-adjusted and don't feel the need to blab about their feelings all the time have disorders?" But he knew she was on to something and was glad that the room was dark. He didn't know how he felt about being seen so clearly.

"It's not in the DSM as a disorder. It's a personality trait. Patterns get set when you're young. It's like one of your birds that has learned to sing. You say that he's crystallized his song, don't you? Once he learns it, it can't be changed."

He felt her lips on his neck, her hand caressing his arm.

"It's not severe, but noticeable. I think it's why you gravitated towards nature and birds."

Sarah was probably right. David had discovered his ability to hear and identify sounds the way some children learned they're good at throwing a baseball. Bird watching gave him permission to be alone, a sense of exploration, emotions that didn't require explanation. From the earliest time he could remember, whenever he heard a sound, he was drawn to its source. Whether it was a bird, insect or squeaky faucet, he listened, made a mental note, and then he never forgot the sound again. At eight years old, he was explaining to his mother the differences between bird, chipmunk and squirrel sounds. By ten, he could identify over fifty species of birds, five or six mammals and a good number of insects. On his twelfth birthday, his parents gave him a microphone and tape recorder.

As a teenager, he walked every morning before school through the wooded area behind his house. Setting out, his heart rate rose in anticipation of what he might see or hear. There was the feeling that he was sneaking up on something mysterious, seeing what no one else was seeing, hearing what others couldn't understand. The world was a detail of sounds, and every year that world became more interesting, the soundscape more complex, his ability to hear subtleties more refined. He learned to distinguish a young robin from a seasoned singer. A mockingbird that migrated to Florida from one that flew instead to Costa Rica. People were impressed, but really it wasn't so hard. Mockingbirds imitated songs from other birds, and only migrants to Costa Rica picked up songs from other Costa Rican birds. Before David met Ed, he didn't know there was another like himself.

The next day Sarah went to a pet store and brought home a parrot which she named Skinner. When David came in from the laboratory, he found her assembling a five-foot cage in the kitchen. Her long brown hair, parted in the middle, hung over her shoulders and covered her face. The bird, nervous in its new surroundings, paced left and right on a perch.

"What's this?" David asked. "A substitute for Ed?"

"Just making sure you keep talking," she said over her shoulder.

David eyed the bird.

"He'll grow on you." She reached out and the parrot stepped onto her hand. She placed him in his new cage and turned to kiss David.

"Truth is," she whispered, "I'm glad you don't go off into the forest like Ed."

David wondered whether she was just saying this for his benefit. What did she see in him when there were other men, ruddy and fit, smart and adventurous, like his roommate? He felt her fingers at his waist, unbuckling his belt. He slipped his hands underneath her tank top and let his fingers move across the waves of her ribs to her breasts. Her personality defied the slightness of her body. He knew he was slow to put words on his innermost feelings, knew he wasn't the best conversationalist, nothing like Ed who could charm a group with his stories of the tropics. The parrot let out a squawk. He hoped he was enough.

"Like I was saying the other night," she said between kisses. "It's a lot more than signaler and receiver. It's about context, perception and collaboration."

A week into the semester, David returned from lecturing and found a young woman with bright red hair at his laboratory door. "Waiting for me?" Clearly, she had disregarded the sign in the stairwell that read: Researchers only. No students allowed.

"Yes. I'm in your class." She fidgeted with her hands. "I want to work in your laboratory."

He laughed at her forwardness. "What's your name?"

"Rebecca."

"Rebecca, I'm sorry. I'm not hiring, but come on. I can suggest other people." He scribbled the names of two labs that he knew were in need of undergraduate help, and could afford it, and handed her the paper, but she shook her head.

"No, I really want to work in *your* lab." She had a small diamond piercing in her nose.

"Why?"

"You said it in class, you know. Birds can tell us about the beginnings of language."

The diamond glinted in the sun when she turned her head and her blue earrings matched her eyes.

"It's more than that." She was flustered. "They fly and sing and nest and seem, I don't know, unbounded in the ways we are."

"Unbounded?" It was an interesting thought, but at the end of it all, he could have told her, everything was bounded and bounded in exactly the same way. "Really, I appreciate your interest, but I truly don't have any projects for undergraduates right now. I'd be happy to suggest some reading material to you."

"I don't mind what kind of work I do." Her neck and face flushed red, and when she turned her head, there was the glint of her piercing again. "I'm drawn to them."

Her honesty and vulnerability were charming. If only more undergraduates could be so moved. He wished he actually had research funds; certainly he could use the help. "That's a sentiment I can relate to. I've always been drawn to them too. I promise to call if anything comes up." But the paper on which he took down her number was promptly buried by other papers on his desk. For the next week he noticed her in the back of the auditorium listening attentively to his lectures, scribbling notes. Once again, she returned to his laboratory.

"You do get points for being persistent," he said. He unlocked the door and they passed through his lab and conference room into his office. He moved a stack of papers from a chair and motioned for her to sit down.

"I just wanted to say," she said. "I mean, what you said in class today." She looked at her notebook and read: "*Speech is a river of breath, bent into hisses and hums by the soft flesh of the mouth and throat.*" She looked up at him. "That's so poetic."

David didn't tell her the sentence wasn't his, but Steven Pinker's, a much more famous scientist.

"And you said, *Birds might reveal the secrets of communication.*"

Anyone who paid that much attention in lecture had the potential to be good in the lab. "Ok, you've convinced me. I'm putting you on the payroll." He would ask the institute's director for emergency bridge funds if it came to that.

A short time after she began working for him, he learned she wasn't a student.

"So what were you doing in my lecture?"

"Crashing the course."

"Why?"

She paused, as if unsure how to answer. "Like I said, I like birds. I'm drawn to them. I looked you up, was taken by what you'd written on your webpage. I thought your work looked fascinating."

"You lied?"

"No, I never said I was a student, only that I wanted to work here."

During the next few weeks David taught Rebecca to care for the birds. He taught her how to properly scrub their cages, how to give them the right amount of food, which supplements to use with different species. The zebra finches were fed peas and boiled eggs every other day. The robins, starlings and white-crowned sparrows got crickets. He showed her how to hold a bird in her palm, with the head between her second and third finger.

"Too firmly and you hurt the bird. Too lightly, and it will escape your hand."

He stood beside her as she learned to put the colored identification bands on the birds. "Go palm up, it's easier," he said.

She turned her palm up and with a forceps slipped a red band around the bird's ankle.

"That's it. You've got it. Now squeeze the band completely shut with these pliers."

She looked up when she finished.

"Well done. Now let's do a few more."

The thin pencils she used to hold her hair in place on the top of her head stuck out like misplaced chopsticks. It made him think of an African grey-crowned crane. *Food for the eyes*, Ed called it after his trip to Kenya. David remembered Ed saying, *In west Kenya, I stayed with an African doctor who runs a small farm, does everything from making methane fuel from cow manure to gravity-fed water systems and organic vegetables. He had a couple of gray-crowned cranes too, loose on the property grazing back and forth in the grass between the cows, and when I asked him why he kept the birds, he said: "People don't just need food for their stomachs; they need food for the eyes."*

Yes, *food for the eyes*. Rebecca was beautiful. There was a vibrancy about her, a confidence in the way she carried herself, though a distinct judiciousness to her speech. In the short time she'd been in the lab, she was proving to be a willing student, meticulous in bird care, always on time, all about the business of work, but she didn't speak unless spoken to. As he stood next to her, he had two rapid, unrelated thoughts. *She's like a bird,* and *her quietness is unsettling.* He didn't know what to make of these thoughts. Was chattiness in humans tied to biochemistry? Recently, researchers in the Netherlands had shown that when injected with testosterone, the females of some bird species would begin to sing.

Regardless of her quiet nature, David was grateful that by the time Anton, the Italian post-doc, arrived in four weeks, Rebecca would be fully trained. David would orient Anton to the laboratory, the surgery techniques and the experimental protocols. By the end of the first month, with Rebecca's clean, organized cages, and a new set of birds, they would be ready to begin a series of intensive experiments.

David's conference room was really a library. There were hundreds of books on every shelf, as if he'd collected any title that included the word "bird." Rebecca liked to spend time in the room, pulling books from their places, flipping through the pages and reading bits of information here and there. She was particularly drawn to the older volumes. She reached up on her tiptoes and took down one that looked quite old. *The Zebra Finch: Notes on a Model Bird.* She opened it to the beginning and read.

> *In the dry central grasslands of Australia, the small finch,* Taeniopy-gia guttata, *lives in colonies of one hundred birds or more. Gregarious and boisterous, these birds can be easily identified by even the casual naturalist. Their upper bodies are gray, their bellies white. The tail is striped black and white, presumably giving the bird its name. Males are distinguished by rust colored cheek patches behind each eye. Both sexes have bright reddish-orange beaks and legs.*
>
> *Zebra finches feed in flocks, landing in one large swooping motion onto the ground, picking at fallen grass seeds, and occasionally, small*

insects. At the slightest noise or commotion, they rise as one and flutter back to the trees to empty their crops. Among them, there is an almost constant chorus of "tet tet" calls, resembling the beeping of a group of children softly tooting toy trumpets.

In the field, they say, birds pair for life and both males and females care for the young. In the field, they breed from October to April, the females selecting nest sites, the males gathering the dry grasses and sticks that the female then uses to construct the dome-shaped nest. In the field, a female lays three to six eggs per nest. After two weeks, the eggs hatch and featherless pink chicks are born. At five weeks of age, the nestlings leave home.

First, the zebra finch was collected because it was pretty, then, because they could be kept in captivity, breeding readily in a cage at any time of the year. They are easy pets and reasonably amusing companions to the curious naturalist. These birds are resilient and of great use to the experimental behaviorist. Bluntly put, one can accomplish a great number of experiments with the zebra finch and it will not die.

She flipped to the beginning to check its publication year. 1952. She shut the book. Australia. The birds were not even on their original continent. She wondered whether they knew this, or could sense it. They seemed happy enough in the lab but they would probably be happier if she stopped reading and gave them their morning peas and eggs.

During the first days, when Anton, the post-doc, arrived at the laboratory, he found Rebecca in the routine of feeding the birds. Zebra finches, flitting on and off their perches, chattered loudly, scattering seed onto the floor. There was the beating of wings against the wire cages, trills of canaries, high-pitched whistles from the starlings, and the sound of birdseed, like the frozen snow outside, crunching beneath his shoes.

He unwound the orange scarf from around his neck, leaving it hanging over his shoulders while he unbuttoned his overcoat, took if off and hung it on a hook over a lab coat that looked like it had never been worn. His body was warm, glowing from the past hour he'd spent in the gym. The scar on his left cheek, usually imperceptible, stood out as a series of small white traces after exercise.

He'd been sixteen, sitting in the living room tightening a guitar string. When he plucked it, the string snapped and hit his face just shy of his left eye. He sat stunned for a moment before he raised his hand and came away with a smear of blood. Setting the guitar aside, he went to the bathroom, washed, and then he stared into the mirror to study the damage. The string had slashed him at the top of his cheekbone. Sound vibration forever imprinted on his skin.

That night at dinner he'd expected his mother to mention the mark, but absorbed in reviewing her newest photographs, she didn't notice. Now the scar was only perceptible to those who came really close, or, he liked to think, like the dots and dashes of Morse code, decipherable only to those who bothered to learn.

"Grüß Gott," he said, directing the greeting at Rebecca.

She turned to him and smiled. "That doesn't sound like Italian."

"It's not." Her eyes were blue and intent. Most Americans, he noticed, didn't hold eye contact for long, but she wasn't afraid to look at him.

"I thought you were Italian."

"Südtirolean." He didn't break the connection.

She raised her eyebrows in question. "So what do people there speak?"

"German mostly. Some Italian. A few people speak Ladin too."

"Latin?"

"No, Ladin. Another language."

"I've never heard of that."

"You've never been to Südtirol."

There was a moment of hesitation. She looked away, clearly frustrated. "But which country do you live in?"

"Depends. We go back and forth, depending on the year, the war, the government." The words didn't come out the way he wanted. Though completely competent in English, his accent sounded harsh and cumbersome to his ear. Although he practiced at night, try as he might, he could not make his mouth and lips move properly around the English words.

"Which war?"

"The latest. World War II."

She didn't say anything before she turned back toward her work. Her red hair was twisted up on her head. A few strands curled around the nape of her freckled neck and he had the urge to reach out and touch them. He removed his blue and orange knit hat. Below, his dark hair was sheared short and even now, in his early thirties, thinning.

"I thought you were Italian," she said.

"I am, half. My mother's an Italian speaker, my father's a German speaker. On the streets people speak mostly German. I speak both but I like German more." He was aware of the fact that whenever he was in her presence there was a tingling on his skin and his English became even more self-conscious. More than once, he'd found himself thinking about her in the middle of the day.

"Your parents don't speak the same language?"

Anton laughed. "Of course, they speak German together." He'd never thought of it quite like that, but maybe language had been the fundamental problem between them. His mother had always insisted on Italian with him, which his father couldn't understand. Her German, though fluent, always seemed strained.

He watched Rebecca slide the gates up and reach into the cages, one by one, pulling out the half empty, feces-coated plastic water containers. She drew out the seed containers too, tipping the hulls into the trash and then tossing all the containers into the large black sink for washing. The insides of her wrists, when she dumped the containers, flashed pale white, the deep blue veins underneath the skin visible for just a second.

She hesitated in front of a cage. "One of the finches has lost his band."

Without the band, the bird would be useless for experiments, there'd be no way to keep track of his movements, no way to follow his song.

"Do you need help?" He moved to her side.

She shook her head. She raised the gate, inserted her hand. The four birds in the cage fluttered up and back, calling out against the intrusion. The entire laboratory of zebra finches joined in their anxiety. She cornered the band-less bird in her palm and removed him. The laboratory went quiet again. She snapped a blue numbered band around the bird's twig-like leg, raised him to eye level and stared at him for a moment before returning him to his cage. The small finch perched for a second, immobilized, as if taking in both his freedom and the confines of his cage once more. He bobbed his black and white striped tail as he balanced on the perch. His eyes were glassy and alert and the orange cheek patches below them jumped with every twitch of his head as if he were still considering Rebecca, only now from this new vantage point.

Anton was close to her and wanted to say something, but what? That he was good at dancing, a better conversationalist in German, Italian or even French than in English? He looked at the birds. She was quiet like his mother. No need to speak when a nod or shake of the head would do. He opened his mouth, but then closed it again without saying anything. She turned to him and smiled and in that second, there was a flash of energy. He felt his face flush. He waited for her to say something else but she didn't.

He turned away to focus on "Red 31," the bird for that day's experiment, the finch that was going to provide the data he needed to publish his first solid paper. He noticed that David hadn't yet removed the food dish from the cage, which violated the protocol he'd been taught, and so Anton pulled the food. Full stomachs didn't go well with anesthesia.

From the other side of the laboratory he brought a cage with female zebra finches and held it in front of the cage with "Red 31." The bird hopped, puffed up his feathers and sang a half-hearted version of his song. "You won't win any contests," he said to the bird in German, "but you're ready for your backpack." He returned the cage of females to their spot on the counter.

Anton took "Red 31" into his hand, slipped a white, elastic belt over the bird's head and around his chest, just below the wishbone, and then, one at a time, he slid the bird's wings free of the belt. Later, electrical wires could be connected to this belt, and then threaded out through the top of the cage, plugged into transformers and computers to measure nerve activity and breathing. He finished positioning the backpack and then released "Red 31" to his cage again, conscious all the while of Rebecca moving around the lab and the fact that both of them were glancing at one another intermittently.

He flipped on the microphone and recorder and went back to the cage with female birds. When he slipped the gate up and inserted his hand inside, the birds flapped hysterically. He cornered one and waited while it fluttered up and down into his hand.

"Males," he'd heard David say, "aren't choosey. Any female will do."

Anton returned to the cage with "Red 31," raised the gate and slipped the female inside. The drab gray female perched next to "Red 31" and pecked him on the head. "Red 31" let out a single, half-hearted bleep, and hopped left and right. Anton took a step back. Single bleeps didn't count. "Red 31" needed to sing a whole song. The female hopped to his side again. Another peck. The male leaned into her. She hopped away. "Red 31" quickly righted himself, and then, with a ruffle of his feathers, he danced right and left blurting a bout of song, a series of harmonic bleeps repeated over and over. Lines of data streamed across the computer screen.

Convinced that the bird was going to perform, Anton left "Red 31" and went through the conference room with its library of books to David's office to tell him that the bird was ready for surgery. He found David leaning back in his chair, eyes closed, his feet propped up on the desk next to the large glass with the grotesque armadillo fetuses. A strange thing to have in one's office and Anton wondered why David had them. And, a strange position for David, who usually was moving around or at the very least, banging the keyboard of his computer writing another paper or grant proposal.

"Good morning, David."

David swung in his chair, as if embarrassed at having been caught in stillness. "Ah, Anton. Finally!"

Anton noted sadness in David's face and glanced away out of respect. ""Red 31" doesn't sing a lot, but he is ready."

"Terrific. I'll meet you there in five minutes."

Out in the laboratory Anton prepared the surgical table and David recounted the article he'd read that morning.

"I'll say it again," David said. "There's no evidence for the engram. Even Lashley, thirty years after he first proposed the idea, concluded that he could not find memory traces. I'm sure you read the paper."

"Of course I read it, David, but Lashley also said in the same paper, that even with evidence against it, learning occurs and it has to be recorded somewhere. And Lashley didn't have the modern tools of molecular and cellular biology that we have." Anton could tell he was having little effect on David's stubborn thinking. He put the scissors and forceps into the pot to be sterilized. "Besides, David, just because you don't see something doesn't mean it isn't there."

"Right, like God?" David asked. He turned on the sink water, waited for it to warm and lathered orange anti-bacterial soap in his palms, allowing the suds to travel up his forearms.

"No, like gravity," Anton said.

David rinsed and dried himself with industrial paper towels before he slipped his hand into the cage and encircled the male zebra finch with his palm. He positioned the bird on the surgery table, his hands gently holding its head while it jerked into anesthetic sleep. He didn't answer Anton.

"Or atoms," Anton said.

David sat down, rolled the chair toward the table and focused the microscope onto the bird. Anton positioned himself at his side and together they began to work on the bird.

"Or sonar of whales," Anton said.

"Whales?" David chuckled. "Definitely lots of atoms there and I can see them."

"But you can't hear them singing. Just because you can't see it or hear it doesn't mean it's not there."

"What's an engram?" Rebecca asked.

David spun around in the chair, surprised by her voice. "Excellent question!" She was nothing like the previous technician who hardly managed to feed the birds and clean their cages and certainly never asked a question. "An engram is wishful thinking." He swiveled back to the bird.

Anton turned to Rebecca to explain. "Engrams are...hypothetical."

David interrupted him, "Hypothetical is right!"

"Hypothetical right now," Anton said, "but theoretically, easy to model. They're shape changes on nerves that store memory—basically, they are memory imprinted on nerve cells. They are something we think, with the right tools, we can see." He turned back to David. "Engrams are why Stanley Sommers will win the Nobel Prize and you won't even be invited to the ceremony in Stockholm."

David laughed. "I hate aquavit and pickled herring anyway." He placed his eyes over the oculars of the surgical microscope and focused closer in on the zebra finch. "And you're always welcome to go work for Sommers and search for invisible memories with him."

"They are not going to be invisible for long."

"Forget engrams," David said. "Single neurons will not reveal memory. The sum of any animal's recall, including a person's, will always be much greater than its parts. Memory has to be a system that grows from emergent properties."

Anton didn't say anything.

David continued. "You'd need to have a way to watch the nerves take on and then lose shapes with different behaviors. If you could do that in an animal with learned language, which you never will, you might get invited to the herring fest. Besides, there are more important questions to be answered, like how and why does a bird learn to sing in the first place?"

"Well," Anton said. "I happen to like herring." He looked over David's head toward Rebecca and gave her a wink.

Rebecca smiled back.

"Are the thermistor probes ready?" David asked.

Anton handed him a probe, and then stepped in to train his eye into the second ocular. David worked quickly and expertly, adding commentary only occasionally. He excelled at this part, the artistry of measuring every aspect of a bird's song. Anton had come to David's lab because he was known internationally for his ability to make birds sing. They sang with weights on their backs and magnets stuck to their beaks, or with half their air sacs packed with sponge. Despite the nerves he cut, the red, blue and green wires he threaded across their skulls, just below their skin, or the electrodes inserted above their hearts, or on their rumps, they sang.

David spoke quietly as he inserted the tiny thermistors into the bird's bronchi, thermistors that would measure airflow through the two halves of the syrinx, the bird's version of a larynx.

"Herring," David said. "You Europeans eat the strangest things. One time in Italy they gave me slivers of white pig fat and expected me to be happy."

"Lardo?"

"Right, lard."

"Not lard. Lardo. It is excellent," Anton said. "Cured in marble caves in Tuscany."

"This is the whole point I'm making, Anton. I'm trying to teach you good taste. If you want to be successful you've got to develop good taste in science. Not pickled herring or pig fat and definitely not engrams."

"Lardo is considered a delicacy."

"By whom? The Romans who ate themselves and their civilization to death?"

Like that of most Americans, David's knowledge of history was mediocre, but Anton refrained from making any more comments.

"Pass me another probe," David said.

Anton put it in his hand. David positioned the probe in place and began to sew up the bird.

"So is that what made you switch from mice to birds?" Anton asked. Like him, David had done his graduate work on mice.

"Is what made me switch?"

"Trying to find out how a bird learns to sing?"

"Well...yes, that and the fact that I took a bet."

"A bet on what?"

"On whether birds would be as good as mice when it came to studying the brain."

"Who did you bet?"

"A friend in graduate school."

"And so, he lost?"

David stopped working on the bird and looked up.

"Indeed, he lost."

"You don't seem happy that you won."

David was still for a moment, as if in a memory.

"Maybe we should make a bet," Anton said. "I'll take the risk and gamble. That's exactly what I'm proposing to do with the engram experiments."

David looked down at the bird again. "Damn it." He pulled the bird from the anesthesia funnel. Anton stepped back. Rebecca rushed toward them. The bird lay limp on the table. David stood and the chair rolled out, hitting the laboratory bench behind him in a loud crash. He tapped his index finger in regular pulses on the limp bird's breast, stopping for a second and then continuing the rhythmic tapping. His head an inch above the bird. "Breathe, Breathe." Although it had been known to work, this bird didn't respond to avian CPR. The three of them stood for a second looking down at the dead bird, until finally David, jaw muscles pulsing, turned and walked away.

Anton stared at the bird for a moment longer before he leaned over to flip off the flow of anesthesia, absentmindedly moving the funnel back into its place, scooting the bird to the right, collecting the surgical instruments in his hand. Rebecca didn't move. A few moments later they heard the click of David walking back, his heels syncopating the tiah-tiah calls from the zebra finches.

"My fault. I'm sorry."

"No one is at fault."

"Another one on my conscience."

Anton continued dusting up feathers. He raised his eyebrows slightly and tried to feign indifference. "It happens."

"Yes, but we needed that bird. Now you have to start again." Every death marked the premature end of an experiment, but some were particularly unfortunate, coming only days before the critical follow-up data had been collected.

Anton brushed the tiny feathers, which had stuck to his palms, into the trash can. "Before that, I would like another cup of coffee." He reached out and squeezed David's shoulder briefly on his way to grind the coffee beans.

David stood for another moment at the surgical table, unmoving, trance-like. Infuriating how quickly a zebra finch could go. One moment, the bird was under anesthesia, its heart beating slowly, the breaths regular, the surgery almost finished, and then suddenly, there were no breaths at all. "I don't know what happened. I've done that surgery a thousand times. I had the anesthesia on low. It doesn't make any sense."

"Maybe the bird didn't want to..." Rebecca said.

David waited for her to finish the sentence and when she didn't, he asked, "Want to?"

"Maybe it didn't want to be studied."

A group of zebra finches erupted into a chorus.

"Of course it didn't want to be studied, but that doesn't explain why it died."

"Maybe it chose to."

"What?" David's voice was curt.

"Chose to die."

"Birds don't *choose* to die. That makes no sense." He took a deep breath and continued. "You're anthropomorphizing, Rebecca. It's a common mistake, projecting human emotions and agency onto animals."

She shrugged her shoulders and continued cleaning the cages.

David stood still looking down at the bird. There was nothing natural in it, nothing of the struggle between predator and prey, no overt brutality or violence. And certainly no choice. Simply a heart going from slow to stop. The air sacs collapsing onto themselves; the neurons, already asleep, now fully arrested. He raised his voice. "How can you think there is choice in this? The bird didn't choose to die any more than I chose to kill it." This was a death for no purpose, and more than anything he couldn't abide subjecting an animal to experimentation for no purpose.

"Do you want me to clean up?" Rebecca asked.

David nodded and walked away.

Rebecca rubbed the black surgical table with soap and then followed with alcohol. She picked up the zebra finch, and put him on a paper towel on the counter and went to find Anton in his office.

Anton was sitting at his desk, hands interlaced, head bowed, the small thinning spot on the top of his head exposed. He heard someone at his office door and looked up.

"Rebecca?" He emphasized the *R*.

"Sorry," she said. "I didn't mean to interrupt."

"No problem," he said.

"Were you praying?"

"Maybe. I do not know." He forced a smile. A funny question. Most people assumed biologists weren't religious. His eyes skirted to the window. "Thinking."

The view from this office was not of the valley to the west and north, but of the snowy foothills behind the institute. At midday the white hillside reflected sunlight into the building. The Alps were never so bright in winter.

"I'm sorry." She glanced out the window to where he was looking.

"Have you noticed?" Anton asked. "We can look out these windows, but no one can look in. From outside, the glass reflects sky, snow, trees."

"Except at night," she said. "At night, when the lights are on, these labs are like fish bowls."

He looked back at her. "True. Except at night."

"Was the bird really important?" she asked.

He shrugged. "Well, it's not suffering anymore." He was conscious of the fact that it wasn't an honest response. Unlike David, the birds did not call to him in any special way. He cared about their well-being no more than he cared about the well-being of beef cattle, or chickens or pigs.

"Does it bother you, I mean, to work on them?"

He made eye contact with her, holding her gaze. "Of course."

There was a flash from the diamond stud in her nose as she tilted her head. Her skin looked pale and perfect against her dyed hair. He wanted to say something to her about his frustration with the bird research, his search to find engrams, his quest—for lack of a better word—to discover how memories were made and where they were stored. Instead he gave another slight shrug of his shoulders. "Mice are worse."

Rebecca placed the zebra finch in her palm, its head drooping between her thumb and forefinger. His body was still warm, a warmth that was expressly unsettling because she knew it was temporary. The hyperactive bird had been stilled and silenced. She held him closer and blew on the soft orange cheek feathers and then smoothed them down again with the tip of her finger. From a drawer she pulled out a plastic bag and shook it open. Why did she feel sad? Was she more sorry for Anton, who she could tell was upset, or for the bird? Was it so bad, the bird dying? Or was it her own discomfort with the conversation and David's anger? She couldn't say, but she knew that death could be a choice. Hadn't she also made the choice to end a life? She slipped the limp bird inside the bag, labeled and stored it away in the freezer.

In the two years since college, Rebecca had been a lot of things: aspiring photographer, waitress, daycare substitute, merry maid, and then aspiring photographer once more before being hired as a technician in this laboratory. She didn't count her other intervening occupation—girlfriend to the famous Chicago photographer. Didn't count the months spent walking the windy streets of the city, confined by forbidding buildings and the glare of tempered glass. Didn't count the blank moments she'd spent under his body or the time she'd been trapped in the deep red glow of the dark room.

A few weeks after she returned from Chicago, she'd found David's lab as she was scrolling through websites related to vocal cords. Her voice had become breathy in Chicago and she wanted to know whether it would correct itself or whether she needed to see a doctor, but as usual, she'd gotten lost on the internet, her attention taken from link to link. A reference to vocal folds had brought her to videos of humans singing opera clips. Someone had stuck cameras down their throats recording grotesque and mesmerizing images of vibrating flesh. That website had taken her to another page that mentioned birdsong and she'd clicked from page to page watching birds sing in slow motion, their beaks moving exquisitely in a kind of ballet, creating songs more complicated than she'd ever thought possible from a bird. And then she'd landed on David's page, which had, just as she'd seen for people, videos of the vibrating vocal folds of birds, and she realized that the lab was here in the city.

On the home page there were six birds on a background and as she scrolled over each bird, she heard its song, the melodies lovely and sweet. Could it be that she'd never truly listened to a bird sing? *We study how and why birds sing.* And below that: *Our work bridges the neural control of a complex learned behavior to its evolutionary and ecological relevance in the natural environment.* She didn't really know what that statement meant. She clicked on David's name and saw a round-faced man with dark curly bangs almost covering his eyes. Her first thought was that he needed a haircut and a better photographer. She discovered that he was teaching and on a whim, decided to go to the class. She sat in the back of a 250-person lecture room, and although she'd never been much interested in biology in high school, his animated lectures about birds drew her in. She returned for the next lecture and the next.

It took her a while to convince him to let her work in the lab, but he finally agreed. She was made to understand that punctuality was critical, and so she arrived at 8:30 sharp. He moved with ease within the regular spaces of the building. His clean-shaven face, quick boyish smile and equally boyish body had a disarming effect. The two of them spoke little but he was patient and kind and quick to laugh. Only now, as she'd just learned, he had a temper as well, a measured rage as he tapped his index finger in regular pulses on the limp bird's breast, hissing a useless command to it to breathe. That outburst unsettled her, as did the conversation about choice afterwards. He seemed angry, and in her discomfort, she sought out Anton. She suspected Anton didn't really want to research birds but the thought made no sense. If he didn't want to research birds, then he wouldn't be doing it, would he?

She looked around the lab. Black countertops, computers, wires, bottles of chemicals, cages stacked on top of cages. Theirs was the only laboratory at the institute that studied birds, the only one that smelled of dust and seed, the only one where feathers floated like snowflakes in a glass paperweight. The other neuroscientists studied mice which were kept in the basement. David had taken her down for a tour and she'd seen the rooms, each with hundreds of twelve by twelve-inch cages. Bred to express one gene or another, only their blood, cells and DNA mattered. Once the right strains were achieved, the mice were guillotined and frozen or ground in a blender. Liquid samples of blended skin or neat slices of brain could then be brought up to the laboratories for analysis. "Unlike our birds," he said, "you don't need to *see* or *hear* a mouse."

She had loved what he'd said in a lecture. "Birds will tell us about the evolution of language. They might reveal the secrets of communication. Unlike you and me, a bird can be opened up. We can see what's on the inside." She liked that idea more in theory, as a metaphor, than she did now in practice.

She heard a white-crowned sparrow pecking inside his soundproof box, a repeated angry sounding tap. *These are angry times,* the photography professor had said with a shrug of his shoulders, excusing himself. Thinking of him brought on the usual frightening sense of defeat.

She made her way over to the birdcages, stepping around computers, microphones and amplifiers, mobile recording stations connected to one another by thick red, black and green wires. The stations were rolled about during the day, moved in front of one birdcage or another during experiments, rarely turned off or put away at night. She looked in at the Inca dove. He was the only one of his kind in the lab and she wondered whether he was lonely.

In the first days of the job, she had tripped again and again over the cables, and David, watching her untangling herself, had said nothing, only raised his eyebrows. Likely he had worried that, at best, her trips would unleash the machines, zero out the electrical signals, stop the collection of data. At worst, she might jerk the birds from their tethers, leave them hanging in midair, fluttering and panicked, undoing the hours of wiring surgery he'd done.

Forget it, she told herself when she returned from Chicago. *Think of it as a bad picture, out of focus, poorly exposed,* but she had not succeeded in destroying the memories. There were still frightful pushing, pulling dreams at night, followed by moments like now when she could hear him speaking and almost feel the heavy breath of his whisper in her ear. *These are angry times.* Days in which she worried a part of him had been left, forever imprinted on her body, that despite the cleaning out of her womb—the suction, scrape and bleeding that followed—he had not been totally removed.

She went down the hallway to the aviary, opened the door and stepped inside. She had no business in the aviary right now, nothing to do here, but she wanted to be alone. In this space, amidst one hundred flying, tooting zebra finches, she knew she wouldn't be bothered because no one ever came in except her and the student who fed the birds on the weekends. She leaned against the wall while birds zipped around one another, the sounds of caged wings echoing off of the narrow, tiled walls.

Photographers should be seen and not heard. His eyes were dark green, waterless. He was a visiting professor, quite famous, who'd been brought to the university for a two-month course. He singled her out after he had seen her photograph and invited her to coffee.

It seems that you already understand that. A pause. *Personality can only come through the photographs.* He'd touched her arm gently. *You don't want people to notice you. It interferes with the work.*

She smiled back, felt his leg muscle flex against her thigh under the table.

Quite remarkable to already know that at your age.

His fame excited her. His attention, in those months focused solely on her, meant she had true talent. He was her reason to leave, her gate to a real city, her introduction to working artists. By the time he left, she'd made plans to move to Chicago.

A zebra finch singing near her stopped suddenly. She watched him cock his head, approach his food container, and then eat a seed. Standing now in the aviary among the birds tooting and bleeping around her, she tried to quiet her mind and remind herself that she was as far away from Chicago and the photographer as she could get. The bird laboratory was a kind of refuge, a place where she was safely in the company of two scientists tapping away at computers, scribbling diagrams on white boards, fighting about whose hypothesis was right. Surrounded by birds. Beautiful, loud, trilling, squawking—but speechless—birds.

She took a deep breath and left the aviary. Back in the laboratory, she sat down at the main computer. Every day after the birds were fed and the cages cleaned, her job was to make three copies of all data recorded the previous day. She stored the cds in large, three-ring folders that were kept on bookshelves in the conference room. She inserted a blank disk, dragged the files and clicked on the green button. While the files were copying, she lifted her head and looked outside. The pink morning had turned blindingly bright, the sun reflecting off the frozen crust of a new snow.

She heard a zebra finch sing a series of songs and looked over at him.

His backpack held wires that were woven up, through, and out the cage. Plugged into computers, they recorded his breaths, heart beats, and any songs he chose to sing. This one was a loud and prolific singer.

When the data were copied, she hit the eject button, removed the disk and used a fine black pen to write the bird's number, the names of the files and the date. She inserted another, dragged, double clicked and stared at the lifeless screen while the computer worked. She heard Anton's whistle and listened to him humming and moving around the lab behind her. She sat up straighter in her chair. He seemed to be in a better mood again.

There was something appealing about him, but she was struggling to put words on just exactly what it was. He seemed simultaneously accessible and inaccessible, strong and vulnerable, serious and light-hearted. The scar on his cheek had twitched as they'd spoken in his office. Was he winking at her again? Was that wishful thinking? She didn't know him at all. They'd hardly exchanged more than a hundred words. She imagined his type was quite common in Italy, or wherever he was from, but she wasn't accustomed to men like him. She didn't trust her feelings.

Since starting to work in the lab, she had begun a new plan. She would save money so that she might travel and take pictures of birds. In her spare time, she read about them, their hollow bones, the air sacs pumping air through their lungs, their funny voice boxes imbedded in the middle of their chests, their ability to fly up and immediately away, migrating to a new place two times a year. She fed them, scrubbed their cages, scanned their nests for eggs. She did as she was told, positioned cages with female birds in front of those with males, tempted them to sing. She was a twenty-four-year-old woman at an interim job. Temporary and safe. And with Anton and his accent, the many species of birds, it almost felt exotic. She had no expectation that she would slip day by day, imperceptibly at first, and then obviously, into love with a man and the sound of his voice, or birds and the world of their bleating songs.

The week his bird died, Anton stayed late at work every night. On Friday he sat in his office, papers spread across the desk, staring down at printouts of songs. The building had mostly cleared out. Rebecca left at five and David had gone to dinner downtown.

Computers were powered down, doors pulled shut, the internal alarm system enabled. Even the post-docs were relaxing. In the bathrooms, women were hanging up their lab coats, pulling on winter boots and lining their lips with shades of red. Soon, like David, they would be stepping into restaurants humming with conversation, sitting down at tables, poring over menus, ordering lamb, pork or steak, clinking glasses of beer or wine. Anton liked to be alone in the lab at night with only the birds, quiet in their cages, and the hums and purrs of computers and machinery.

He was glad to have the space to himself, never inclined to join them because he usually ended up feeling confused like an old man who was hard of hearing. Crowds and background noise made understanding English, not to mention being understood by others, more difficult. Instead, he often worked late, returning to the laboratory after dinner, walking from his apartment up and across the empty campus in the dark. He would swipe his card through the security system, wait for the green light to flash, and enter the institute.

He took out a piece of paper and began to write an over-due letter to his mother. He could see the blue envelope of her last letter on the table at his house, where it had been for weeks, and tonight he finally felt like he could cross the distance and write. She wanted to know what this western American city looked like. He could have just taken a picture and sent it to her but he'd always refused to buy a camera. Instead, he wrote:

> *The city is constructed of boxes. The institute that houses our labora-*
> *tory is a transparent, well-guarded rectangle. Inside this rectangle*
> *there are smaller spaces, mostly squares. The outer walls of the build-*
> *ing are constructed of red brick and glass, the inner walls of the*
> *same. Rooms are delineated by plasterboard, doors and glass. Half-*
> *walled small spaces define work cubicles for students. My office is a*
> *perfect square. In the conference room, the walls are cut into parallel*
> *lines by the bookshelves and each book a small rectangle of its own.*
> *Down the hall, the aviary is a dirty, noisy square. The experimenta-*
> *tion room, lined with thick, white Styrofoam, where I spend most of*
> *my time, is soundproof. Outside the walls, the desert is grey and flat*
> *and leads to another mountain range. I do not know what's on the*
> *other side.*

The problems with his research worried him. He didn't know what it meant but lately there had been a lot of dead birds and the death of the bird this week was a major set-back. He took down the blue binder and flipped through the pages until he found the one for "Red 31." In her neat handwriting, Rebecca had printed the date and next to that the word *deceased*. He studied the bird's history looking for clues as to why it suddenly had died, and without finding any, he closed the binder. He wrote:

I'm not as sure as David, who came to neuroscience through a love of birds and their songs, that we are uncovering the truth of birdsong, and at times I doubt that it can even be done. Unlike him, I just want to understand circuitry, the wiring of memory. Truth is, I don't care much for research with birds.

It was funny how the act of writing made feelings more concrete and the act of writing his mother, in particular, with whom he'd shared more words on paper than in person, brought out his loneliest self.

Birds. Anton didn't like them much. Plain and simple, though they'd been a constant presence in his life. His grandfather's nightingales. The storks he worked on for his master's thesis. And now this work. He avoided looking at their eyes and at the sloughing epidermis where their beaks met their faces. He didn't like the scaly feeling of their spindly legs or the way their toes sometimes curled around his pinky finger when he held them. He didn't like the feeling of their quickly beating hearts or warm bodies in his hand, and the truth was, he resented them deeply when they died.

All I want to do is use the bird to understand how memory works. Measure it. Distill it. How does our brain memorize patterns of sounds? If we can memorize, does that also explain how we can forget? Is forgetting the opposite of learning?

The talking part, at least, was relatively easy for him. There were other, larger, problems. Computers crashed. Expertly placed electrodes failed to record a pulse. Some days his hands shook and he couldn't be trusted to open a bird, or like this week, the bird died for no apparent reason.

Rebecca had suggested that the bird had died by choice.

"Surely, it's an absurd notion," David said to him later, "but I don't have a better reason for that bird's death."

Choice. An interesting concept. He continued writing.

Everyone knows that birds don't migrate east and west. South American species come north. European birds fly south. I feel I've been blown off course, like one of those confused "accidentals," mistakes that bring delight to the bird fanatics who spot them. Just like those birds, I fear I'm destined to die of starvation, disorientation, or both.

What would his mother make of this letter? They'd never talked much when he was a boy, but since coming to the States, their letters, for Anton at least, seemed to function as a type of journal. They never responded directly to what each other had written, though they continued writing back and forth in an old-fashioned way with pen and paper and stamps.

He heard a soft whistle coming from a tiny microphone in one of the white-crowned sparrow coolers. Enclosed as they were, they didn't know day from night. He listened for more. There was a buzz and trill, a tremolo of sorts, and then the descending sweep. No outside stimulus seemed to be needed. As it was, in its solid enclosure, this bird could only be singing to itself.

Anton had been in the States for almost five years and he was ready to go home. He'd come at the urging of a professor, and then finally, his mother.

"One of your professors stopped by today." She was at the table sorting through photos while he arranged cold cuts and cheese on a plate.

"Which one?"

"Gianetti. He said he admired my work." There was a slight smile on her face.

Everyone admired his mother's photographs and he wondered what else Gianetti admired about her.

"He said that the USA is the only place to do neuroscience."

Anton cut a slice of cheese.

"He said that here his technicians spend their days washing pipette tubes, but in the USA they use them and throw them away like bottle tops. A garbage can-full a day. He said his lab needs another fifteen years just to catch up to what they're doing over there."

Anton placed the plate on the table beside her, careful to not get the food too close to her photographs. Their lab was not fifteen years behind and he doubted Gianetti, with his quiet but constant ego, would have ever admitted such a thing even if it were true.

"He said you're too talented to stay here. He needs you over there."

The first post-doc, four years in St. Louis, got him a couple of scientific publications and landed him this second post-doc with David; but now he needed results worthy of publication in *Science* or *Nature*. Dead zebra finches were not a ticket home. He heard David say, *This is how science is done. Baby steps that add up over the years.* Anton didn't have time for baby steps. He needed the elusive engram that David didn't believe in.

The world of neuroscience had grown quickly. When David was a post-doc, there had been about six thousand neuroscientists, but by the time Anton went to his first meeting, attendance had doubled, and now they were predicting that there would soon be twenty thousand neuroscientists worldwide. Whereas David was on the forefront of the first wave, Anton was a late arrival. If he had any hope of a career in neuroscience, he needed to sprint. He needed a big win, a World Cup goal.

The white-crowned sparrow sang again, and Anton half-heartedly sketched how the song would look if digitized. Whistle, buzz, buzz, trill, trill, downward sweep.

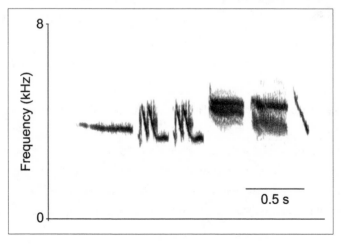

Tremolo always preceded by a trill. Auditory awareness of one thing seemed to bring on the other. Was that fixed in the brain?

Everyone knew that auditory feedback was important. The definitive experiments had been done long ago. Take out a bird's ears and not only does he go deaf, but slowly he loses his ability to sing. What if he could turn that tidbit of information about deafness into a tool to find engrams? What if Anton could take away the bird's ability to sing, but not the ability to hear? What would happen if the bird sang but made no sound? He ought to, if predictions held, forget how to sing. Could he then see changes in the bird's nerve cells as it began to forget its songs?

He reached for a piece of paper and began sketching the syrinx, the bird's voice box, imagining how it might be possible to temporarily keep it from vibrating, devising how he might be able to mute a bird.

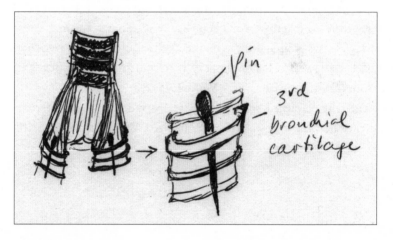

He labeled the parts. A syrinx was an awfully small place to work, no bigger than a rice grain. How would he keep the bird from making sounds?

He heard rattling at the window and looked outside. A storm was moving across the valley. Frozen rain pelted the windows and the glass blurred. He'd arrived in the city on a night much like this one, cold and black, huge snowflakes coating the road. David had picked him up at the airport and given him a quick tour of the downtown, bright and shiny in the night-time snow, the Temple Square, still lit in red, blue, gold and green, though Christmas had already passed.

He looked back at the drawing of the bird's syrinx again, and suddenly he saw it. If he could keep the labia from moving, then theoretically there should be no sound. He thought he knew how he might do just that. He jumped from his chair and went to fetch a zebra finch. Even though the finch's song was less interesting than the white-crown's song, he wouldn't try to mute a white-crowned sparrow. Those birds were reserved for David's syntax experiment.

He slid the finch into the plastic funnel and waited for the anesthesia to work. When the bird was asleep he sterilized the tools. He cut tiny pins from pieces of metal, flipped on the microscope's light and lined up everything on the table.

A few weeks after he'd arrived in Utah, he met Francesco, who owned the Italian deli downtown. Francesco leaned over the counter and spoke in Italian as if he were revealing a secret. "The church cranks out married couples every Sunday like ravioli from a pasta maker. The pope is supremely jealous. The Vatican only dreams of practitioners like these—no sex, no wine, no coffee...".

"No coffee?"

"And ten percent of your paycheck, too."

The religion didn't bother Anton. What did affect him was the openness of the desert, the space and barrenness of the West. If he kept his vision on the mountains he felt at ease, but looking across the flat, gray valley or driving into the desert was disorienting. Just west of the city the salty lake hovered like a mirage just inches above the horizon. If you were at its shore on a sunny day, the white salt reflecting sunlight could blind you.

Space seemed to be one of the main things that made Americans different from Europeans. Anton had come to believe that fundamentally, the American experience was based on just that: dealing with loneliness in vast areas of land. Where Europeans had high density, medieval cities and two thousand years of ruins to temper their loneliness, Americans, especially those in the West, had horizon, massive rocks, thorny bushes, and a few ugly cities that looked like they'd been constructed overnight.

"Don't you feel lonely out here?" he asked David once.

"Often," David said, "but I love space. It's liberating to be on a frontier where no one can tell me what to do."

David didn't mind telling others what they could and couldn't do though. He'd forbidden Anton to work on engrams. *Not my lab, not my funding, not my birds.*

The zebra finch lay on the table before him, breast exposed, slow pulses up and down, breaths in and out. He had made a small opening in the bird, pinned the skin back and now he was looking down at the syrinx, a forked section of cartilaginous rings, the valves inside no bigger than rice grains. He meant to weave the tiny pins in one side of this ring and out the other. Picking up a pin with the forceps, he steadied his elbow on the table, moved in closer and held his breath.

"What's it like?" his friends at home asked.

"Like a giant Ferris wheel."

They presumed he was making a joke, laughed, lifted their glasses and sipped their wine, but he'd been serious. Coming to the States for the first post-doc was like stepping into the small cabin and hearing the door click shut. He remembered the beginning weeks of panic, disorientation, loneliness. Forget the fact that he could read and write in English, he could only make out half of what they were saying. Everything in the American accent sounded garbled and mispronounced. Language, he learned quickly, was a clear line, and you either stood on one side or the other. Making out the words was not enough. You either understood what a person was saying, or you did not.

The big wheel had begun to turn and then he'd experienced something new, the freedom of leaving Südtirol, his life there, his old self, behind. On the way up there was one new perspective after another, the horizon always larger, his vista longer. There was a brief time when the wheel stopped at the top, and he'd been perched there, feeling the gentle swing of the cage, enjoying it all, but then the wheel had begun to turn again. Heading to the bottom once more, he wasn't so enamored. He felt caged, saw the bars more than the horizon.

He looked down at the bird. It appeared as though he'd succeeded in placing a pin through each labium of the syrinx but he wouldn't know until the bird tried to sing. He tied off the last stitch and doused the suture with a bit of surgical glue. While he waited for the bird to wake up, he cleaned the table and tidied up the instruments. He wouldn't say anything to David. If it worked, he would have to see that this was the definitive test. The engram would appear.

By the time he trudged down the hill from the laboratory, head bent against the wet snow, orange scarf wound around his chin, eyes squinting into the shimmer and dim glare of streetlights, he was feeling almost giddy. He looked into the sky, felt the snow hitting his cheeks and blinked the drops away from his eyes. In a few more hours everything would freeze once more, the slush turning to ice in the early hours of the morning. Tomorrow he'd be slipping and sliding as he walked up the hill toward the institute.

When he opened the screen door to his house, a small box wrapped in brown paper tumbled out. He bent to pick it up and squinted in the dim light to make out the return address. It was from his mother. At least, she was in Südtirol. For months he'd been following the Italian newspapers and the stories of the unrest in Somalia, the battle of Mogadishu, looking as always, for her photo credits. Feigning ignorance on this side of the world, he'd written. *Can you give me an update? Over here, the news is fifty percent weather report.* She'd understood what he really wanted to know and said she wasn't on this assignment, but Anton hadn't known whether to believe her or not. Lately, as if trying to make up for his childhood years, she seemed to have become protective of him.

He unlocked the door and went inside. He set the package on the small table, and passed into the kitchen. He filled a pot three-quarters full with water and put it on the stove. His mind was still turning on the possibilities of muting. Everyone said that once a bird settled on a song, once it crystallized, it couldn't change, but he thought they were wrong. That was too simplistic. What if he could watch the birds lose song when they no longer made sounds? See the changes in the nerves when they forgot how to sing? And then later, if he could reverse the muting, would they get their old songs back? He would figure out how memories come and go.

From the cupboard he took down the sea salt, opened his palm to the white crystals and spilled them in a stream into the water. He dusted his hands over the pot, opened a drawer, removed a sharp knife and went back into the living room. He ran the knife along the side of the package, slit the thick paper. Underneath he found a thin cardboard box. He peeled back a piece of tape and opened the top. Inside there was a book. *The Conference of the Birds*. He studied the cover, a group of birds—a falcon, some ducks, parrots, herons, a peacock with tail flared—stood at the edge of a stream, their beaks and attention directed toward a strange-looking bird called a brown-crested hoopoe that stood before them.

He sat on the couch and opened the book's cover. On the title page was his mother's careful handwriting, in Italian as always, never German as he preferred:

Caro Anton,
Lines 2643-2649:
"The world, as far as I can see,
Is like a box, and we are locked inside,
Lost in the darkness of our sin and pride;
When death removes the lid we fly away—
If we have feathers—to eternal day,
But those who have no feathers must stay here,

Tormented in this box by pain and fear."

--Tua mami

The book his mother had sent was a Sufi tale, written in Persia in the 12th century, a long poem about birds searching for a god. He wondered how much had been lost in the poem as it was transcribed over and over through the years and in various languages. And why had she pulled out that quote about having feathers and the ability to fly off to eternal day? She'd never been religious or spiritual. His mother remained a mystery to him and he knew that if he asked her straight out about the lines of the poem, he wouldn't get a satisfactory answer.

He closed the book and looked at the cover once more. She'd certainly never been shy of putting on feathers and flying away. She'd left the house when he was eight, leaving him with his father and grandparents so that she could wander Africa, photographing the news anywhere she could find it, making trips back for months between assignments.

Feathers for *eternal day* versus *pain and fear* for the flightless.

Both his mother and father had suffered from a sort of muteness. His mother had avoided conversation by fleeing; his father had been able to achieve the same end by staying. And now Anton was trying to mute birds to reveal the relationship between memory, sound and communication. The irony was unavoidable, and on this cold, wet night in the Western USA, reading this Persian poem, the thought made him feel particularly misplaced. He studied the book's cover for another moment before setting it on the table, and then returned to the kitchen to prepare the pasta sauce.

The next morning, Anton boarded the train to see a photography exhibit at the library downtown. He wished he had invited Rebecca to join him, but he had no idea whether she would enjoy such a thing. He got off the train, stepped into the bustle of the small square and crossed over to the library. He passed through the massive revolving glass door and stopped at the entrance. Inside the library's common area, sounds and voices were carried upwards disappearing into the air high above, leaving only a low hum below, a rumble that was quickly absorbed by the travertine floor. Even David's shoes, which clicked back and forth in the laboratory during the day, would be quiet here. The glassed-in elevators to his right ascended and descended in silence. Somewhere in the great hall, a child was crying.

Avoiding the elevators, he climbed the curving stairs to the exhibit on the third floor. There was one other person in the room, a white-haired woman with glasses and a notepad moving methodically from photograph to photograph. He stopped in front of a picture of a man holding a potted plant. The man was smiling, his face shadowed by the faint, blurry trace of fencing, which on a closer look seemed to be prison fencing. Prison. Boxes. Working in the lab had become a sort of box as well. He felt condemned to failure. *But those who have no feathers must stay here, Tormented in this box by pain and fear.* Next week, he resolved, he would overcome his fear. He would invite Rebecca to lunch.

On weekends in the laboratory the Bengalese finches, starlings, and robins fluttered and called and ate and slept in the private space that the weekend created. Except for those attached to recorders, the birds were not being watched. The animal-care technician, a laconic, pale, too-thin student, came early in the morning. He was supposed to change the newspaper lining the cages, refresh the water, replace seeds and add egg whites, peas and carrots to the dishes, but on Saturdays, when no one was checking his work, he just added some new seeds here and there, filled the water containers if they were low, and left most of the cleaning and feeding until Sunday. No one knew that on Saturdays and Sundays, the birds danced and sang less readily. Nor did anyone suspect that when they slept, they dreamed of singing.

On Sunday, just before daybreak, David took Anton to the Great Salt Lake. "Bird watching is the appropriate Sunday alternative for a scientist."

"Some people say birdsong is the voice of god," Anton said.

"Of course it is."

David drove north out of the city past the refinery, its tall towers rising like giant cigarettes giving off intermittent puffs of black smoke, past the few remaining fields of wheat and soy, past the shopping malls and fast food restaurants. When they'd left the city, the sky above the foothills had just begun to lighten; now it was turning quickly from deep blue to white.

"You know, this whole valley used to be covered in water. A big freshwater lake, the water as high as that smoke stack out there. As big as Lake Michigan."

"What happened to it?"

"It drained about fourteen thousand years ago. The earth dam holding it in, up in Idaho, gave out and all the water rushed to the ocean, up and out through Oregon and Washington."

It was easy for David to be with Anton because they had science as a broad point of contact. David knew he wouldn't spend as much time with Anton if Sarah were home, but he felt a real affection for him. Underneath his accented English, European arrogance, and misdirected obsession with memory engrams, Anton was basically a sweet guy. Coming out of Gianetti's lab in Italy, one of the best in Europe, he was more adept at math, physics, experimental design and techniques than most Americans, and he had an ability to remember intricate details of papers he'd read that reminded David of Ed.

David saw a hawk-shaped bird in the sky and wheeled the car to a fast stop at the side of the highway. The maneuver would have been dangerous, even deadly, any other day of the week, but on Sunday, without the heavy traffic, it was reasonably safe.

"Eagle," David said.

Anton raised his binoculars to his eyes while David peered over the steering wheel.

"Looks young, still has whitish wing linings," David said. "Probably last year's."

They sat together, heads crooked sideways, necks craning to look out of the front windshield watching the eagle fly upward. "One time I was out at the bay and it was wicked cold, the water completely frozen except for where the stream comes out of the culvert. I saw three or four eagles flying low and a bunch of California gulls and they were making a ruckus."

"Ruckus? What does that mean?"

"Loud squawking noises. So I walk over to see what's going on. There are small fish in the water and the gulls are fishing them out, only every time a gull gets a fish and hops up on the frozen bank to eat it, an eagle swoops down and steals it away. I watch for a good twenty minutes and see this happen over and over. A gull grabs a fish, flops it onto the bank, takes a peck or two of flesh and then loses the entire catch to an eagle."

"Is that the behavior that makes eagles a great American symbol?"

David shook his head and laughed. "Our natural ease with competition you mean?"

"Or stealing," Anton said.

"One doesn't exclude the other." David put the car into gear, glanced into the side mirror and accelerated quickly onto the highway. "Boy do I love this car, even if it is German."

"It is strange," Anton said, "how you Americans love many things."

"It's a manner of speaking."

"I know, but it is funny to be always saying you love everything."

Recently Anton had written to his mother: *Americans like verbs and adverbs. Italians prefer adjectives. This is another difference between us.*

"Well, I don't love everything," David said. "Only my car." He giggled to himself and then popped a CD into the machine and they began their usual diversion of listening to bird songs and naming the species.

"There used to be this program on television," David said. "Back in the '70s, called 'Name that Tune.' They would play the beginning few notes of a song and whoever guessed the song title fastest, won."

The bird songs played and David named them all instantly.

"I think you memorized the tape," Anton said.

"Okay, for your benefit, then, we'll scramble." David pressed another button and the songs were now played out of order, but he still named them all.

"I give up. You're too good," Anton said.

"Nothing like Ed."

"Who is Ed?"

David slammed on the brakes and jerked the car off the road again.

"David! You'll crash!"

"Sorry. I thought I saw a rough-legged hawk." He put the binoculars to his eyes. "Nope. Wrong. It's a red-tail."

They drove out along the causeway that connected Antelope Island with the mainland, the question of Ed momentarily forgotten. The water was low, the shoreline white, not with snow but salt.

They parked the car at the base of the mountain. "Every time I come to this place I feel like I am on another planet," David said. He especially felt this way on the backside of the island where the air was heavy and white, the horizon misty, the rocks red, where all you could see was salt, the shimmering blue of the lake and sky. Bison roamed the lower fields, looking like prehistoric beasts with their heads weighted down with thick curly locks. David raised his binoculars to see them better and only then did he notice the small group of pronghorn antelope in the background. Red and brown, perfectly camouflaged, invisible to the naked eye. "Later we can go look for the foreigner," David said.

"Foreigner?" Anton covered his short hair with his orange knit cap and wrapped a scarf around his neck.

"The chukar."

"What's a chukar?"

"It's like a grouse, introduced from Asia. Sounds something like a chicken."

They spent the day climbing the mountain, stepping around the early spring grasses and wildflowers that were sprouting between the rocks. David took off his sweater and tied it around his waist and unbuttoned his shirt. They searched for the chukar, but with no luck. They sat down on the red rocks, looked out over the murky blue water, unwrapped their sandwiches and ate in silence.

On the hike back to the car, Anton said, "House sparrows and starlings from Europe, chukars from Asia, all adapted in this place, not able to remember home."

"Does that seem so bad? Perhaps not worth remembering," David said.

"Francesco down at the deli told me that when you go to live in another country, you give up home forever."

"That's interesting." David wondered whether Ed would agree. There was no way to ask him.

"He said that even the language changes; you lose the rhythm of your mother tongue."

David stopped and turned to Anton. "I guess I've never thought about how hard it must be for you to be here."

"That's not what I meant, but it is really different," Anton said.

"Since it wasn't bird watching that got you into this sound business, and landed you in our foreign land, what was it?"

"Guitar. Classical guitar, and then later, physics." He might also have said a house that was too quiet. "But there were birds in my past. My grandfather was a bird singing judge."

"A what?"

"He lived in a village in the mountains and every spring he kept the custom of collecting a bird, a young one, and he raised it up for singing competitions. There are villages in the mountains where all the men come to coffee every morning with their birds. They set the cages on a long table and the birds listen and learn from each other. During a competition, the judge goes down the line of cages with a stop watch, timing how long each bird sings."

"You're kidding me."

"No. My grandfather always had good birds, but the people loved him for his judging. His fingers clicked the stopwatch very quickly. He was fair and honest. He was always asked to judge."

"What birds?"

"Nightingales, mostly. Finches too. Even after my grandfather went deaf, he judged, measuring the song by watching the beak."

"What kind of finches? Were they bullfinches, as in Nicolai's finches?"

"I don't know."

"You've heard about Nicolai and bullfinches, haven't you?"

"I studied guitar and physics."

"But still, how could you not know about Nicolai? He was German."

"You are forgetting, David. I am not German. I am from Südtirol. Why do all you Americans think Germany, Austria, Switzerland and Südtirol are the same place?"

"Nicolai was a famous animal behaviorist," David said. "Everyone should know about him. The bullfinches he studied have almost no song, just a *who who* sound, but if you take them young and train them, like Nicolai did in the 1950s, you can teach them complicated songs. Nicolai had them singing German folk songs, but the odd thing was that they always transposed the song up a half step. If the song was in F, they sang it perfectly, but in F#. The other strange thing was that the birds bonded only with Nicolai and his male assistants. After they were trained, he would sell them as pets, but the birds only sang for men. If bought by a woman, they became mute."

"I understand," Anton said. "They are afraid of saying the wrong thing."

David laughed. "Right. With women, it's usually better to say nothing at all."

They arrived at the car. Each man knocked his salty boots against the tires and got in. Driving back along the causeway, David stopped and they got out to set up the telescope. There were small groups of ducks—goldeneyes and green-winged teals—along the shore, but the peak migrations had not yet started. Soon they would be seeing ibises, avocets, stilts, phalaropes, the birds coming along the north-south flyway, from Argentina, Chile, Brazil and Mexico, stopping off at the lake for a little rest before continuing their travels north to nest and breed.

On the way home, the bird songs played again, only now David just listened to the songs, not bothering to say the names.

"So who is Ed, the guy who is better at birdsong than you?"

David waited a moment before he answered. "Edward Matheson III. The best birder ever known." His fingers clenched hard on the steering wheel. "And, incidentally, the man who came between my wife Sarah and me."

"Believe me," Sarah was saying, "if a person develops a vocabulary for loss when they're young, they're pretty much immune as adults."

Ed, who was driving, turned his head briefly away from the road and raised his eyebrows to Sarah who was sitting next to him in the front seat. Sarah ignored his challenge. Ed was back for two weeks to defend his dissertation, and the three of them were going on a camping trip for the first time. David sat in the back with the parrot Skinner calmly perched in his plastic green cage. It cocked its head at him and so David cocked his head back.

"It's the difference between learning a language when you're young versus when you're old," she said. "I'm not saying that it makes you immune to loss as an adult, just that you don't stumble. Loss and grief don't derail you if you've gone through it young."

Ed downshifted and then pulled into the left lane to pass a truck. Skinner let out a loud squawk.

"See?" Ed said. "Skinner also thinks that's bullshit."

"Sounded more like he was agreeing with me," she said.

"I'm wondering if it's weird to be taking a bird on a camping trip," David said.

"He needs to be out where he can hear other birds, not just cats and dogs," she said.

"What if we lose him?" David asked.

"We're not going to lose him. I'm not even going to open the cage."

"We could tether him out. He'd be good bait for an eagle." Ed was not fond of the parrot. He waited to feel the punch on his right shoulder. A smack from Sarah now and then was the only physical contact they shared.

"I was thinking he'd be better butterflied on the grill, a sort of appetizer," David said.

Sarah turned to the back seat and spoke to the bird. "Don't listen to them, Skinner. They don't mean what they say."

David and Ed had been on many such trips in the years since they'd met early one summer morning at the beginning of graduate school. David had been walking a trail in one direction, Ed was going the other way. Recognizing in one another the look of serious birders, they stopped, chatted, reviewed their lists and in the course of talking, realized that they were both grad students at the university. David in psychology. Ed in biology. Soon after, they began sharing an apartment, and whenever Ed was in town, going on bird watching trips to Northwest Florida, Big Branch Marsh and Corpus Christi, trips in which they left at nightfall and took turns driving through the dark. They birded from sunrise to early afternoon, compared their lists, and then slept a few hours before driving home again. In between, they worked on their dissertations. Ed flew to the tropics in Peru, Ecuador, and Colombia to study birds. David stayed in Louisiana and put mice through their motions, ran them blindfolded through mazes, froze them, sliced open their brains.

David met Sarah a year after he met Ed. Having arrived early to class he took a front desk near the window in the classroom, hoping to spy an odd bird during lecture that he could later gloat about to Ed. He was staring out the window, watching for movement in the leaves when a woman behind him spoke.

"Would anyone be interested in sharing books this semester? Splitting the costs?"

He turned his head slightly, surprised by the sweetness of the voice, mildly southern, but far from the girlish lilt of the local women. When he turned to look back, he saw her legs first, long and tanned, and without thinking about whether he wanted to share books or not, his arm shot up.

Sometimes in class, he would hear her talking with others and only single words reached him, but that was enough to evoke images for him. He heard her say "Spanish dancer" and instantly had the image of a young woman with black shoes tapping on a wooden floor. When she said "swan," he saw the ripple of smooth water as a white bird glided away. He had no idea what she was talking about or where the words fit into her conversation, but he realized that he'd stopped paying attention to the birds outside and was holding his breath.

Six months after meeting, they moved in together. At first, it was like the sharing of books, an economic and convenient arrangement. Ed, who was off in the tropics much of the time proving with his ears that indeed there were more bird species out there than people had believed, didn't mind letting out his room. "I can use the extra cash. Besides, you two will start sleeping together and then I'll get my room back."

Ed was right about Sarah and David. And he was right about birdsong. There were roughly ten thousand species of birds on the planet, and of these, over four thousand were songbirds. Only one man in the world, Ed Matheson, could recognize every species by call or song alone. Despite their competitions, David had only awe for Ed, whose ear was tuned far better than anyone else's. His ability to listen, assimilate and identify sound bordered on the super human.

"How do you do it?"

"Practice."

David shook his head. "I practice too. It's something else you've got."

"A good memory maybe," Ed said.

Ed could put a name on a singing bird in half the time it took David. He did it without thinking, as if his ears, brain and mouth were a computer, the hard disk chock-full of animal calls, the processing mechanism inhumanly fast, but Ed was more interested in the diversity of those sounds than in his own peculiar ability. "There is a funny feeling you get in the tropics," he told David. "Every time you turn and walk a few more feet you see or hear another species. I mean, how did so many birds and so many different songs evolve? It's eerie. I'm no mystic, but it borders on the spiritual."

One time, Ed came back from Peru, thin but energized after having rediscovered the white-cheeked tody flycatcher, a small bird with big eyes—a bird that had been thought extinct for one hundred years. Ed opened the refrigerator and took out two beers, popped the tops and handed one to David.

"Imagine this," he said. "A two-mile radius. In sixteen hours, me and Esteban saw or heard three hundred twenty-four bird species."

"Okay, I'm imagining."

"You can't," Ed said. "That's the point. You have to be there to believe it." He stopped talking and then finished his beer in one long gulp. David noticed that his face looked more weathered than before, older.

"It's different from here, nothing like forests in Louisiana or Ohio, Washington or California," Ed said. "It's weird. You get up before dawn and go out. In the forest you feel vulnerable, part of the food chain even, but then at the end of the day, once you've washed up and are sitting reviewing your lists with a whiskey in hand, everything has flipped and you feel invincible. Maybe it's the isolation. No electricity, no running water, no phones. Nothing keeping you in. Totally free. I don't know, maybe it's knowing that you could walk out into the forest, keep going, and no one would ever find you.

This was the first time Sarah had come with them on a camping trip. They pitched the tents, one for Sarah and David, the other for Ed, and put Skinner on the ground between them. The men woke at 4:30 a.m., sprayed themselves with mosquito repellent, looped binoculars over their heads and took off bird watching. In the woods at the crack of dawn, each man quietly moved around the other, using the same strategies, a step, a cocked ear to listen, a few more steps, a few more moments, checkmarks on paper. There was no need to speak, only a mutual nod when they'd both heard and recognized a song. Both experts, both talented, only unlike David, Ed was never wrong.

Sarah got up later, intending to spend the morning hours studying. She opened her folder and spread the papers on the picnic table. Skinner's cage was next to her. The bird hopped onto his perch and then stepped toward the edge of the cage and peered out at her, as if asking her to open the door and let him out. When she tried to focus on the clinical study before her, the words blurred. A mosquito buzzed at her ear and she swatted it away. A drop of perspiration fell from her forehead onto the pages below. By afternoon, when the men returned, she was in her tent, flushed with fever. They packed up and drove back. At home, she was diagnosed with mononucleosis.

"I can't believe this," she said to David. "Two weeks before my exams and I get the virus you get from kissing in junior high."

"Does this mean you've been kissing junior high boys lately?"

"I'm not sure what's worse, the chills, fever, and muscle aches or the fact that I'm too tired to study and now I'm going to fail my exams."

David stationed himself next to her bed, took the research paper from her hand and began to read out loud. She lay next to him, her eyes closed, listening to the outline of the experiments, the results, the conclusions. David offered commentary to each one, articulating exactly what she would have responded if she'd felt better. When he had to go back to the lab, Ed took his place, and during the days that followed, the voices of the two men intertwined, David's melodic voice with Ed's skeptical reading of psychology. The night before her exams, David looked up from his reading and saw that she'd fallen asleep. He set the paper aside. Sarah had read them all before, and would pass her exams effortlessly. Across-town he could hear the whistle of a train and then the rumble of boxcars powering down the rails. That was Sarah. Unveering. Sarah, he thought at the time, would always stay on track.

David wrote in his notebook. *The theory of sexual selection is all about sex, which males get it and why. Theory says that if song is a signal that gives female birds information about a male's merit, then it should cost him something. Food, time, energy, increased risk of predation. Nothing is free.*

David stopped writing. He looked up from his desk and out the window. It was still dark outside and he was the only one in the lab. Cost. He'd been thinking lately of the cost of song. The tradeoffs between singing and not.

Often, standing in front of a classroom of undergraduates in an attempt to get them to see that they were animals too, he would apply the same logic to explain human mating behavior. Signal, he would tell them, is something like guys cruising the strip on Friday night. As such, not all cars are created equal.

"Listen now, ladies. You all are aware, I'm sure, that a BMW is worth more than a Ford, and by the sexual selection theory, the man who drives it earns more than his Ford counterparts."

As he talked, he would reach into his pants pocket, remove his hand slowly, revealing his keychain, allowing the BMW sign to swing. "That is," he would continue as they laughed, pausing long enough for them to become quiet again, "unless the man is in debt." Here the comparison petered out. In nature, David reminded them, there was no debt. In nature, debt was equivalent to death.

He started to write again. *For a bird, this theory means that all songs shouldn't be equal. Better songs should cost more to sing, and males with these better songs should be superior in territory, health, genes, in some way that matters to the babies.* But it wasn't so straight-forward. How could you measure which songs were better? Some males, when trying to pair up with a female, sang several thousand times a day. Maybe time spent singing was like time spent cruising State Street—no matter what kind of car— only the really fit guys could afford the time. He put down his pen. Or the bums, he thought. No, it wasn't black and white at all.

Measuring the cost of speech in humans was easy and the proverbial "talk is cheap" was about right. You stuck a plastic mask over a person's nose and mouth and asked them to speak softly, then loudly, slowly, then quickly. You put them on treadmills, ratcheted up the speed and asked them to recite poetry while running. You corrected for air in and air out, measured oxygen and carbon dioxide. You got an answer. It cost almost nothing, no extra oxygen, to speak in a normal voice at a normal rate. Singing took some extra effort.

David heard the telltale whistle announcing Anton's arrival at the lab, heard him settling into the day. He expected him to show up at his office door in a few minutes. This wasn't the first time David had thought of cost. At night he lay in bed ticking through possible methods to measure cost in birds much like other people counted sheep. You couldn't ask a bird to wear a mask and run on a treadmill. In graduate school he'd written in his notebook:

How much energy does it cost a male bird to sing his song?

Below that, in the margin, Sarah's careful handwriting:

Less than it costs a female to lay an egg!

At one point in their relationship, she had begun to filch his notebooks and slip comments into the margins. He looked forward to finding her notes, these inside conversations that happened on top of or alongside other conversations they were having. She asked questions about his questions, and noted references for papers she thought might interest him. Sometimes, she'd draw portraits of owls, kingfishers or robins. Once she had printed: *You're the only one I really talk to.*

Now they weren't talking at all. David sensed Anton at the door and looked up from his notebook. "Good morning."

"Rebecca's not here?" Anton asked.

"Sick."

Anton nodded. "Coffee in an hour?"

"Sounds good."

Anton turned and left to set up a new bird for the thermistor experiment. Midmorning, he poured them both cups of coffee and slid one toward David.

"Funny how she doesn't say much, but you feel her absence," Anton said.

"Who?"

"Rebecca."

David smiled. "You interested in the technician?"

"I was just making an observation." Truth was, Anton was acutely aware that he was passing the day without the normal eager sensations that he felt upon seeing her.

"You're right, though. She's quiet." David said. "I always find quiet women suspicious."

"Suspicious? Maybe I don't understand what the English word means."

"No, not suspicious. That's not the right word, just aberrant. You know: women talk, men listen?"

Anton laughed.

"Anyway, my advice is steer clear."

"Why?"

David shrugged, took a sip of coffee. "You know I've been thinking about the *one* thing that no one has ever measured about birdsong."

Anton raised his eyebrows.

"Cost. How much does it cost one of these guys to sing?"

"Can't you just measure it?"

"How?"

"Oxygen consumption. Seems pretty trivial."

"You'd think so, but it isn't. First off, you've got to figure a way to measure oxygen consumption in a bird. Second, even if you manage that, which I can't figure out how to do, how do you measure tradeoffs?"

"Tradeoffs?"

"Ecological tradeoffs. In the spring, male birds can sing thousands of times a day and while they're singing, they can't be eating. What does it cost to sing that many times in terms of energy usage and then how much does it cost to do that instead of eating? I can't figure out how to replicate it in the lab. They never sing as much in here as out there."

"Then just model it with mathematics."

David laughed. "The physicist's solution to everything."

Anton had been sketching while David talked. He'd drawn a bird's head and a balloon mask over the beak, held in place by a sort of helmet. "What about this? I think if you fixed something like this, a collar over the bird's head, and you attached the balloon to that, the bird could still move its head around pretty freely."

"Maybe," David said. He liked the idea of the helmet, and it might work with a zebra finch, but still, would he ever get a bird to sing enough with that mask on?

"You would have to have an inlet and outlet tube," Anton said, "but you might be able to measure small changes in oxygen and carbon dioxide."

"A good project for retirement," David said.

Anton continued drawing the inlet and outlets for the oxygen and carbon dioxide and was trying to work out an equation to measure the volume of air so that he could determine how sensitive the measurements would have to be.

"There is one big unanswered question, Anton."

"I know. It's volume. You need the balloon space to be as small as possible."

"No, the big unanswered question is whether Rebecca will go for you!"

"Stop."

"Seriously. It's the one question you don't have a mathematical equation for. I want to know essentially the same thing. Of course I want to know how much it costs a bird to sing, but what I *really* want to know is why do females think that some males sing better than others?"

At the end of graduate school, David was invited to interview for a post-doctoral research position in Pennsylvania. The position meant a move from Louisiana to Pennsylvania, from mice to zebra finches, but despite his love of birds, he hesitated. He would be studying communication, not cancer. There was less money for research on birds than mammals because the genome in birds hadn't been sequenced as it had been in mice, and so there was no way to knock out sections of the genetic code and test hypotheses. His research questions, at least in the beginning, would be crude. Appreciating a bird in a tree was one thing. Trying to take apart the mechanics of singing in the laboratory was quite another. With doubts, he flew to Pennsylvania for the interview but from the first moment he was put in an aviary with the small chatty birds, he immediately forgot his hesitation. He realized his skill and practice in bird watching might be useful for studying the neuroscience of song, and within just a few hours, he began to recognize the songs of different males, much like the voice of a friend could be picked out of a group of people talking. Questions bombarded him and he spent the next two days in constant conversation with the laboratory director. On the plane ride home he filled his yellow note-book with questions.

I want to know how birds sing. How do the muscles and nerves and breath work together to make sound? Do all birds do it in the same way? He wondered at his own inability to describe his emotions. Why did he find it so hard to put words on his emotions when other people seemed to know exactly what they were feeling all of the time? *Do the variations make any difference?* Did the fact that others could say how they were feeling mean they really knew? His reticence might be, as Sarah said, a disorder, but he thought it might also mean that he understood how difficult it was to understand the human brain and body, how almost-impossible it was to truly see into one's own self. His reluctance to describe how he felt might represent deeper insight and honesty.

He wrote: *I want to understand language. I want to know why I choose some words and she chooses others.*

When he came home from the interview, he did what he would have previously thought impossible. He canceled a long-planned expedition with Ed to search for the probably, but not certainly, extinct ivory-billed woodpecker. Ed understood, unpacked half the food he'd already stuffed into a duffle bag and gone off to paddle the swamp alone. Meanwhile, David slipped into the world of neuroscience and sound, passing nights in the library where for once the quietness did not worry him because his brain was a mass of noise, making out the words in books, unpacking the research.

Ed returned a week later with foot fungus and an impossibly long bird list.

"This is amazing. Did you sleep at all?"

"A bit," Ed said.

"I don't see the ivory bill listed here."

"'Fraid that one's gone."

David knew that sleeping "a bit" meant that Ed had crawled into a tent only after the owl hunting was over and risen a few hours later, always by

4:30 a.m. He would sleep a few more hours midday when the birds were quiet before dismantling his tent and paddling the rest of the afternoon to the next day's location.

At eighteen Ed had broken the North American record for seeing the most birds in one year. Few people understood what sort of ability and dedication that took. Most birdwatchers wouldn't have the stamina to rise every morning for a year at 4 a.m. to hike miles in the cold or wet, ticking off bird species and then after a short nap, jumping into a car and driving, sometimes hundreds of miles, before falling asleep in the back seat, often too tired to undress or crawl into a sleeping bag, but never too tired to forget to set an alarm for the next morning. Day after day for one year. David knew that for most people this would be hell. For Ed, it was one of the best years of his life.

"Obsessive," Sarah said when Ed described his schedule that year.

"There now, Ed, you've got it from the clinician herself," David said. "You've been diagnosed obsessive."

Sarah looked at David. "I might add, the word works just as well in the plural."

David had been spending days and evenings in the library, shoulders hunched, neck crooked over an open journal, the tight dark curls falling over his face. He felt like a detective, retracing the steps of scientists, piecing together the history of birdsong from ecology, physiology to the present-day neuroscience. He loved the work, felt a certain confidence living within the collective mind of the scientific community. Sarah came to the library and implored him to come home.

"I'm not tired yet."

She brought him food and a change of clothing.

"You're scaring me, David."

"Scaring you, how?"

"By this obsession."

"It's not an obsession. I'm simply interested in what's been done before me. I need to get up to speed before I can start the post-doc."

"It's not healthy. The books will still be there after you sleep."

When he finally fell into bed after two straight days and nights in the library she said, "You know, you're experiencing a sort of pseudo-manic phase."

He pretended that he was asleep, snuggled up against her, and hoped she didn't say more.

nton went into the makeshift experimental room that he'd created for the secret bird he'd tried to mute. He flipped through the files on the computer, all were blank. The bird had recovered from surgery but he couldn't tell whether his attempt to immobilize the syrinx had worked because the bird hadn't yet tried to sing. He would add a bit of enticement. Back in the main laboratory, as he was wrapping his palm around a bird, David walked in.

"What are you doing?"

"Testing a bird."

"What bird?"

He stopped, his hand still stuck in the cage, the noisy birds fluttering around it. "A new one for a replicate of our last experiment." He tried not to look at David for fear he'd recognize the lie.

"Why not take the whole cage? Multiple females usually work best."

"This is easier." The experimental room where he'd hidden the muted bird was really just a tiny closet and too small for the big cage. "Besides, I thought you said that females aren't choosey."

"Quite the opposite," David said. "Of course they're choosey. It's the males who tend to be indiscriminant."

"Well then he should sing to this female as well as any other." Anton really meant that he hoped the bird would *try* to sing and he hoped that when it did, it would be unable to make sound.

Back in the experimental closet, he stood off to the side and watched as the female bird hopped around the cage. The male seemed oblivious to her presence. Why couldn't David see that learning song, the process by which a bird mastered that miraculous feat of memorization, and by extension, the process by which any human memorized sounds and meaning, was the real question? How was memory formed? Where was it encoded in the brain?

Early on, philosophers had thought that memories were stored in the heart and that the brain was more of a cooling system. Others believed that memory was stored in the kidney. It wasn't until Descartes that people started understanding that memory, and all other cognitive processes, happened in the brain. Still, how to find definitive proof for a specific memory trace or engram?

He decided to leave the female in the cage and come back later, only when he returned an hour later, the male bird lay at the bottom of his cage, limp and dead, the wires strung up and out of the cage, the computer measuring a flat line reflecting lack of breaths. Anton's mood sunk. The female looked out as if accusing him of something. "It's probably your fault," he said to her. "He didn't like you and so he *chose* to die." It felt good to voice Rebecca's anthropomorphic ideas just then, but still he felt defeated, as trapped as the birds. He unhooked the bird, unplugged it from the computer, and without looking at it, slipped it into a bag. Back at his desk he tossed it into the top drawer. He needed to get out of the lab and so he went to David's office to tell him he was leaving, and in that moment, he decided what he would do. "Do you have Rebecca's phone number?"

David smiled. "Ah, I'm so often right. Maybe *you* can get her to talk."
He sorted through papers looking for her file, jotted the number on a slip
of paper and handed it over to Anton.

The thought of Anton with Rebecca irritated David and he immediately felt irritated at his irritation. Ridiculous emotions. She was twenty years too young for him. He heard Sarah. *Jealousy is a teenager emotion.* It was during an argument after she'd returned from Peru, though even she must have known that she was wrong. Emotions didn't have ages.

He thought back to a time when they lived in a house full of birds. First, the parrot, Skinner, and later, during their post-doc years, canaries, zebra finches, conures, doves. David came home from the laboratory one evening and found her perched on a ladder on the front porch, staple gun in hand. She stretched the mosquito screening along the wood frame, leaned over and placed a staple. She looked down when she noticed him. "Hi." She quickly stepped off the ladder, scooted it over and mounted it again.

He could tell she was happy. "What's this? Trying to save us from the mosquitoes?"

"An aviary for the zebra finches. I might even get some more tropical species. It will be like we're following Ed to Peru and Ecuador, all those great places he goes."

David was quiet for a moment while she inserted another staple with a bang. He felt an irrational fear in his gut. He knew she held Ed in high regard. Of course he did as well, but her descriptions of Ed and his work seemed tinged with special emotion.

"Zebra finches aren't tropical," David said. "They're a temperate, grassland species. From Australia. Ed's never seen them in the wild."

She looked down at him briefly, and blew him a kiss. "Better yet. Another continent altogether." Again she stretched the screening, slid the staple gun down a few inches, pulled the trigger and then checked that the staple had been inserted well before stretching the screening some more.

He wondered whether she harbored a secret desire to be with Ed, the adventurer. *He's discovering new species, documenting the world's diversity,* he heard her say. *What could be more important than that? And he comes home with the most amazing stories.*

That evening she introduced the birds to the enclosed porch. One by one, she reached into the cages, cornered a bird and then walked out to the aviary where she opened her hand and waited while it flew into its new space.

From that day on, he lay in bed in the early mornings and listened as she stepped outside to collect the seed and water dishes, whistling short melodies up and down, trying to mimic their songs. Back inside she washed the dishes, filled the water cups, smashed peas and generously doled out broccoli and chopped eggs. In the winter she moved the birds inside and situated the cages throughout the living room. For months of every year, the house became a clamorous, chiming aviary with two quiet people living inside.

Anton arrived at Rebecca's house with a bouquet of flowers. She was paler than normal. Her hair, usually pulled up, hung down to her shoulders.

"You're not well." He handed her the flowers.

"David told you," she said. "Thank you."

"You're not dressing for winter. You need a hat, a scarf. How do you feel?"

"Terrible." She sat down on the sofa and pulled a blanket around her.

He reached over and touched her forehead. It was cold. "You have a fever?"

She nodded.

"Are you taking some medicine?"

"Yes."

They were silent for a moment.

"How are the birds?"

"Fine." He didn't want to admit the new death, afraid he might tear up at the thought of another experiment gone wrong.

"They don't miss me?" she smiled.

"Of course they miss you." *And me too,* he could have said. She had come to occupy large portions of his mind and he had no explanation why. He looked around the room. "Is that you?" He pointed at the framed photograph of a woman perched naked, folded over on herself, at the edge of a cliff. Behind her was an expanse of rock, canyon, sky, an enormous valley. The woman's head was turned away, out to the horizon. There was black hair that gave evidence of wind. A broad back, arms encircling her legs, her hands lightly balancing on the rock at her feet. She was crouched, ready to take off and fly.

Rebecca shook her head and reached for a tissue. "No, I took it."

He looked at her again. She was even more beautiful with her hair down and he wondered whether she always wore it up or only in the lab. "Why do you feed birds when you can do that?" He resisted the urge to reach out and touch her forehead again. He wanted to crawl under the blanket with her.

"Because that doesn't pay rent, and I like the birds."

"But there are other jobs for photographers—newspaper, magazine, weddings...". He wanted to ask her whether she had a boyfriend, but had no idea how to do that.

She started to laugh, a congested garbled sound. "That's exactly what I used to do—weddings—and I got fired."

He got up and stepped closer to the photograph.

"Once I made the bride look fat, cartoonish. On purpose."

He took in the rest of the room, the collages of photographs cut and pinned on the wall. For a moment, he was overwhelmed with the memory of his mother's darkroom, remembering the smell of fixative, photographs clipped to string, others laid out on the countertop, the sound of water dripping slowly from a faucet. He could see his mother's back, her head looking down as she studied which photographs to keep, some having already been discarded into the trash at her feet. He remembered standing quietly behind her, waiting, never speaking until she turned to him, as if darkness and silence went together. He scanned the animals on Rebecca's wall. There were multiple exposures of the same dog, cat, some chickens, all against a background of desert. "Why didn't you study photography?"

"I did study photography, well sort of, fine art, but I did all my projects on photography."

"Not biology?"

"No. I never liked science much."

He shook his head. "Only in America."

"You seem disappointed. Only what in America?"

"Only here does a photographer work as technician in a laboratory. That would never happen in Europe. There, biology technicians are biologists." He nodded toward a framed black and white photograph, three men, two of them holding handkerchiefs in front of their faces. "Is that a Weegee?"

"You know him?"

"Yes. 1930s, New York crime photographer." He turned back to her, but kept his eyes on the photograph above her sofa, afraid to look directly at her, afraid his intense attraction and vulnerability would come through.

"How come you know Weegee?"

"My mother," he said, "she's a photographer too."

Anton could tell that Rebecca was tired, but he didn't want to leave. He talked, a kind of nervous low chatter, telling her about the birds he'd seen with David when he was at the lake, the way the water shimmered and appeared bare but when you put up your binoculars you realized that there were thousands or millions of birds, black dots, scattered across the horizon.

Her eyes looked heavy. "I will let you rest now," he said.

"No please don't go. I mean, unless you need to. I feel lonely when I'm sick."

"Of course. I'll stay."

"Tell me something else." She smiled at him. "Maybe in one of those languages you speak."

And so he began to speak German, telling her about the book his mother had sent, which he'd begun to read, conscious of the fact that she did not understand, and conscious of the fact that in talking about the book he was trying to understand it himself. She nodded off and slept. He stopped talking and pulled the book from his bag, looking from time to time at her resting, the pale skin, freckles, bright red hair.

When she woke an hour later, he made her tea. While she drank it he went to the kitchen and despite that fact that there was little food in the refrigerator, he managed to make a simple soup that his grandmother made when he was ill. Broth, tiny chopped carrots, sprinkles of oatmeal and a beaten egg. He served her the soup, promising that it would work wonders, but secretly hoping that it wouldn't, that he'd be given another opportunity to cook for her, to serve her, speak in German, and remain at her side while she slept.

Not wanting to go home after leaving Rebecca's house, Anton went back up to the lab. He sat at his desk listening to the hum of the laboratory, the late night occasional bleeps of the zebra finches. He had not been given a word of explanation when his mother left. One morning she was there, as always, warming milk for his breakfast, checking that his books were in his school bag, dressing for work. That afternoon he watched as she packed a suitcase, spreading skirts and blouses out onto the bed, folding them in half and pressing them flat. She did not explain. When she finished the suitcase, she closed it with a click and looked up at him.

"Shall we get started on your homework?"

Later that evening she left the house and his grandparents moved in. If there were fights, he didn't hear them. If there were tears, he didn't see them. There was silence and separation.

She'd abandoned him in the time when there was no divorce, opting for her own freedom, the world of journalism and her camera. Over the next ten years, from eight to eighteen, he would come home from school to his grandparents, his father arriving much later in the evening, often not in time for dinner.

On Friday afternoons, when she wasn't in Africa on an assignment, she would pick him up from school in her battered car and he would spend the weekend at her house in the mountains, which had also been her parents' house, a cold and dark place in the winter that became glorious in the summer. She gave him liberty to explore the overgrown garden, the abandoned village houses and the mountains beyond, never making him stop playing to come inside to eat as his grandmother did, but instead she served cold sandwiches outside in the little garden. At night, she rinsed him off, slowly rubbed his hair dry with a towel and gave him a cup of warm milk to drink.

Anton filled the quiet space of these weekends with his own chatter, invented stories, fights between bad guys, good guys rushing to the rescue. He became a boy who knew how to play alone. The boy who could wash his own scraped knees. The boy who knew when to talk and when to keep quiet. He remembered his fascination with the mystery of breakdown, burying things in the garden and then later digging them up. He covered pieces of cheese, hard bread, once an entire apple, and returned weeks later to dig them up, wanting to see how fast they had changed. His mother was never far off with her cameras, attaching lenses, snapping photos, setting up pieces of material to create shade. He didn't know that she was also watching him, taking pictures of him. Years later, in a catalog from a photography exhibit, he found a photograph of himself as a child. She'd captured him with an inquisitive look on his face, sitting in the dirt, legs spread wide around the rotten objects he'd unburied.

He opened the drawer and shook the dead zebra finch from its bag onto his desk. How had he gotten it wrong? He picked up the bird and went into the main laboratory to the surgery station. He would try an autopsy and see whether he could learn something about why this bird had died. He flipped on the microscope light, lay the bird on its back and opened him up with a scalpel.

From his fascination with decomposition in early childhood, he'd moved on to guitar, electronics and the physics of sound. He didn't know why sound physics interested him so much. At first he thought it came from guitar but later he realized that there might be other reasons. He'd come to believe that sound and guitar became especially important because they were what filled the silence with his mother. During his adolescent years, their time together consisted of the lunch hour. His mother had a dislike for cooking and so he learned to cook, refining his skills year after year, setting the table and calling her from her studio to eat. During lunch, she used language sparingly, as if she were on a diet, never saying a word that didn't need to be said, and so he learned to become an entertaining talker. She spent hours every morning in the darkroom, emerging only to eat, and then she would return to her room and work until very late at night. He fell asleep early so that he could rise at first light to hike in the mountains.

He peered into the opened bird, refocused the microscope down lower and looked at the red fleshy labia of the syrinx. On the left side, he could see the pin he'd woven through the two sides, but on the right side, there was no pin.

He remembered a time when he was a child, perhaps ten, he'd called her from her studio.

"There is something funny about sound," he told her.

She waited, probably not sure what he was talking about.

"Come and look."

She followed him into the living room.

"I put my tuner here in front of my guitar and play. See? The light blinks for the different notes."

"Yes?"

"But now look." He went through the living room and back into her studio. She followed. "I put the tuner here, on this side of the wall. Wait here."

He left her with the small note tuner and went back into the living room. He played his guitar.

"Do you hear the guitar?"

"Yes."

"Is the tuner making light?"

"No."

"See? You can hear it, but the tuner can't."

His mother told him that she'd once heard something about sound being like waves, but then said that it probably had more to do with the sensitivity of the tuner. Coming back into the studio, he stopped her before she could say anything more.

"I'm going to study that," he announced. "I'm going to study sound, how it moves and how it stops. Then I'm going to write a book about it."

The book, of course, was forgotten, but his interest in guitar and sound continued through high school and into the university. He studied Bream, Segovia, Domeniconi and de Lucia. Classical music, pure unaltered, non-synthesized, non-amplified sound. Sound. How it moved and how it stopped.

He began to hunt inside the bird for the missing pin, finally finding it lodged in the heart tissue. Maybe he hadn't secured it in place well enough. Next time, because yes, he had just determined that he would try it again, he would use a longer pin and more surgical glue. Convinced of this decision, he flipped off the microscope light and sat in the darkened laboratory.

What he remembered most about their weekends together was the slip and click of the camera's shutter, the metallic ting of a lens being screwed on. Without a camera in her hands, his mother was a nervous woman, constantly scratching at her arms and legs. At times her calves were raw and bleeding. Later, he learned that she'd been suffering from microfilariae, an infection of threadlike worms that were transferred through the bite of an African black fly. Once inside the body, they burrowed under the skin, replicating and sending out tiny copies of themselves. Quiet inhabitants who only made their presence known at their death, after which there was inflammation, intense itching, and if they traveled to the eyes, blindness. She never explained any of this to him. She never complained. She took her medicine and eventually after some years, managed to rid her body of the infection, but even after the worms were gone, she continued to scratch at her legs out of habit, shedding layers of flaky cells. For his whole life, he would associate those dry, rasping sounds with his mother.

In the first days of March, David prepared to leave for a week-long symposium in Florida. "They're using birds as test subjects for cochlear implants in deaf humans. I'm not much interested, but this is where all the money is," David told Anton. "If we sell our projects right, we can use this human funding to get more of the auditory feedback work going. Maybe you should come too."

They stood at the counter in the laboratory where they had carved out space for a coffee maker. Anton poured out two cups. "I will leave the conference to you." He spooned sugar into his cup and stirred. "I'm not much good in crowds."

"You sure? It's Miami, warm tropical breezes, salsa dancing, seafood..."

"Right." Anton took a sip. "You'll spend all your time in the conference center eating American doughnuts, drinking watered coffee from paper cups and then you'll eat dinner in the top-floor restaurant of the hotel. I won't miss anything."

David laughed. "You're probably right. Anyway, I'll fill you in."

On the plane to Miami David leafed through a yellow notebook. He had written:

Why can mockingbirds learn new songs during their entire lives? In winter, they migrate from Pennsylvania to Costa Rica and come back singing a good rendition of some tropical bird's song. Why can the mockingbird do what the zebra finch cannot?

As soon as he began serious work on zebra finches he knew—instinctively—that he would win his bet. Ed had said that songbirds were too complicated to be useful for neuroscience, but Ed had been wrong. Complicated enough to be interesting, not so complicated as to be impossible to understand, birds offered perhaps the only clear, non-human window into learned communication. Unlike owls, hawks and the like that were born screeching and cawing, songbirds had to learn to sing. A baby bird was like a child at birth. Just like human babies, they needed to listen and practice. They needed to be spoken to.

He had written: *When do learning and recognition flip over into memory and instinct?*

Early on, people had thought that language was mystical. Everything that passed from one human being to another, the grunts, hisses and spurts of sound that became words, the transmission of ideas magically passed from one head to another was supposed to be impossible to understand. David didn't think language was mystical at all but it was true that its origins, communication by sound, sound into speech, grammar, dialect, remained an unanswered question and David intended to understand it from the inside-out.

Why can Ed keep learning and fine tuning his ability to recognize songs whereas I am finding it harder and harder to learn more?

When David and Sarah moved to Pennsylvania, Ed stayed on in Louisiana and took a job leading birding tours to the tropics. Between sessions with clients, he recorded birds, learned songs, wrote papers. Within a year he had founded the Rapid Assessment Program or RAP team, as they were called, the best group of tropical biologists ever brought together. Every few months, Ed was off on a RAP trip to another remote location. His team of experts would swoop into a forest, spend eighteen hours a day—light and dark—making fast inventories of plants, mammals, birds and insects.

The botanist walked hundred meter transects, back and forth, recording the canopy trees one way and then returning, more slowly along the same line to identify the understory. He looked, touched, smelled and wrote down the name of each plant, easily topping two hundred species per transect. The ones he didn't immediately know were, by definition, species new to science and so he collected their leaves, seeds and flowers for future identification.

The entomologist stretched out a plastic sheet below a tree and blasted the canopy with insecticide fog and then waited while the insects rained down. Too numerous to be identified in the field, it would take him months back at the Smithsonian to even estimate the insect diversity.

Before dawn, Ed set up mist nets and stood sentry. When a bird hit the net, he untangled it, figured out which species it was, looked it over for sex, health, and then let it go. If it was a bat, he radioed the mammologist to come and do the same. Eighteen hours a day, weeks on end, no showers or beds and barely enough food to eat, they listened, sorted, counted and recorded. For many tropical areas, their surveys were the first time biologists had ever visited. In several cases, their visits meant the difference between deforestation and protection.

David envied Ed's trips, but only in a distant way. He imagined the exotic locations Ed described, thought about the birds he must be seeing and hearing, but despite many invitations, he'd never gone along. He was too busy with his own birds, he always said, but there was another, unspoken reason. He was never sure whether it was purely a reluctance to leave his work in the lab, or whether he unconsciously feared the chaos of the forest, the ways it might upset the ideas he was forming about birdsong.

And then, there was always the unstated fear that the reason he'd declined was that he didn't want to confront Ed's genius, preferring to admire it, without competition, from afar.

The day after David left for Miami, Anton arrived earlier than usual to the laboratory, coming through the door just as a white-crowned sparrow escaped from one of the top isolation chambers where Rebecca was working. The bird buzzed toward the wall of windows and then veered left, stopping just short of slamming itself against the glass. Sensing that he could not get to the world beyond, he landed in a panting plop at the corner of the desktop. He struggled to find a grip, but his claws splayed on the smooth, slippery surface.

Rebecca stepped off the ladder to follow him, but Anton beat her to it, the desire to help her outweighing the distaste for the sensation of a bird in his hand. When she took the animal from him, he felt a tingle of electricity. He wondered whether she felt it too. She clasped the bird's head between her second and third fingers.

"I didn't need the help," she said on her way back up the ladder.

"I know." Anton watched as she returned the sparrow to his cage. "Perhaps there is an ulterior motive."

"Perhaps?" She smiled down at him. The metal gate slid shut over her hand and this time she made sure it closed completely. The sparrow hopped to the plastic perch and peered out with his tiny black eye. She stepped down off the ladder and turned to Anton.

He placed a hand on her shoulder. "How are you this morning?" She didn't move away.

"Besides two escapees, I'm fine."

"I thought you might come to lunch with me."

"That's the ulterior motive?"

They took the train to Francesco's deli downtown and sat at a small wooden table for two. Speaking in Italian, Francesco asked Anton what they wanted for lunch.

"Doesn't he speak English?" Rebecca asked when he'd walked away.

"Yes, of course, but he doesn't like to." Francesco had told Anton that after thirty years he'd grown tired of never being able to say what he wanted. *In English,* Francesco said, *nothing sounds right.*

Two plates of food arrived. Layers of see-through meat rippled across white ceramic plates, tomatoes cut in half, bits of celery sprinkled like cheese. Francesco drizzled olive oil over each plate. Anton began to eat and then realized that Rebecca was not eating. "You do not like bresaola?"

"I'm vegetarian," she said.

Well, she had one flaw, then. She'd joined the American vegetarian fad. In the five years he'd been in the States more and more people, especially young people, seemed to be rejecting meat, milk, cheese. He'd even met one who wouldn't eat honey. He hoped she wasn't one of those and he hoped his disappointment didn't show. "I'm sorry." He picked up her plate, scraped the meat onto his own and then went to find Francesco. He returned with bread and a plate of roasted vegetables.

"Thank you."

"Try this bread." He broke off a piece of crust and popped it into his mouth and broke off another, larger piece, and handed it to her. Instead of taking it, she leaned over, took hold of his wrist and bit into the bread directly from his hand. She nodded her head as she chewed. He was acutely aware of the effect that her gesture had on him. He waited and then broke off another piece and held it out to her knowing he'd sit there all day feeding her if he could. Why did he feel so comfortable? So far they'd shared only a few hours and yet here they were flirting and courting, saying little but making their desires and intentions clear to one another and probably anyone else who happened to be watching.

"I looked Südtirol up on the map," she said. "Your home."

"Yes? What did you find?" He liked the surprised expression in her eyes when she spoke.

"Mountains, churches, blue lakes."

He laughed. "We have lots of those. You're interested in the Alps?" The prominent blue veins under her pale skin were like roadways on a map.

"I'm interested in—" she hesitated. "I've never traveled anywhere, never been further than Chicago. I guess I just wonder what it's like on that side of the world."

When they finished eating, he ordered espresso but she declined. He stirred in the sugar. Normally, he would drink the sweet coffee in two swallows, but he took sips wanting the lunch to extend for as long as possible. He told her about the bells, how he missed the ding of the goats being led up into the fields in the mornings and the clang of cows moving from pasture to pasture during the day. In the evening there were church bells and children laughing, and nightingales singing into the dark. "I could take you there," he said. The idea seemed more wishful than a possibility. He'd begun to doubt he'd ever get back there himself.

"When?" She laughed. "I can go anytime."

Back at the laboratory, they were both flush with energy.

"Come, I want to show you something." So far, he'd done just one muting and now that David was gone for a few days, he intended to do more. He prepped the table for a surgery. They stood side by side. There was the scent of lemon and roasted garlic. His own breath carried hints of espresso.

"I have not told David yet. I want to see if it works, but I think I know how to test the engram idea. I mute a bird…"

"Mute a bird? That's terrible!"

"No, no, I fix it afterwards." He turned to the cage on the counter behind him. Slipping open the gate, he inserted his hand and, with a flick of his wrist, caught a gray, black and white striped zebra finch. "I'll show you."

With the bird in his left palm, he turned the knob for the anesthesia with his right. When the drug was flowing, he inserted the bird's small head into a plastic funnel and held steady while it fell asleep. Black and white dotted feathers poked out from underneath his hand. He was aware of her arm next to his, the warmth of her skin.

"Birds are like humans," he said. "Like babies, at first, they listen. Later, they babble. Finally, they learn to sing."

He positioned a small piece of clay, like a pillow, under the bird's neck and the limp head fell back. Air coming from the anesthesia funnel ruffled its wispy, white neck feathers. Their forearms touched but she didn't move away.

"If you keep a baby bird isolated and don't give him songs to listen to, he won't learn to sing." She was peering so intently at the quivering bird that he wasn't sure she was listening. "Like a child. If you don't talk to them, they don't learn how."

Anton hoisted himself onto the high chair and scooted closer to the surgery table. "Once their song is memorized, people say it can't be changed, but I'm not sure. I want to see if adults can change their songs."

"Like learning a new language?" she asked.

He could feel the breath of her words in his ear. "Right," he said, his eyes still on the bird, "learning, but also memory, how we remember the things we learn."

The bird's dark legs kicked out and stiffened. Anton pinched a toe to see if it was fully asleep. The bird didn't flinch. "It's the same with human speech. A deaf human baby will be mute." He adjusted the chair and then moved the microscope and light so that he had a good view of the bird. "Maybe you don't know this, but when you speak, your brain is listening, judging the sounds you make against a model for how they should sound."

With a Q-tip coated in brown antiseptic he dabbed and smoothed the gray chest feathers out of the way. He picked up the forceps and plucked out four small feathers that were still in his way. Underneath the feathers, the bird's rosy skin was thin and wrinkled, almost translucent.

He sat back from the microscope for a moment and turned to her. Their faces were close. Her eyes beryl blue. Small freckles dotted her cheeks. The tiny diamond stud in her nose glittered with each nod of her head. "I am trying to understand how much birds use their own singing to sing."

He leaned in again and looked into the scope. With his right hand, he turned the focus knob. "If I understand auditory feedback in birds, I might understand how song is learned and memorized and then forgotten. Right now, it's all unknown. I mean, is it recorded like a music score, note by note? Or is it laid down in one big chunk, and if you lose it, the whole thing is gone forever?"

The same questions could be applied to human memory, he thought. No one knew how memories were formed, let alone why some parts of life became embedded in intense, beautiful, and sometimes even unwanted detail, whereas other moments, days or years, just slipped away like the hairs from a head?

With his left hand he pulled the bird's skin taut and now he could see the hollow bones and tissues below the skin. With the tip of the forceps, he punctured a hole below the bird's rib cage and inserted a short piece of clear plastic tubing into one of the bird's air sacs. One stitch and some surgical glue, and he would be able to record the bird's breathing, breaths in and breaths out.

"What's that for?" she asked.

"Breathing patterns change during song. This tube in the air sac will tell us whether he is singing or just breathing normally, even if he does not make a sound."

She was quiet.

"Come, look through this ocular. You'll see better." He repositioned his ocular higher up on the bird's body and turned his attention to its chest. As he worked, the instruments, Q-tips, forceps, scissors, appeared and disappeared from view.

"It's interesting," she said, "when I'm looking into the scope with this tunnel vision, the lab gets louder. I hear the birds singing around us more clearly."

Anton made a straight slit, and suddenly, they were looking down into the red insides of a bird's chest, the tendons pulsing rapidly with each breath.

"He's beautiful," she said.

He positioned the pins through one side of the tissue, into the syrinx, the bird's voice box, and out the other side. His right fingers stopped moving. He took a Q-tip and dabbed at the blood.

"The pins keep the flaps from vibrating when air is pushed past. No vibrations, no song. Afterward even though the bird can't make sound, he will try to sing. I'll record his muscle movements and respiration as he silently beaks."

"Isn't it like cutting out a person's tongue?"

"No," he searched for the words, "more like long-term laryngitis. Later, I think I can take out the pins and make the muting go away, and when he sings again, after not hearing himself for a long time, I can see whether he is singing his old song. I can see how much song memory he lost when he couldn't hear himself."

He felt a touch on his arm, her fingers lightly clasping around his bicep. Unsure of what this meant, he continued working.

"I wish I could do this on humans. We know nothing about memory." With forceps he brought the bird's sticky skin back together and then began to stitch the wound closed with black silk thread. More than ever, he willed this bird not to die. He tied off the final stitch and with tiny scissors snipped the black thread just above the knot. He removed the bird from the anesthesia funnel, took a deep breath and leaned back in the chair. It was the second time he'd done it. Hearing her shallow breaths, Anton was afraid to look at her. Her hand still around his bicep, they waited together for the bird to wake.

"You know," he said, "they say that babies can hear in the womb, that the waves of a mother's voice travel through skin and fluid." Finally, the bird flicked its foot, uncurled a toe and quivered on the table. He turned to her then and she slid her hand from his arm. "They also say that hearing is the last sense to go at death." Her eyes were glassy, as if from exhilaration, and he knew that like her, his own brow and upper lip were also dotted with sweat.

The next morning Rebecca hurried down the long hall to the sound-proof room to check on the muted bird, passing refrigerator-sized machines, all humming and purring at their own frequencies, the sounds of shaking and jiggling, the soft clinking of glass flasks being agitated on electrical stir plates. Sometimes other researchers greeted her as they passed in the hallway, more often they nodded silently, while some never even managed that but averted their eyes at the last second as if they were strangers on a city street rather than people who worked together daily. She had learned to meet their silence with silence, countered their bent heads with her own. The bulk and purr of the machines, the faces of the other people, had become familiar. Non-communication, a comfortable habit. She didn't need to talk with them because she knew what they were doing when they opened the massive subzero freezers or when they slipped tubes of liquid into the centrifuge circle. They hoped that the bits of blood, protein and flesh they carried in their gloved hands back to the labs, would reveal secrets about the inner workings of the mind.

She unlocked the experimentation room with her identification card. The acoustics inside the foam-lined room were altered. Sounds were absorbed, echoes lost. There were three birds: a starling, a robin and "Blue 27," the muted zebra finch who had not yet sung. The microphone was angled toward the cage, the amplifier stacked on top of the computer, everything was set to go. All they needed was for "Blue 27" to get excited and try to sing. So far, he'd refused.

The door behind her opened and Anton stepped in and smiled at her. Because the microphone was sensitive and because it was important to have as little background noise as possible, neither spoke. Anton unplugged the wires coming from the bird's backpack, untwisted them and plugged them back into the amplifier again. Since it had turned five circles since the previous afternoon, the wires had gotten tangled up and needed to be unwound. Anton leaned in to the screen as he clicked through the empty computer files.

Rebecca began to feed the birds. A few moments later, she felt Anton's fingers on the nape of her neck. She turned to him and he brushed her cheek lightly, and then quickly, he leaned toward her and touched his lips firmly to her forehead. When he moved back he placed his index finger to his mouth, backed up, and left the room, clicking the door softly behind him.

Rebecca stood still and alone in the soundproof room. The stuffiness of the small space usually reminded her of the dark room, making her sweat so that most days she came in and out as quickly as possible, but today, the excitement of Anton's kiss overpowered the fear.

The muted zebra finch, as if frustrated and desperate with his condition, ruffled up his feathers, opened his beak and let out a series of soft, almost imperceptible toots. Wave-like traces rushed across the computer screen, the measure of inhalations and exhalations that always accompanied song. The bird closed his scarlet beak and the respiration lines returned to their regular pattern: lines swooping down for inhalations, up for exhalation. He ruffled once again, opened his beak and sang a series of almost silent syllables once more. She felt a sense of elation, though she couldn't be sure whether it was because Anton's experiment had worked, and the bird seemed unharmed or because of the fact that she could now rush to deliver him the good news in his office.

"Your bird has begun to sing."

"Shoot."

"No," she said. "I don't mean sing as in sound. I mean sing as in trying to sing, opening and closing the beak."

Anton jumped out of his chair and rushed to the soundproof room. She followed him and waited as he clicked the mouse and reviewed the recorded files. "Yes! The bird's song is silent. David will not believe this!"

He looked at her. "We did it!" He wrapped his arms around her, picked her up for a split second and kissed her on each cheek. They stood close looking at each other, and in the next instant, lips touched lips and tongue met tongue. Next to them, "Blue 27" breathed out another silent song.

MEMORY

The lights inside the laboratory made it brighter than the overcast day outside. Zebra finches tooted at one another, scattered seeds, flitted up and down. A male, wired for research, hopped along the perch in his cage and cocked his head. He twisted around, faced backwards and then twisted back again. Ample food, water, predictable temperatures. Regular daylight. Regular darkness. The hum of computers, keyboards and human talk, all familiar sounds to generations of birds accustomed to life in the laboratory.

Outside, a flock of waxwings landed in a serviceberry tree, their plump bodies and crested heads scattered among the branches. A male called out a high zeee whistle. A female tipped her head, answered the call with her own, and flew up. With a red berry in his beak, the male hopped toward her, turned his head to the left and presented her with the berry. She leaned in and took it into her beak and then hopped away. At the end of the branch she turned and hopped back with the berry once more. The male inched closer, accepted the berry when she offered it, mimicked her dance to the opposite end of the branch and returned. Around them, the other waxwings made hissy, high-pitched whistles. The sun was low in the sky. The valley stretched beyond them. The two birds passed the berry back and forth a few more times, and then, quite suddenly, the male swallowed the berry and the entire flock took flight into the gray afternoon light.

Zugunruhe. From German. *Zug* meant movement or migration; *Unruhe* was for anxiety, restlessness. *Zugunruhe* was everything a bird did before migration. After the fat had been added to muscle, the restlessness began. It was the energy before flight, the anticipation of mating season. It was what made the robins crazy to sing. And then months later, when the days got shorter and the singing stopped, when the babies had—alive or dead—left the nest, *zugunruhe* described a bird's behavior before it flew back to its wintering ground. It was an orientation towards a home, either north or south. It was a frenetic jumping, hopping, a mad fluttering of wings, birds in love with life.

Anton and Rebecca spent the next seventy-two hours together, walking to the laboratory after coffee, cleaning cages, setting up experiments, checking on "Blue 27." Late at night, they raced, hungry and elated, down the hill to Anton's house. He cooked dinner. They ate and drank with the eagerness of children and then afterwards, he put on traditional Südtirolean music and taught her to dance. She loosened her hair, laughed and mimicked his moves.

He told her about the book his mother had sent him. "The birds must pass through seven valleys before they get to their god. And one is the valley of love."

"There's a valley of love?" Rebecca leaned over his shoulder. Lemon. Always the scent of lemon. She nuzzled against his neck but she was too close to his ear and he couldn't decipher her muffled words, only felt her gently bite down on his ear lobe. She leaned in and kissed him, holding her lips to his for a long moment and then they moved a few inches apart. She ran her hand over the scar on his cheek.

"What's this from?"

"Guitar."

"How?"

"I was sixteen, tightening a guitar string. It snapped and hit my face just here." He didn't tell her that his mother hadn't even noticed. "Now I have sound vibration forever imprinted on my skin."

"It's not very obvious."

He pulled her close. "I like to think it's like the dots and dashes of Morse code, comprehensible only to those who bother to learn the code."

They stared into one another's eyes in the evening light, not speaking, just touching. There was a freedom in their togetherness, a mutual relaxation, an implicit understanding that neither had experienced before, as if they were a set of mirrors, seeing themselves anew, seeing how the other could see. They did not begin, as some lovers do, to tell each other of their pasts. Setting their conversations only in the hungry immediacy of the present, the past was left to involuntary recall.

When Anton turned eighteen, his father took him out for a night on the town. He would have avoided the evening if he'd been given some warning, but there was no one to warn him. His mother was in Africa, absent as she was so often during those years and his grandmother was surely oblivious to the plan. They were to go to dinner, which they did, and to a movie, which they did not. Instead of a film, he took Anton to a hotel outside the city, where he ordered more drinks, and as it turned out, women.

The women were in their thirties. Forward. Uninhibited. One woman sat on Anton's father's lap at the bar, her skirt high up on her leg, her lips red, as if she were acting a clichéd part in a movie. Anton disliked her immediately. He'd never seen his father with a woman and couldn't imagine him liking a person so different from his mother, who was reserved, sophisticated, smart. The other woman drank, smiled, and laughed at whatever Anton's father said. Anton didn't speak.

Anton remembered protesting when his father told him they'd be staying the night. Pushing him into a room, he said, "What's wrong? You a fag?" Anton remembered the woman, who both scared and excited him. Breasts. Wetness. The scent of fusty, overly-perfumed sweat. It was all over quickly. Afterward, she laughed and caressed his face as if he were a child. He slapped her hand away. She continued laughing and left the room. There was knocking on his father's door. Anton got up, showered and then got back into bed, lying awake long into the night, overwhelmed by a rage that surfaced toward his mother. And then he fell asleep.

The next morning, the women were gone. He and his father breakfasted in the hotel restaurant, coffee and toast, read the newspaper and then drove back home in silence. The mutual, but awful, experience was concluded by a hard thud delivered by his father onto his back as they entered into the house. Anton could not say now what she had looked like. Whether she'd been tall or short, blond or dark. Until Rebecca, he had associated sex with that night, sex with shame and anger. The memories, fragmented by wine, whiskey and a will to forget, could still make him shudder.

Anton woke from a dream and found Rebecca beside him, her fingers lightly touching his arm.

"I fell asleep," he said.

"I know." She smiled at him.

"I was dreaming."

"Was it bad?"

"Yes. How did you know?"

"You twitched. Your face was sad. What was it?"

"I think it came from the book I've been reading. In the dream, I was in the book, going through the valleys with the birds, but I got stuck in one place. It's hard to explain now, but it was really frightening. There were parrots but they didn't act like parrots; they buzzed around like flies and I kept having to duck out of the way so that they couldn't bombard me."

"Like Hitchcock's movie?"

"Sort of, but the parrots were yelling. They told me that I would never be able to leave, that I would suffer, that I would have misfortunes, that I would fail."

"You're not going to fail. Besides, that's why we say 'it was just a dream,' right?"

"Indeed," he said. "Just dreams." Strife and grief. What was the dream trying to tell him? That he had to stay in the United States? He couldn't give up on the muting. That he didn't really have a choice? He pulled her close. "Please stay with me tonight."

She inched closer to him. "I'm going to stay with you every night."

Rebecca spent the week at Anton's apartment, but he didn't want David to know.

"I think he is alone." They were eating cheese and olives at the kitchen table. "Only the laboratory and birds, nobody at home. Someone told me that his wife moved out." Anton leaned over and kissed her. "I am afraid David will be jealous."

She laughed. "Anton, he doesn't even look at me."

"I am Italian and male. I know things you cannot."

"I thought you were Südtirolean."

"In this, we are all the same." He held an olive up to her lips and she took it into her mouth. "Women, I think, understand very little about men. Like boys, we do not know how to handle feelings. Jealousy is a dominant gene. The weaker the man, the more he needs power. Our parents learned this during WWII: Hitler, Stalin, Mussolini."

"Hard for me to see how Mussolini applies. We're talking about a bird laboratory and a boss who doesn't much notice me, not international history."

"Very relevant." He popped an olive into his mouth, talking around the pit. "Question of scale."

"Scale?"

"In Tuscany, there is a village called San Gimignano up on a hill and surrounded by a stone wall. When you go there, you see towers." He spit the seed into his fist. "There are maybe twenty towers today, but one time this village had one hundred towers. Each family showed their riches by building towers taller than their neighbors, and sometimes they had fights tower to tower. Everybody who goes to this village today laughs at those people, their small view and all that money put into building pointless towers, but I think nothing has changed." He took a sip of wine. "Every man likes a tower."

She rolled her eyes. Anton went into the living room, came back and handed her a book. She looked at the title. *Theory of Sexual Selection*. "What's this?"

"Everything you need to know about men, and it will tell you why male California quail have the curled feathers on their foreheads, which you like."

"Great. A guide book to birds and men."

Anton left her at the table with the book while he began chopping an onion for dinner. "It's what I'm telling you about San Gimignano. A biological explanation for men and towers. Why we should not say anything to David."

She opened the book and glanced at the pictures of birds.

"Besides," Anton continued, "American men are even more childlike than Europeans."

"How so?"

"They play games. In the laboratory where I did my first post-doc they had this small basketball hoop stuck to the door. The students and the professor had competitions every day tossing a ball into the basket. They hooted and clapped and slapped each other."

"Did you play?"

"In the beginning, yes. Later, I made excuses." American men didn't know how to sit and talk, share a story, a cup of olives and a beer. They passed one another quietly in the hallways, only coming verbally alive with their hoots during games, needing these physical activities to break tension, bond and reestablish dominance. He had always secretly chided them for their adolescent manners, but lately, he'd begun to think there might be advantages to their stunted maturity. A certain freedom. He'd written to his mother:

> *I like the Americans. They're curiously free, almost childlike, not hemmed in by a sense of cultural history or historical responsibility. I wouldn't want to live here forever, but there is a certain creativity that can come with this naiveté, this release from history. The food, by the way, is only good when I cook.*

"Don't you ever have the urge to let them go?" Rebecca asked.

Anton had lost himself in the memory of the letter to his mother. "Who? The Americans?"

She laughed. "No. The birds: zebra finches, sparrows, canaries, let them go."

There was a sudden sting in his eyes so he stopped mincing the pungent onions and turned toward her. "Of course not. These are domesticated birds. They haven't been free for generations. They would fly straight for the windows and break their necks."

"Right, but maybe they shouldn't be subjected to experiments and small cages."

He turned back to the stove. "A cage is a cage." He scraped the onions from the cutting board into the oil. There was a loud sputtering and then a low sizzle.

"What does that mean?"

"To some extent, aren't we all in a cage?"

"I'm not talking metaphorically," she said.

"Suffering is relative."

"Relative to what?" she asked.

"You're questioning whether we have the...right?"

"Yes, I guess I am."

He was silent for a moment. It seemed impossible to say it well in English, but really, it was simple. "Humans are a species, one of millions on the earth. We just happen to have unique technological and intellectual abilities. Big brains, opposable thumbs, curiosity and consciousness. We have the right to appropriate these abilities and skills just as any other animal does, just as any other animal would be expected to do."

She took a sip of wine and was quiet for a few moments. "I don't think that's right."

"What is right?" He added garlic to the pan, stirred and waited for her to answer, and when she didn't, he turned down the stove, went over to her, lifted her chin and kissed her. "This is right, no?"

She smiled. He went back and added chopped tomatoes and basil to the sauce. A few moments later she asked.

"Do you think they're saying anything to each other?"

"The birds?"

"Yes."

"What do you mean saying something? Like humans? Talking?"

She nodded.

"No, I don't think so. But you know, everyone wants to think they do. Aesopus, Democritus, Anaximander and Tiresias were all supposed to have understood the singing of birds. Francis of Assisi quieted loud birds. In the Talmud, Solomon is wise because God lets him understand bird language. There is the same idea in folk stories, the hero is given a gift so that he can understand birds, and the birds, like magic, save him from danger or lead him to treasure." He poured the pasta into the boiling water. "There is something sacred about language, I think. We need to communicate. People hope that birds, because they sing and fly up to the heavens, will bring us closer to god. And god will help us understand."

She cocked her head as she thought. "I don't know. I think there is something more to them."

"You're not alone. In Sufism, the language of birds is magical." He went to the living room, came back with the book his mother had sent and flipped through the first pages. "First the birds decide they need a king, but they don't know how to find one. The hoopoe bird..."

"Hoopoe? Seriously, that's the name of a bird?"

"Yes, a funny bird. Later I'll show you a picture. You find it in Africa, and in summer, in Europe. This hoopoe wants to be leader, and he tells the birds that they must go on a long trip to get to their god. The birds agree that the hoopoe should be the leader, but then they all get scared and say they cannot go on the trip. The finch is frightened. The heron loves the sea. The nightingale can't leave his love. On and on. The hoopoe says no, no, they must go. It's funny. He tells the duck: *Your life is passed/In vague, aquatic dreams which cannot last.* Finally, after all the bird species have complained and the hoopoe has told them they must go, they agree to the trip."

The poem could just as well be talking about doing science as finding the way to god.

> *How featureless the view before their eyes,*
> *An emptiness where they could recognize*
> *No makers of good or ill—a silence where*
> *The soul knew neither hope nor blank despair.*

As he read to Rebecca, Anton thought about the fact that he had no idea whether the zebra finches would tell him anything about memory. He had no assurance that the muting would be the tool he needed to demonstrate that engrams existed. He just hoped that it would be. He saw nothing of the emptiness ahead. Nor how that emptiness would obscure his ability to recognize the makers of good or ill in his life.

Rebecca crouched down and peered into the bird's cage. She'd been checking on "Blue 27" every few hours for a couple of days and each time he seemed increasingly pathetic. He acknowledged her presence by hopping left and right and then sometimes by opening his beak to try to sing. Was he protesting what had been done to him? Or singing to her? What was he saying?

"Anthropomorphizing," is what Anton and David called it but she didn't care what they said. She knew the bird wasn't human but that didn't change anything. He was trying to communicate and she was trying to listen. It was much the same between people. Anton was trying to communicate and she was trying to listen, and in turn, he was listening to her and she was regaining her courage to speak. She wasn't sure what to do with all these thoughts because on the one hand, she was thrilled. They'd done it together, and in the doing they'd become a team, spending every hour of every day together, and when she was with him she felt new and confident, the Chicago photographer far away. On the other hand, what they'd done together was in front of her with a backpack wired up and out the top of a cage, hopping and turning around on himself, perhaps struggling as much as she to understand. What they'd done together had made a bird mute.

Chicago. Sometimes she wondered whether she might have grown to like the city. She might have learned to withstand the biting wind that blew off the lake in winter, picking at her face and freezing her nose. Or the wet that chilled her even in bed. She would have accustomed herself to the skyscrapers, reticent soldiers along the lake, if it weren't for that one night.

She had grown up with persistent feelings of constraint, spending her teenage years arguing loudly with her parents about vegetarianism, politics and the proper vocation for herself while making quiet plans to escape. During the summer, when the population in town tripled, she worked as a waitress. She listened to the tourists, the cadence of their German, French, Spanish, Japanese and other languages she couldn't identify, and wondered what they were saying. She noticed how slowly they ate, how much they conversed, the way the women seemed to inhabit as much space as the men. She saved her money, and to her parents' dismay and parting words of discouragement, she left to study photography at the university in the capitol city. Before long, though, she discovered that the city was really only a large town, and the art department had just two photography professors who happened to detest one another. Until the Chicago photographer arrived as visiting professor, she'd felt isolated.

He was famous, had showings in San Francisco, Chicago, Europe. He commented on her work and encouraged her in a way that no one ever had. She listened carefully and then spent days trying to do what he'd suggested before running back to ask for a new opinion. Her world opened into something different. She expanded in his presence to fit her own, secret belief in herself. Around him she believed she could be out in the world and become a photographer and she might take pictures that mattered. Two weeks after he left, she agreed to follow him to Chicago.

When she first arrived in the city, they spent days touring the Art Institute where he gave her tutorials in room after room. He saw the paintings in a way that was entirely foreign to her, stepping in close, peering at the work and then talking as if he was talking not only to her but to the artist as well. She pointed to one painting after another, and for each one, he told her about the painter, the technique, the reason it was special. He would slip his hand from the nape of her neck to her back and whisper lovingly in her ear. And then in the next moment, he'd turn to look at another piece of work, gone into a world of understanding that she hoped, with his influence, she might gain access to.

In those first weeks, they zipped around town in taxis from one reception to another, arriving late when the rooms were already full of happy, brilliant people. Artists and intellectuals. Gray-haired men with green eyeglasses, young students with ripped jeans and tattoos. He introduced her as his "muse," which at first, flattered her but as the weeks went on, she noticed that people glazed over at her name, nodded their heads, but didn't make eye contact. One night, she corrected him. "Not muse, nor concubine."

She moved away from his side and situated herself within the younger group. She engaged a painter whose freckles matched her own. The photographer noticed her absence and raised his eyebrows to her from across the room. On the way home in the taxi, he laughed. "Concubine."

The next night he went out without her, suggesting she take the time to use the dark room at the house to work on her pictures. What she didn't know at first, was that he'd locked the door, but later when she'd tried to leave and realized she couldn't, she became flush with anger and fear. Her only response, she realized, was to focus on her work. He would return, she told herself, and then she would get out and then they would talk. She focused on her negatives and their development, but then he came home drunk, not stumbling, but changed, vibrating, buzzing. He swung open the door of the dark room and flipped on the light switch. "How's my concubine?"

There was a voracity about him as though he were expanding like bees spreading out from a hive and she instinctually backed away. He came toward her and reached for her face, taking her chin in his hand and raising it. "You're so pretty." He smelled of whisky.

She swatted his hand away. "You just ruined my pictures!"

He bent to kiss her and she tried to turn her head but he forced his lips to hers and pushed her mouth open, his fingers pulling hard against the corner of her mouth. He rubbed his unshaven chin against her chin. She pushed at his chest, tasting blood at the corner of her mouth. He stopped for a moment.

"What are you doing?" she said.

"I want you."

His breath was bitter. She tried to get away, but he kept her against the countertop.

"Please," she said. "You're drunk."

"I want you."

"Okay, not here. Let's go to the bed." She thought in appeasing him she was making a choice but the bed didn't soften his touch. She tried to call out but his hands clasped around her neck. She gasped. Her tongue flapped around inside her mouth. He clamped down on her throat, and then she didn't think anymore. Denied air, choking on her tongue, she struggled to breathe. Finally, with a long low grunt, he stopped, and collapsed next to her, panting.

She took a series of shallow breaths. Too afraid to move, she lay motionless until she heard the congested breaths of his sleep. When she stood her legs shook and so she steadied herself against the wall. Liquid ran down her leg. She was raw inside and out. She wanted to scream, to muster tears and cry, but she couldn't make a sound. She crept out of the bedroom, wrapped herself in a velour shawl on the couch and slept. When she woke a few hours later, she dressed and went out into the summer morning, walking for hours downtown. At midday she sat on a bench in Millennium

Park and cried. How could this have happened? He had been charming and attentive and caring. She had never considered the possibility of him being cruel as well.

A male bird presented with a female, sings automatically, a hard-wired response, biology-speak for how the genetic code can govern behavior. In the experimentation room, Anton hooked up "Blue 93" by plugging wires from his transducer into a battery and a voltage meter and then he checked to see that the bird's respiration was being recorded. He hoped "Blue 93" was a good singer. If he were, he would record his song now, mute him next week, and if he was lucky, the data would come fast. The muting was going extremely well. One more bird and he would be able to share it with David and then David would have to see how muting and auditory feedback could be used to find engrams.

He hummed as he turned on the microphone and recorder, and then whistled into the microphone to test that everything was connected properly. Satisfied, he went to collect a female zebra finch. When he slipped her into the box, she perched next to the male and gave him a peck on the head. The male made a single mee-mee call, hopped right and left. Anton stood back. Short calls were useless. He needed long songs. The female bird hopped to the male's side again. He ruffled his feathers preparing for the dance that zebra finches often did right before they sang. The female ignored him and hopped away. The male responded to her withdrawal, as if automatically, with a long song bout, singing the same motifs over and over, his wings fluttering as he danced left and right. Yes! This one was a ready singer. The horizon might include the Alps after all. Switzerland, Austria, France or Italy. He had his preference, but he wasn't going to be picky.

David returned from the symposium in Miami excited not about the prototypes for cochlear implants, but because a research group had revealed their findings on the FoxP2 gene. Known to be important, in some still undetermined way for human speech, FoxP2 had just been found in birds. Sitting in the auditorium at the conference, he'd experienced the tingling in his fingers and arms, an excitement he'd often felt as a graduate student and a post-doc, but one that had been absent for the past year, especially since Sarah had left. He in no way thought FoxP2 was "the" grammar gene in humans as the newspapers had reported it, distorting and exaggerating findings as they usually did, but its having been found in birds meant that the world of song and genetics was opening up. There was a new frontier to be explored. The "Decade of the Brain," he realized, could be followed by one specifically for language. Soon, he thought, they might begin to understand the evolution of communication itself.

He heard Rebecca out in the main laboratory busy with the morning routine. His first inclination was to get up and say hello, but they were always a bit awkward around one another when they were alone. He would wait until Anton arrived.

While he'd been gone, the laboratory had been organized and cleaned as if they were preparing for an inspection. Research equipment had been put away in neatly labeled drawers, the black counters had been wiped clean, and the seeds swept up from the floor. The birds had never been cared for so well, the cages cleaned and lined with newspaper folded neatly into perfect squares at the bottom of the trays. The birds looked fit, their feathers healthy, colors lustrous, and they sang. He would make a point to tell her this.

An hour later, hearing Anton's whistling, David came out of his office. "Do I hear that it's coffee time?"

"Yes, sir. How was Miami?" Anton took down two mugs.

"Tropical breezes, girls in bikinis, mangos on the beach."

"Like I thought," Anton said, "you never left the hotel."

David laughed. As it turned out, he hadn't needed to leave the hotel. "What about here? You're looking particularly happy and healthy."

"Healthy?"

David stepped back and looked Anton up and down. "Yes. There's a sort of glow to you. Anything new?"

Anton shrugged his shoulders and poured the coffee. "Just—what do you always say—baby steps that add up over years."

David laughed again. Anton had taken on some of his expressions and they sounded amusing in his accented English. He told Anton about the newest results in deafness, implants and the genetics of birdsong, hoping that the FoxP2 might distract Anton from his interest in engrams and memory.

"I thought you weren't interested in human applications," Anton said.

It was true. FoxP2 and cochlear implants weren't the only reasons for David's enthusiasm. At the conference, he'd watched a woman interpreting for the deaf. Of course, this was nothing new; there were always interpreters at these conferences. He even knew a bit of Sign Language because he'd studied it at Sarah's urging.

Sign language appeals to me, she'd said. It flips our assumptions, puts more effort on the person watching, or listening, than the speaker.

But there's a reason no one chooses that form of communication, he'd told her, unless they're forced to. It's unnatural for us given we can speak and hear.

Come on, it can be our private language.

They'd gone to enough classes to pick up the basics, and he understood more than he could sign, but in the end he wasn't motivated. Harder than learning a foreign spoken language, he knew there was no way he'd ever become fluent. Besides, they weren't children and they didn't need a secret language.

The young interpreter had coal black hair pulled into a short ponytail and was dressed in a white blouse, a beige knee-length skirt, no socks and red tennis shoes. Besides her odd tennis player outfit, what drew his attention was the way she used her body to sign. Her hands moved, of course, and often her lips. That was normal but she also used her cheeks, eyes and eyebrows too. His attention repeatedly slid away from the projector screen toward her in the shadows on the side of the stage. He listened to the speaker but watched her. She swayed left or right with the words. A zebra finch song became a jutting out of elbows. A canary's long trill was a hand to her ear and then a fluttering of the eyes. When she meant to emphasize a point, she lightly stamped her foot. Her rising eyebrows alerted the listener to the main points, the summary statements, what the speaker believed were his most interesting results. She gave motion to the speaker's intentions.

Afterwards, when he caught up with her outside the conference hall, her shirt was damp, beads of perspiration speckled her hairline as if she'd just walked off the tennis court after a strenuous match, which incidentally, he thought, she would have won.

"Is this your first time?" he asked. Guessing at her age, he interpreted the perspiration as nerves.

She laughed, her flushed face smiling. "No. I've been doing it forever." She dabbed at her forehead with a tissue. "It takes a lot out of me, though."

He was surprised at the slight lilt to her speech. "Not American?"

"Half-breed." She plopped into a chair. "My mother is American, deaf. My father, Lebanese, deaf, but we left Lebanon when I was sixteen."

"That explains it."

She crossed one leg over the other, raised her eyebrows and waited.

"The native signing, the slight accent in English. You look thirsty. Can I bring you some water?"

She nodded. When he came back with the plastic cup of water, she took it and drank it in one swallow. People were still trickling out of the auditorium in groups of two and three. The importance of the FoxP2 paper from the day before was being debated around industrial-sized coffee pots. Camps were forming. There were those who believed FoxP2 to be the holy grail, the genetic tool that would allow bird research to flourish as mice research had, and there were the skeptics who cautioned restraint. Tomorrow there would be break-out sessions to discuss the implications of the gene. Normally, David would be standing side by side with them at the coffee pots, debating as well.

"I recognize most of the interpreters here. That's why I thought you were new."

She shook her head. "Not new, just lazy. I only work a few months a year."

"What do you do the rest of the time?"

She laughed. "I live." She glanced at her watch. "Show time."

He hadn't planned on going to the next session, but he followed her and watched her move with the words, mimic the sounds and lack of sounds with her body. Her trance-like exhaustion returned him to a nagging question, and he began to wonder about effort and cost. At the end of the session, David's brain was in hyper mode. He often watched male zebra finches move down the perch toward a female, swinging their bodies left and right and grasping and then un-grasping their toes as they went. They would stop in front of the female, ruffle their feathers, cock their heads one way and sing. Did that hopping, courtship dance, which he'd always ignored, have anything to do with their song? How much energy might the dance take? Did it add to the cost of singing? These were the thoughts he was thinking when he noticed that she was also looking at him. When she signed "follow me," he stood up and followed.

"You were watching me," she said.

"Not a hard thing to do." He blushed.

They made their way through the crowd of scientists, people identified by name, institution and rank with white nametags pinned to their chests. They waited at the elevator, looking at one another before glancing at the mirrors flanking the doors, each watching the other's reflection.

"You understand sign language?" she asked.

"Some." He hoped she didn't ask why or where he'd learned.

Inside the elevator she pressed the button for floor ten. "It's the perfect job for me. I sign better than I speak. The direction is natural." They walked down the hallway and she stopped at the door of her room. "A drink." It wasn't a question, just the utterance of a confirmation, something already understood between them.

Once at her room, she gave him options: vodka, whisky or gin. He chose gin, she drank whisky. Quickly, he noticed. She excused herself to the bathroom. He took in the room, incredibly bland, marveling at how it countered his state, the excitement he'd felt during the previous day's sessions about FoxP2 and now with her. When she came out a few minutes later, her hair still in a short pony tail, she was dressed in a robe and then, as if she'd known him for months, she slipped it off.

Shocked at her naked body in front of him, he began to speak, the beginnings of an utterance, but she quickly raised her fingertips to his lips. "No." she signed. "Undressed, no talking allowed."

She held out her hand for him. He stood. She smiled, unbuttoned his shirt, undid his belt, removed his pants, his shoes. She pulled back the bedspread and sheets, signed "lie down." He stretched out cautiously on his back. She sat next to him on the edge of the bed. She spoke slowly, signing out what he should do, how he should touch her, how she planned to touch him. These were the words he understood. There were other phrases he was less sure about, and might have imagined: Mouth over you, your tongue in me. And there were movements he didn't recognize as words, the way she brushed her fingertips over herself, touched her own breast, her lips. He reached out and took her hands in his, stopped her from saying more. They remained motionless for a moment longer, her sitting on the bed next to his prone body, hand in hand, eyes on eyes. Language rendered useless.

The intensity of this memory created a quick flush in David's body. He took another sip of coffee, shook it off and focused back on what he'd been telling Anton.

"A family, the KE family, was brought to some British scientists. For over three generations about half the people in this family can't speak properly. Their speech is essentially unintelligible and they're taught sign language instead."

"What's wrong with them?"

"It's incredible, a single mutated gene."

"A single gene controlling speech?"

"That's what the Brits said and so the popular press and science magazines were swarming all over the conference. They were calling it the language or grammar gene."

"But you don't believe that?"

"No, of course not. There can't be one gene for grammar or language, just like there can't be a single answer for memory." David's voice went up an octave, "Engrams do not exist."

Anton didn't respond.

"Seriously Anton. Anyway, it doesn't need to be *the* language gene to be interesting. What's cool is that this gene has a forkhead, and the fork codes for a transcription factor and because transcription factors turn things on and off, it has the potential to affect the expression of *a lot* of genes."

"And?"

"Having a mutant means there's the potential for experimentation. Once the research progresses a bit further, we might be able to use FoxP2 in our auditory feedback experiments." David laughed. "You should have been there, though. It was a feeding frenzy. The reporters were saying they found the reason for the evolution of humans. Supposedly, this gene enabled us to speak, which in turn allowed us to evolve into the superior creatures we are. Utter rubbish, but I guess everyone, not just you, Anton, is looking for some kind of holy grail."

"Not a holy grail, David. Just some data, a few published papers, maybe eventually a job and someday a vacation to one of those tropical places where I really will hang out on the beach."

David laughed and set down his empty coffee cup. He thought of Sarah. "Vacations are overrated."

David woke in the faint blue gleam of his office, taking a moment to remember where he was. He lay for a few more seconds allowing his eyes to adjust before unzipping his sleeping bag and getting up from the cot. He didn't think that anyone knew he slept in his office two or three nights a week and he preferred to keep it that way, although if he were ever asked, he could always use the winter weather as an excuse for not driving up the snowy canyon to his home.

Outside there was a layer of late spring snow and the dark city was sparkling. From the institute, nestled in the foothills, he could see the flashing yellow lights of snowplows working their way through the streets. He loved the fleeting stillness of the laboratory when he woke in the morning knowing that in a few moments, when he flipped the light switch, the birds would come to life, fluttering and squawking. Silence to sound. And then later at night, when he turned out the lights again and there was only the glow of the computer screens, the birds would quiet once more, tucking their heads to the left or right to sleep.

He rolled up the sleeping bag, tied it, and stored it in a bottom cupboard. He folded the cot in half, balanced it against the wall and then opened his office door to keep it in place. He switched on the light and checked his watch. 6:30 a.m. He glanced at his calendar knowing already that Rebecca and the undergraduate students would come in two hours, and he noticed, once again, the unopened letter from Sarah postmarked from eastern Peru where she'd gone back in a futile search for Ed.

Taking a clean shirt and underwear from a drawer, he went through the dark lab, unlatching the double bolt quietly, careful not to disturb the sleeping birds. He walked down the hallway past the aviary and the experimentation rooms to the shower. When he returned a few minutes later, the dirty clothes bundled under one arm, the red light was flashing on his phone. He punched in his code to listen to the message.

"David, hi, it's me. Sarah. Look, I'm worried. I've been calling for months and despite the time changes, I think I've managed to call at every hour of the day. And you never answer, which means you're not at home even during the hours when you should be, which means you're working absurd hours at the lab, but now I'm calling the lab and you're not answering either." There was a pause. "And well, I don't know what that means. So please, send me an email or something and I'll try again." Another pause. "Okay?"

He heard the click of the phone and then pressed the number four so that he could listen again. Despite being in Peru, her voice sounded clear and crisp, as if she were in the next room, and as always, the clearness brought longing because it had been her voice, the timbre and cadence, that had drawn him first. As a graduate student he would arrive at class early, close his eyes and wait, trying to decipher if he could hear her coming down the hallway and entering the room. Usually she was laughing. In the beginning there was so much anticipation in knowing he would hear that voice and talk with her every day. After they'd begun living together, her verbal ease became the perfect counterpoint to his difficulties with expression, and he became so accustomed to her presence in his life that he'd never feared losing her, her voice, or the ease he felt with her. And then one day, she was gone. The machine's recording came on and he listened again and this time when he was offered the option to delete or save, he hesitated, and then without choosing anything, he hung up the phone.

His stomach growled. He needed a coffee and something to eat, but that could wait. Sarah frequently complained about his thinness. *There's nothing on you, no reserves. How is your body to keep working when you get ill?*

"I rarely get ill," he said out loud.

Once, just before they'd begun living together, he had recorded her. He'd gone to the university library where she was leading a study session for undergraduates and hidden behind a shelf of books. It was the end of the semester, the undergraduates were nervous about the final exam, and Sarah, being Sarah, felt a great deal of responsibility for them. She had always given more than anyone asked. Even with him, he realized now.

Removing a book, he spied her through the shelves in jeans, a tank top and a man's white shirt, unbuttoned, sleeves rolled up, her hair pulled back in a ponytail. He slid a small microphone through the space and then hunkered down on the stepping stool to record her speaking, then laughing. Later, he'd filtered out the other students and noises so that he was left with the purity of her voice. He had listened to it over and over late at night back then, like one listens to a great piece of music or a favorite song.

He hadn't thought of it in years. Where was that recording now? He rummaged through cabinets in his office, emptied the contents of his desk drawers onto the floor. The tape had to be somewhere. Without cleaning up what he'd dumped on the floor, he went into the conference room to scan the bookshelves. He opened the glass cupboards and looked among the scraps of old recording machines he no longer used. There was a rising anxiety at not being able to locate the tape. He tried to remember when he'd last seen it. Had it been the year or two years before? He'd found it and played it for Sarah and they had laughed at his early shy approach to her.

"You were stalking me!"

"Not you, just your voice."

"I should report you."

Out in the main laboratory he heard the canaries and zebra finches making the first tentative sounds and he remembered that he planned to record their early morning songs today. He could do it another day. The tape was more important. He opened the door to the laboratory, flipped on the lights and the birds let out a single burst of sound, their songs overlapping, mixing and then echoing off the walls and windows, creating a dissonance that mirrored his anxiety. He pulled out drawers, fumbled through their contents before slamming them shut again.

Could Rebecca have filed the tape away? He moved from one laboratory bench to another, opening each of the cupboards below the counters and looking through the shelves. The birds called, sang and fluttered against their cages just above his head. Would Rebecca have known it was something precious, not to be thrown out in one of her organizational cleanings? What if the tape was there, on one of these shelves, but in his haste, he'd missed it? He went back and looked in every cupboard again. He was sweating now, not from exertion but fear.

The birds had quieted by the time he finally gave up his search. Next to the laboratory bench, his back against the wall, he shut his eyes and tried to imagine how her voice would look if it were digitized by the computer. He could call up visual images for at least a dozen birds: harmonic stacks for zebra finch songs, trills for canaries, whistles and buzzes for white-crowned sparrows, but not her. There was the soft call from the Inca dove, the one that said *no hope, no hope*. Sarah's favorite bird. He stood and went to its cage, removed the food dish, dumped the old seeds into the trash and filled the dish to the brim with new seeds. Back in his office he sat down, and for the first time since he was a boy, he cried.

David remembered how much Sarah wanted them to visit Ed in Peru. There was no reason not to take the trip, but he hesitated. "I can't. I've got all this stuff to finish. A grant deadline coming up. A paper to submit. You go."

And so Sarah had flown to Los Angeles and from there to Lima. In Lima she boarded a small plane that went up, stopped briefly in the Andes and then down into the forest at Puerto Maldonado. For the first time in years, they did not have daily contact. David rose alone in the morning, fed the birds at home and went to the laboratory, relieved that he could remain there for however long he liked. Other than knowing the date and arrival time of her flight, he gave little thought to her return. He had assumed that the space between them was temporary.

When Sarah came back from Peru she said, "The forest sounds like a mess of jumbled noises, but Ed can distinguish them all."

"I'm not surprised." *It's the only place where I can forget myself,* Ed once said. *Everything falls away, and I simply become ears that hear.*

"He's so gregarious. You know the weird thing? He speaks Spanish, fluently. Of course, if I'd ever thought about it, I would have expected him to, but before getting off the plane in Maldonado, I'd never heard him say a word in anything other than English. Have you?"

"Come to think of it, no," David said.

"It's really beautiful. The first morning I went into the forest just as the sky was beginning to lighten and within a few minutes there was this explosion. A bunch of parrots came flying over me. You can't imagine how loud they are. Skinner is one thing, but all of these together is quite another. A blitz of sound unlike anything I've ever experienced. Awful really. I don't know how any animal can hear another."

As he listened to Sarah talking about her trip, the towering trees, the mud, the jaguar tracks they saw early one morning, David's mind kept shifting, two conversations merging, Sarah's voice and phrases from Ed in the past.

"Intimacy is established so quickly," Ed had said. "Perhaps it's the humidity or the small groups, or the isolation. People come immediately closer."

David imagined Ed, his eyes continuously scanning the skies, casually noting when a bird passed by. He imagined Sarah watching him as they motored up the river. He wondered about sudden intimacies.

"He asked about you," she said, "and I told him that you're focusing on neurons, trying to get to the smallest unit so that you can understand the initial generation of song."

"And what did Ed say?"

"He said you're the best at what you do."

Once Ed had told David about the time he brought a wealthy man and his son up the Tambopata River. "Finnish or maybe Norwegian. I can't remember. They were quiet, shy people, hardly speaking with one another and so I didn't try to force the conversation. We'd gone about two hours upriver, the boat cutting through water, the sky hazy, the green forest to each side, when all of a sudden, the driver cut the motor and said my name. I turned and saw that a male jaguar had positioned himself out on a big snag over the water. He was relaxing with one paw over the other, eyes half closed. I could see his eyelashes. We were that close! In thirteen years in the tropics, seeing footprints occasionally, I'd never seen the real thing, and here he was. I took about five hundred pictures in thirty seconds. The Finnish. You know what they did? They took out their cameras, clicked a couple of shots, looked through their binoculars and smiled over at me. I don't think they had any idea what they were looking at. I think they thought this was normal. You know, you go to the tropics and it's like going to the zoo. You see animals. You take pictures. You buy a hotdog and go home."

"Are you listening to me?" Sarah asked.

"Of course." David refocused on what she was saying.

"I was saying that I felt weirdly lonely there. Small, but a different kind of small than I feel around mountains."

"Ed once told me that the rainforest was the one place in the world where he didn't feel lonely," David said.

Sarah was silent for a moment and then she began to cry.

"Sarah, what is it?" He reached out for her, putting his hand on her shoulder, but she shook her head and stepped away.

"It's nothing, sorry. I'm tired. It was a long trip. I think I need to get a good night's sleep."

That night she had slept in the spare bedroom.

In the small conference room off the laboratory, David sketched a diagram on the white board. Rebecca and the undergraduate students, Sasha and Stephanie, sat at the table, blank pieces of paper before them and waited while he drew. He turned to face them.

"Nerve pulses originate here in the HVC." He circled the region on his sketch in red and drew arrows over what he'd just drawn, outlining the pathways that controlled vocalization. "What we hear as song starts out as information passed as action potentials from one group of cells to another. These electrical impulses travel in super speed down the axon from cell to cell." He circled the HVC region again. "So, the action potentials start here in the HVC, pass to the RA, and then to the syringeal motor nucleus in the brain stem, which then sends a signal along this motor neuron to flex the muscles around the syrinx."

He glanced at them. Stephanie and Sasha nodded their heads, but looked lost. Rebecca, as usual, was following without difficulty. He began to re-label the diagram, spelling out high vocal center for HVC, sketching out a new image of the trachea that branched into the syrinx.

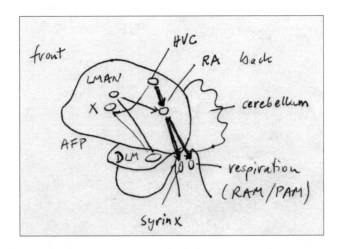

"The bird's syrinx is like your larynx," he told them. "When you exhale to speak, air is pushed from your lungs past flaps of skin in your larynx. The flaps vibrate and create waves of sound."

"Here, Rebecca," he said, placing his fingers softly against the front of her throat. "Pretend you're in a doctor's office. Say 'aaaa.'"

She voiced "aaaa." He lifted her hand from the table and exchanged her fingers for his. "Do you feel the buzz?" She nodded. The other students began to "aaaa" as well.

"The buzz comes when the vocal folds partly cover the opening in the larynx called the glottis. Now make the sound lower. Now higher."

The students did as they were told.

"For lower frequencies, the flaps are further apart, vibrating more slowly. For higher frequencies, they come close together and move very fast."

Whether in humans or birds, every exhalation was a potential sound. The folds pulled in and vibrated. Or they did not. But unlike in humans, in birds the right and left sides of the syrinx could be controlled separately by nerves coming from left and right sides of the brain. David could snip a bird's left syringeal nerve and instantly, the low frequency sounds were gone and the bird's song shifted higher.

"From the syrinx," he continued, "waves of air travel up and out the beak." He drew a blue line for air from the syrinx, up through the trachea and out the beak. "Beaks function something like our mouth, tongue and lips to filter out certain frequencies, to create resonance." He noticed that Rebecca had straightened herself in her chair. "Beaks held wide open enhance high pitched sounds. When the beak is more closed, the sounds are lower."

His ultimate goal was larger. It was true that he wanted to know how a bird sang, how the impulse to make sound had been organized throughout millions of years of evolution, how air was pushed past the syrinx making it vibrate, but those were only the technical parts of the story, the relatively easy things to know, the questions he could pose in grant proposals and be sure, at least up until this year, to secure funding for. These were the questions that had kept his laboratory running for the last decade, kept the students busy with projects, but not the ones that kept him awake at night, not the ones that had drawn him to biology.

As a teenager he had walked a daily loop around his neighborhood. Behind the row of new houses, there was a field of undeveloped land bordered by a copse of trees, a small stream and a pond, the relics of a farmer's property. He knew what he was likely to see and hear, knew at which spots the chipmunks and squirrels would rattle at him, which thrushes would flush from the ground as he approached. But some days there were surprises. Once he came upon the pond and found a purple gallinule standing still, one bright yellow leg bent, the other in the water. He stood frozen and watched as the gallinule made its way across the pond, poking its head into the water to eat, staying until the bird stretched its iridescent wings and took off. The next day he set out with great hope to see the bird again, but it was "an accidental," a bird blown off course. He would have to wait until graduate school in the south before he would see a gallinule again.

"Rebecca, I have a project for you," he said later that day.

"The aviary? I cleaned it yesterday."

"No, a research project. You can do more than clean cages. You ask good questions and you're good at handling the birds. I have to go to New

York to give a seminar but when I return, I have a project for you about the cost of song."

"What do you mean, cost?"

"Probably one of the biggest unanswered questions in birdsong. Imagine you're a male bird singing to attract a female. How much oxygen and energy does it cost for you to serenade?

"It would depend on the lyrics, wouldn't it?"

David smiled. She had the same freshness, ebullience, curiosity about the world, and raw smarts as Sarah.

"True. That's what people have been looking for. Song structure, complexity, but what if structure doesn't matter? I mean what's probably more important are the indirect costs, not the oxygen consumed, but every moment spent singing is one less moment for foraging or nest building. Not to mention the fact that every time he sings, he's giving up his location to the predators."

"I get that, but what I meant was," Rebecca said, "maybe a trill is more expensive than a whistle."

David looked at her again. No one had ever considered the cost of different syllable types, and he didn't have any idea how he'd test such a thing, but she'd made him think. "Interesting," he said. "Very interesting. I'll think about how to test that on the plane tomorrow and we'll get started when I get back."

At five hundred miles an hour, the plane burned through the clouds, the jet engines leaving a trail of iced water behind. Stanley Sommers, his friend from their post doc years, had invited him to New York for a seminar. Outside the window he saw white.

He had just read that women preferred men with lower voices, especially around their time of ovulation. A curious finding. The evolutionary psychologists would have had a field day with that, concluding in their strict Darwinian way, that the preference was easily explained. In ancient humans, low voice equated with bigger men and bigger men were bound to be better protectors. As easy as that. In birds, he didn't think pitch had much to do with it but maybe trills. Yes, Rebecca reminded him of Sarah, only Rebecca was quiet where Sarah was expressive. And then he reminded himself that Sarah's gift for verbalization next to his inability to talk about his feelings, was probably half the reason she was gone. The other half, he didn't want to think about.

The airplane was trembling, bumps of turbulence, pockets of higher and lower pressure air shook the plane like a toy. He looked away from the window and closed his eyes to the shaking. Was a female bird really more attracted to one song than another? Could she tell the difference? If so, how did his singing bring her in? The shaking stopped. He opened his eyes and looked out. They had come out of the clouds and he could see the land below. At this time of year, the tilled fields of the Great Plains were dark brown sprinkled with snow. From the height of the plane it looked as though a gigantic starling in white-spotted winter plumage had spread its wings upon the earth.

David's seminar was a success, only he made the mistake of agreeing to stay with Stan, his wife, Helen, and their two children in their small New York City apartment. He was required to sit through noisy dinners in the cramped space with pre-teenagers and answer Helen, who bombarded him with questions. She asked about Sarah first, of course. David answered that she was fine. And she was. He just didn't see the need to explain that they were no longer living together, that Sarah was probably, right now, hiking through the rainforests of Peru, tanned and sweaty, some ruddy, equally sweaty man by her side. He was grateful that the two couples hadn't known one another better in Pennsylvania, the post-docs having divided out neatly into those who had children and those who did not. A lie of omission was unlikely to be found out but Helen wasn't satisfied with bland answers and kept on with more questions. Like a dog on the trail of a pungent wild pig, he wondered if she could smell his loneliness. Fortunately for David, Stan was bored with Helen's personal questions too. "So, David, let me tell you about the spin-off we've set up. You remember the paper I published in 1985? About the configurational changes to neurons during memory creation and retrieval?"

Helen excused herself.

"You mean the theoretical one about engrams that you've never been able to shore up with data?" David asked. He reached for the bottle of wine. Perhaps he'd be able to tell Anton that Sommers himself was giving up on the idea.

Stan laughed. "Right, that one. Although that's about to change too."

David set the bottle down quickly, his glass still empty. "You've got them? You've seen it happen?"

Stan was nodding. "Crystal clear. I'll show you tomorrow, but it's under the radar. This time we're going to be extra sure before we release it." Stan was smug. He reached for the bottle, took it from David's hand and refilled both their glasses.

"But that's not what I'm talking about. I'm talking about business ventures. Ever since Bayh-Dole, it's been worth our while to invest in business, only most of us didn't realize it. Now there's real *incentive*. On top of knowing you've found a way to beat big diseases, there's actual money to be made."

"I've never been interested in business spin-offs, Stan. You know that."

Stan took another sip of wine, letting a brief silence precede what he was going to say next. "We've got a new drug that enhances memory. It's passed Phase I trials and has been accepted for Phase II, and you know what, David, it really works. It's going to revolutionize the way we treat all sorts of age-related memory loss. Attention deficit disorder, too. In a couple of years Ralph and his research team will be done, dried up."

Ralph Krest, premiere neuroscientist, memory expert and Nobel Prize candidate, had said Stan's configuration theory of neuronal memory—the existence of engrams—was nothing more than wishful thinking. David had always agreed with Ralph but he'd never voiced his opinion to Stan.

The wine had made Stan more exuberant than usual. He might be getting a little ahead of himself, but his vehemently competitive spirit reminded David how pleased he was not to be Stan's direct competitor. As it was, he knew Stan felt him to be a non-threatening colleague, a smart one to be sure, but someone who'd chosen the wrong animal to study. Stan believed that unlike mice and rats, birds would never reveal the essence of the human mind.

After three days with Stan, David was sick of New York. He didn't understand how people could make it through the winter locked in by the tall buildings, the sky as grey as the wet streets. He was relieved when he boarded the afternoon flight out of JFK. Weary of questions from under-graduate and graduate students, he looked forward to the comfort of his own lab. They had asked: Where would neuroscience be in ten years? Would there still be enough subject matter for a student today to build a career on? Did he think there would be a neurological cure for Alzheimer's? He'd forced himself to answer politely, to not say what he really felt, which was he didn't know anything about an Alzheimer's cure and he didn't care that he didn't know. He didn't care about human diseases or how neuroscience could make life better. All the while he was responding to their youthful eagerness, he was hearing Stan in his pompous way.

"I tell you what you do. Forget the post-docs. You get three grad students for the price of one post-doc, four depending how your department supplements the funding, and you put them all on impossible problems. You shoot buckshot and chances are you'll bring down something."

Buckshot. He wanted to tell the students about Stan's philosophy. Don't you know you're nothing more? Go find a lab where your time and energy isn't the whim of a gambler. Sarah had never cared for Stan. *A classic narcissist. He talks about himself constantly, his research success, his new house, even his physical workout schedule!*

David didn't know whether Stan was a narcissist or not, but he definitely was a bore. What he thought now, as the plane passed over the Rockies, was that he might have told the students the truth—that the only question worth knowing was this: *How much does it cost a bird to sing and why do females think that some males sing better than others?*

Rebecca hadn't touched her camera in months but today, after she left Anton sleeping in bed and scribbled a short love note to him on the counter, she'd gone home to get it and carried it with her to the institute. She swiped her identity card through the magnetic strip and when the green light flashed, she pulled on the door and entered the cold stairwell. With a flick of her head, she knocked back the hood of her spring jacket and went up the stairs, her footsteps echoing in the hollow space, the crisp air pushing at her back. Three flights up, she opened another door and stepped into a broad hallway flanked by massive windows. This six-floored, rectangular glass building felt like a fishbowl. Down the hallway she passed four black leather chairs set around a pink granite coffee table. In the months since she'd been hired, she'd never seen anyone sitting in the chairs. Three science journals lay in a fan across the table, the cover of the top journal showed a bird singing. Outside the laboratory door she dug into her jeans pocket for a key, but even with the door closed, she could hear the muffled calls.

"Uncovering the rules of speech," was how David explained the work. She pulled on the heavy door, propped it open, and stepped around empty cardboard boxes and outdated electrical equipment.

The zebra finches, noisy, feathered holders of this speech secret, stacked two stories high along one wall of the laboratory, chattered loudly with her entrance, flitting on and off their perches, squawking, eating and fluttering, scattering seed grains everywhere. She was mesmerized by these small gray and white birds with their quick robotic movements, intrigued by their calls and songs, their necessity to make sound. *Do they understand each other at all?* Today when she was done feeding them, she would take some pictures.

She dug into her bag and pulled out the chocolate bar she'd brought for Anton. In his office, she drew a large heart on a piece of paper and placed the chocolate on top.

Back at her cubicle she took off her coat and looked out through the massive western-facing windows, glazed with gray film to protect against the afternoon sun. From this perch on the foothills she could see the entire valley: the university campus below her, the white dome of the state capitol, the Oquirrah Mountains to the west. The Great Salt Lake, on this clear morning, was a whitish blue line. She gathered her long red hair and twisted it up along the back of her head, holding it in place with two pencils from her desk, and tucked the shorter strands around her ear.

As she approached the row of cages a zebra finch opened his scarlet-orange beak to sing and the rest of the males, as if on cue, joined in, repeating the same nasal harmonic bleeps over and over. She watched them for a moment before she began to slide the cage doors up, one by one, to reach in and pull out the half-empty, plastic water containers. She drew out the seed containers too, tipping the seed hulls into the trash and then tossing all the containers into the large black sink for washing.

While the water filled the basin, she went back to one of the zebra finch cages, having noticed that one of the birds had a strange looking feather. Checking that he was okay, she raised the gate and inserted her hand. The four birds fluttered up and back, calling out against this intrusion. The entire laboratory of zebra finches joined in their anxiety. She easily cornered the bird in her palm and removed her hand, too quickly though, rubbing her wrist on the way out against a sharp wire on the cage door.

The room went quiet again. Flutter like shutter, she thought. The shutter of a camera, brought about by the pressure of her finger as she let out a breath, her left eye accepting the momentary blackness of a long blink. It had been a while since she'd assumed that posture, a while since she'd looked at the world one-eyed through a camera lens. She squinted now at the bird in her hand drawing out his wings to inspect each feather. A bead of blood had seeped from the scrape on her wrist and she brushed it away.

Being in a space with the birds these past months had made her realize how mysterious their world was. She'd become convinced that they had secrets to tell and not just about communication. She was sure of it. They were made of air. Air moving constantly through buoyant air sacs, waves vibrating through the syrinx, up the trachea and out the beak. Their hollow bones were light for travel. They were sound ruffling through feathers. Their physiology was more dinosaur than mammal. Beacons of the past, they were meant to be free.

What had Anton said? Humans had a brain and an opposable thumb and technology and just having all of that made it alright. She would ask David what he thought when he got home from New York, how he justified the rights he had and the work he did. Certainly he'd have a better way of explaining himself than Anton. More of a visual thinker than a talker, she couldn't quite put words on her thoughts, but deep within her she felt that Anton was wrong about the birds. It couldn't be as simple as he made it out to be. He had shrugged his shoulders, as if he didn't care, and said, *We're all in a cage to some extent.*

She stopped scrubbing the seed and water dishes and looked around the laboratory. She closed her eyes so that she could hear better. What were they trying so hard to say? That they should be free to live and die as they chose? Now with the muting technique, they wouldn't even be able to make sound and so she couldn't hope to understand. She felt the stirrings of a new, fiercely awful thought. A feeling of dread. She'd been wrong about someone before. What made her think that she had any more insight now? And if Anton was wrong about the birds, then was she wrong about him?

STUTTERING

David arrived home from New York in a snowstorm, brushed off his car at the airport and drove slowly up the canyon and then even more slowly for the last mile of winding road, realizing as he neared his house that the plow had once again piled the snow in front of his garage door. He spent the next hour shoveling, listening to the sounds of his heavy breaths and the blade cutting into the wet snow, thinking of the letter of complaint he would write to the company. While moving pile after pile of snow he composed it, conscious of the fact that this was as far as any letter would ever get. Once he returned to the laboratory and the salt melted the snow, his irritation would disappear and the plowman, who never got it right, would be forgotten. Until the next storm. As he shoveled, he contented himself with the thought that despite his ambition he'd never used people as Stan did, never succumbed to firing human buckshot at anything. His relationships with all his previous graduate students and post-docs were supportive and congenial.

During the summer months he was happier for this mountain home, the idea for which had come from Sarah.

"I mean really, David, can you imagine yourself pushing a lawnmower, planting a geranium?"

"Maybe not geraniums," he said, "but impatiens and irises."

She rolled her eyes at him.

"No reason to kid ourselves into thinking we'll ever be the gardening types," she continued. "The more natural the better."

It was all part of her "real" campaign, what she called authenticity psychology. She wanted to get to the basics of each person's self, scrape the layers of defensive constructs out of the way, get rid of anything that wasn't genuine.

"Grass in the West is ridiculous," she said. "It's inauthentic. I even think it might be responsible for some of the depression I'm seeing in women here."

"I hope you're not saying that in public. You might lose your license." The connection between gardens and psychology and authenticity eluded him, but he was happy not to rake, dig, mow or water. Sarah, he admitted, begrudgingly to himself as he straightened his back and appraised his midnight shoveling work, would actually write and send the letter. Sarah would fix the recurring problem of the inconsiderate snowplow.

The next morning he rose at his usual early hour and had his normal breakfast of fresh squeezed juice from three oranges and then a bowl of cereal eaten standing at the sink. When he finished, glass, bowl and spoon were rinsed and put in the half-full dishwasher, which he ran once, or at the most, twice a week. He didn't bother with coffee, waiting instead to drink a cup with Anton at the laboratory mid-morning. He dressed quickly, went down the steps into the garage and started the cold car. He let it warm a few seconds before backing it out into the dark morning, hearing the crunching of snow and ice under the tires.

Before Sarah left they'd always kept the house clean and neat and that's the way he kept it now, not out of any effort, but mostly from absence. Some days, arriving from the laboratory in the evening, the empty house surprised him, as if he'd forgotten she was gone. Maybe it was because she was so present for him during the day when he imagined her analysis of every experiment, knew the language she'd use to ask questions about his work, questions that made him think more. He talked back to her in his mind. That sort of conversation, the kind that continued even in the absence of the other person, had never happened with anyone else in his life.

He pulled onto the canyon road and shifted into a lower gear. The plows had not passed and the road was covered with a film of snow. A conversation before she left played in his head.

"Birds in cages, like men in prison, tell lies," she said. Her face and voice were neutral, letting him interpret the words however he chose. He couldn't help but think that her clinical training after graduate school had made her difficult to read, her blank open stares receiving whatever information the patient chose to present. He knew that with her patients, she was delicate, the heat on low.

The lights of the city appeared, a halo of blue, just before he rounded the last curve in the canyon.

"Process," she said. "Patience and process. You need to empathize first, understand what's really going on before you can say anything helpful. That takes time. In a way, I'm trying to do the opposite of you."

"Please explain," he said.

"You're trying to understand how birds, as a proxy for people, learn to sing. Learning and language. Sound and song. I'm trying to ignore words, see past what people say and help them unlearn thoughts and behaviors so that they can create new ones."

Before she left, she had said, "Sometimes, I wish I believed it were as easy as you do."

"What's that supposed to mean? When did I ever say it was easy?"

"I mean, I wish I believed I could stick an electrode in them, get them to talk and believe that whatever they said was important."

He arrived at the institute, parked his car and crossed the dark parking lot quickly, the cold air stinging his face, freezing the moisture at his nostrils. At the time, her words had felt harsh but now with distance he could acknowledge that she'd had reason to be upset. He listened for calls, but heard only the crackling of frozen snow, the urgent whine of an ambulance approaching the hospital. He went into the building and at the top of the stairs he unlocked the double bolt and when he flicked on the lights, the birds came alive. The tiah-tiahs of the zebra finches mixed with the hushed machine gun sounds of the Bengalese finches and the muffled coo of Sarah's Inca dove.

Just after Rebecca started working in the lab, she asked whether the birds could have bigger cages, and he told her no, but then he noticed the old gray dove hunkering in its cage, its feathers dull and sparse, and he told her to give the dove a bigger cage. And all the food he would eat, too. Extra seeds, fruit, calcium supplements, boiled eggs. The works. The bird was nearing his end. He heard its second muffled coo, but avoided looking at it. He scanned the cages of experimental birds, checking for anything new since he'd been gone to New York. There was always the same anxiety when he returned from a trip, a sense of tension that did not fade until he had checked everything and assured himself that all the birds were as they should be. *My worrying man*, Sarah had whispered sweetly as she watched him counting the birds in their aviary on the front porch every night and then again in the morning. She would wrap her arms around him and together they would stand beneath the fluttering animals. She had understood how much the birds and their songs meant to him.

This morning the laboratory appeared in order. He shook his keys, found the right one and went through the conference room to his office. He unlocked the door and bent to pick up the mail that had been shoved underneath during the days of his absence. There was another letter from Sarah. He put it aside and spent the next hour catching up on the previous week's issues of *Nature* and *Science*. At 8 a.m. he heard Rebecca arrive and got up and went into the laboratory to say hello. In the moment he saw her, the long red hair twisted up on the top of her head, chopsticks holding it in place, he felt a distinct pleasure and the feeling surprised him. She'd always been attractive, but today there was a different aura about her. He hadn't realized he had been looking forward to this moment until it happened.

She glanced up at him and smiled, "Good morning." From his side of the counter, her face and torso were half hidden by cages, bottles, plastic containers of seeds. There was a tattoo on her upper shoulder that he couldn't remember noticing before. He saw her jaw moving slightly as if she were grinding her teeth. He paused to give her a chance to ask about his trip, but she looked back down at her work and didn't say any more.

No chit-chat or questions. What would Sarah make of her? Rebecca was so quiet that sometimes he forgot her, but luckily she was there, a smart dependable, responsible lab technician doing exactly what she was supposed to do. There was that old adage "beware of those who talk too much." He'd always thought they'd gotten it wrong. It was the silent ones who were hard to know, hard to predict. He couldn't read Rebecca. Nevertheless, he was happy to see her after the cold days in New York. He wanted to tell her that he had come to rely on her and appreciate her, but these were not sentiments easily expressed. Was it the potential for her misunderstanding, or his own, that assured his silence?

He heard Sarah again. *You are afraid of people.* It had been a late night in graduate school. They'd been drinking and Ed was there. She was laughing, her eyes crinkled in smile. The conversation, having begun with the discussion of a new clinical study, became a tongue-in-cheek analysis of their respective fears. Ed had eventually left them to go out to look for owls and he and Sarah had ended the conversation in bed. Silent or not, fearful or not, he thought, Sarah and her theories about him were now irrelevant. Rebecca's steady competence in the lab was gradually replacing Sarah's presence in his mind.

"When you get a chance, can you find "Blue 17"?"

She looked up again, her hands soapy, her yellow apron splattered with wet seeds. "Sure. Where do you want him?"

"Bring him in here. We've got the space. We'll use him for our cost experiment." He heard the soft coo of the dying dove. "Or you can swap out the dove."

With the sound of Anton's whistle mid-morning David came out of his office into the laboratory. Rebecca and Anton were standing at the coffee maker.

"Coffee time?"

"Yes, sir. How was New York?"

"Cold, dark, cramped, and I got back at eleven and had to spend an hour shoveling my way into the garage. Somehow in only three days, my body adapted to Eastern time. I managed less than five hours of sleep."

"Any good science?" Anton poured a cup of coffee for each of them.

"Not much. Heard a lot about Stan's new business venture. Memory drugs. He thinks he's going to get rich on the fact that all of us baby boomers are getting old and no one wants to forget anything."

"Viagra for the brain?"

David laughed. "Perhaps."

"Sounds promising," Rebecca said. "I can think of all sorts of good uses for such a drug."

"Such as?" David asked.

Rebecca smiled but before she could give an answer, Anton interrupted.

"If they have a drug for memory, it might be another way to see the engram."

"Anton, you're like Ponce de Leon looking for the fountain of youth."

"I don't know who that is."

"A man," David said, "who was searching obsessively for waters that would restore his youth."

"That's an old version of history," Rebecca said. "Now they teach us that he was ill and confused, or purposefully mislead by the natives."

David laughed. He did not mention to Anton the memory engrams that Stan had showed him. They were not "crystal clear" as Stan had suggested during dinner and David was left unconvinced. The last thing he needed was the already idealistic Anton getting distracted by Stan's blurry pictures.

"I don't want to always be young," Anton said, "but I do know that once we understand memory, we understand more about humans."

"That's absurd," David said. "All animals, or almost all, I'd wager, have memory. It's not special to humans."

"That only makes it more interesting," Anton said.

"Besides, memory is mostly projection," David said.

"What do you mean by that?" Rebecca asked. "I've always thought that memory was like a photograph."

"Far from it," David said. The ideas and thoughts were Sarah's but the words came from his mouth as though they were his own. Sarah had worked to figure out how to help people un-memorize, un-learn. For her, memory was unstable. "I take notes," she'd once told him. "The story that a patient tells me one week can be very different from the story she tells me the next week, although she is sure it's exactly the same. There's a processing that goes on, and we're not aware of the fact that we're changing our stories."

"I don't think anything matters more than memory," Anton said. "If we don't have memory, then we don't pass on information from one individual to another, from one generation to another. Without memory, there is no culture. We have to understand how the memory forms. We need to know the process, whether it's physical, chemical or something else."

"Something else?" David said. "Like what? I think we're more like mirrors, unconscious momentary projections and reflections, and somehow our minds fool us into thinking our experiences are real, and so we call that memory."

He'd rendered Anton speechless. Of course, at some level, David knew this was an absurd notion because memory did matter, but he really didn't think it mattered as much as people thought it did. Thoughts could overwrite memory. Thoughts could be controlled. Too bad there wasn't a drug on the market for the opposite, a drug to take away bad thoughts, make one stop creating unpleasant images, like the one he'd formed of Sarah in the rainforest with another man, a drug to make the sting of her absence disappear as easily as she had.

Rebecca crossed the laboratory and went into the conference room to find the blue notebook where she recorded information about all the birds, filing them by species, number, and if she knew it, parentage. She flipped through the pages and wrote the bird's number and color, "Blue 17," in a column and made a note: *moved to individual cage*. Back in the laboratory she fastened together a new cage by clicking the metal roof onto the sides, and then she folded a sheet of old newspaper to fit onto the tray for droppings. She positioned a wooden perch crosswise inside the cage and then went down the hall to the aviary.

The birds were identified by tiny colored bands, plastic rings marked with black numbers around their legs. Blue, Red, Yellow. The colorful males were easy to distinguish from the gray females. She waved the net and caught a bird with a blue band. He fluttered in the mesh. She slid her hand into the net, and going by feel, slipped her index and third finger around his head and pulled him out. Wrong number. She let him go and tried again. After the thirteenth try, repeatedly swinging and missing, the birds fluttering in a panicked mob from perch to perch, their feathers and claws grazing her hair as they passed, she found "Blue 17." In the main laboratory she slipped him into the cage. He hunkered down, legs splayed, belly low on the newspaper. He seemed fearful, not the least bit accustomed to life in a cage.

From the lab she went to the experimental rooms where she noticed that the robins and starlings were hopping nervously around their cages, pecking at and then gulping down the crickets and worms as soon as she fed them and following every meal with a burst of song. Spring was coming on and they were loud now, unstoppable, as if unable to be silenced. She liked all the birds but was particularly fond of the sad, quiet robins who watched her with timid turns of their heads, cocked one direction and then the other as if they were studying her as much as she was watching them.

She moved on to the soundproof boxes where the white-crowned sparrows lived in isolation so that they couldn't hear each other's songs, only the one version that was pumped in via speakers twenty times a day. And, of course, they could hear themselves sing. The white-crowned sparrows didn't jump and flutter when she neared them as the starlings did. They were shy like the robins, but quieter. She opened a cage and suddenly, a sparrow darted out, but instead of flying toward the window or the light fixtures as the zebra finches did, it landed on the black countertop. Just as she was about to move toward it, the bird reoriented itself and flew straight back to the platform outside its box and then a moment later, it crawled inside through the open gate. She snapped the chamber closed, hearing his five-note song muffled through the box. At least this bird appeared comfortable in his cage.

The birds were all so different. She couldn't read them, couldn't say what they might or might not feel, but she knew that the more she worked with them, the less sure she was.

Anton came into the laboratory. "Rebecca!"

"Ciao Anton."

"You speak Italian now?"

"I figured I could manage that one word. Is it true that you say it for both hi and bye?"

Anton laughed. "Yes. I guess Italians are always saying hello."

"Or goodbye," she said.

"Ciao," he said, and went back to the soundproof room to copy the data from his muted bird.

Rebecca continued down the row of white-crowned sparrow chambers, feeding and cleaning and checking on the birds. In the last chamber she found a dead bird. Its beautifully black and white-striped head lay at the bottom of the cage as if he were sleeping. Though it certainly wasn't the first dead bird she'd found, she recoiled and stepped back. She didn't know why she was hesitant to touch this one, but finally she reached into the cage and removed him. She looked him over but she could find no obvious reason for his death. She carried him in her palms into the main laboratory over to David at the surgical table.

David stood up, his shoulders rounded toward her, a curl of hair falling in front of his face. "Oh no, my favorite bird."

Sadness took Rebecca by surprise. Her shoulders rose and fell and she tried to suppress her tears.

"Rebecca, it's okay." He took the bird from her hand.

"It's not okay. It's awful."

"Unfortunately, it happens. It's hard for me too."

Silence. She bowed her head. David reached out to her shoulder and then moved his hand to her chin, lifting it so that her eyes met his.

"It's not fair," she said. She'd never been this near to him, but she suddenly had the sense that he might find her attractive.

"No, it's not fair. The flourishing of one is never independent of the other." His hand, pleasantly soft and warm, moved from her chin back to her shoulder.

"What does that mean?" She wanted him to explain himself, to make the research with the birds, the need for the cages, and her own feelings, make sense.

"We depend on the birds. We ask them to tell us how they work. A bird sings, we record him. He dies, we stop. Through the process, we do our best to listen carefully and understand." Anton entered the lab and David pulled his hand away.

"In every experiment," David said, his tone of voice dropping, his hands hanging awkwardly at his side, "there are risks, unknown factors, unexpected results."

It sounded to Rebecca as if he was trying to convince himself as much as her. She glanced over at Anton, but he was gone.

"We're responsible for them," David said.

She looked to David and hesitated. "I have to tell you something."

"What?"

Her neck reddened. "I don't want to do the cost of song project."

He crossed his arms. "It's alright. Tell me."

"I don't want to hurt them."

He smiled and stepped closer to her, and placed his hand again on her bare shoulder. "You and I have this in common."

She shook her head and lowered it.

"And yet we sometimes harm those we love."

Rebecca looked up at him. That was too much like the photographer's: *Pain is part of love.* She stepped back abruptly. "But if you still do it, it's on purpose. That's worse than not caring at all." She felt herself become enraged. She turned and ran from the laboratory.

W hen she didn't return, David finished feeding the birds, and went back to his office and shut the door. The letter from Sarah still lay unopened on his desk.

The day he'd driven her to the airport, there had been a wet snow, the first of the year. They didn't talk and the air inside the car got thick and heavy. The windshield wipers whined against the glass clearing the view only momentarily in front of their eyes. He hoped she would say something, anything. If they just could take some air into their mouths and lungs, he thought, the in and out movements might relieve the thickness. Afraid perhaps that they would suffocate, he rolled down the window.

He had not answered her calls or letters. He knew she was worried about him. He was worried about her too. Neither had siblings and the bond between them and with Ed had been the most family they'd ever known. The feedback loops that he liked to talk about had been damaged.

He got up and cracked open the door to his office and listened for the sounds of Rebecca in the lab, but she hadn't returned. He shut his door again and sat down. Outside, spring was coming to the valley, though none of the trees had budded yet. He thought about the spring shortly after he had first become intrigued with the idea of auditory feedback. He and Sarah had gone together to the foothills behind the institute and hiked into the scrub oak where lazuli buntings were establishing their territories. They stopped near a brilliant blue and rust-colored male furiously singing and dueling with a nearby male. David pulled recording equipment from his bag, held the microphone out toward the bird and pressed record. "Watch this," he whispered. A few seconds later, he pressed rewind, held the machine out to the air and played the sound he'd just recorded. Immediately, the bunting flew toward them and landed on a perch directly in front of them. The bird cocked his head right and left and hopped on the branch.

"Curious fellow. He's never heard this particular male," he said.

"You mean himself," she whispered.

"I mean himself as he sounds to others." The bird hopped closer toward them to investigate the sound coming from the recorder, stayed for a few moments and then flew up to perch on a higher branch. David turned off the recorder. The bird sang his song. There was a response from the male in the next territory.

"What happens," David said, "when the sound producer and the receiver are one and the same?"

Thinking about it now he realized he'd hit upon an interesting question. When producer and receiver were one and the same, was it like looking in the mirror and experiencing instantaneous recognition? Or was it utter confusion? And what could one really learn from instantaneous recognition anyway? With Sarah, their differences had pushed him to know himself more, while their similarities had led to collaboration—not cancelling out.

What David hadn't told Anton after his trip to New York was his increasing concern for purpose, his drive to understand the reason for song. Of course, birdsong was about communicating signal, transferring information, but what information and at what cost? He struggled against the presentiment that true measurements of cost, which would explain mate choice, might always elude him. And then there were the waxwings in which both sexes looked alike and sang the same song. How could any theory of sexual selection account for that?

He thought of Aisha, the interpreter, and the conversations they'd had over the two days at the conference, sharing secrets because they had no fear and no need to hide from one another. He had told her about Sarah and Ed. She told him about the husband she didn't love at home. He thought of their silent lovemaking, the energetic rise and fall of her eyebrows, and then he had a thought he knew he'd never share with anyone: birds sing first because they can and second just because they like to hear their own songs.

At dinner that night Anton asked Rebecca about the dead bird. "Another sparrow died?"

"Yes."

"What happened?"

"I don't know. I just found him in his chamber."

"That's odd. What did David say?"

"He doesn't know either but I think they're getting tired of the laboratory, especially the soundproof chambers."

"Tired? What do you mean?"

"Tired of life in a box."

"That's not possible, Rebecca."

"Why not?"

"Birds don't die like that."

"How do you know? You'd go crazy if all you did was listen to yourself all day."

"I saw him touching your arm."

"So?"

"So, I don't know. It made me uncomfortable."

"You sound possessive. Not a good quality. I'm not an animal in one of your books on sexual selection theories." Though she'd hardly eaten, she moved her dish away. "What's the real reason you haven't told David about the muted birds?"

"I told you. He will not understand." Anton served himself another helping of pasta, aware that the answer wasn't exactly truthful.

"David has different ideas about the research, the right to work with animals than you do," she said.

"What are his ideas?"

"You'll have to ask him yourself and while you're at it, you should tell him about the muting before I do. You know, my job is on the line here too. I'm responsible for all the birds, for keeping track of them. If any go missing, he's going to blame me."

"He won't blame you. He likes you. Maybe you've thought about that? Maybe you like him too?"

"Oh my god." She stood up, went to the window and looked out. "I'm going home."

It was the first time she had left without making love.

Anton couldn't find the right words to explain why he couldn't tell David about the muting yet. As he rinsed their plates he thought about his master's project where he had studied storks, voiceless birds that communicated not through song, but by tossing back their heads and then clattering their bills. For two years Anton listened, recorded, measured the length of their bills and the frequency of bill beats. He had figured out that certain tapping frequencies carried different messages. One for courtship. One for alarm. One for nestlings. He had broken the code. Until he told others, he was the only one who knew.

And he could still remember the exhilarating sensation he'd felt the first time he slipped an electrode into a nerve and heard the bang-bang of a neuron firing realizing he could hear inside a cell. Although he certainly hadn't been the first man to do that, the experience had been singular. There was a before and there was an after. He couldn't explain that feeling in any language.

Now this new ability to mute a bird was potentially big. Making a discovery in science was like being told a secret that no one else knew. Something to be enjoyed alone. He didn't want to share it just yet.

He put on his jacket and walked back up to the institute. The night was clear, the moon nearly full and bright. He had been working late, exercising more, sleeping little. David had said he looked happy and healthy. Was it Rebecca or the new muting work? When Anton arrived, he saw that David's office was lit. He was sitting at his desk, his unruly hair like a halo around his head. What was he doing in the lab so late at night? Anton watched him stand, walk out of his office through the conference room and into the lab. The main lab lights came on. Anton followed him, walking around the building to see what he was doing inside. Strange that David, who usually insisted on a strict daytime/nighttime light regime for the birds, would be turning on lights and interrupting their schedule like this. He watched him stop in front of a birdcage and position a microphone. Birds didn't sing at night. David reached in, took out a bird and then carried it over to the surgical table. With David in the lab, Anton's plan to mute another bird was dashed, but he didn't feel like going home either. He turned his back to the city and looked toward the white slope in the moonlight. He jammed the toe of his shoe into the hillside and began to run up the hill, feeling his heart beat faster and the cold air burn his lungs.

"Risk, risk, risk," David had said during one of their Sunday birding excursions. "Science is like falling in love."

Anton had laughed at him then, but maybe he'd been right; Anton was trying to find his first love again, trying to regain that high. Science had always been the one effort he could count on to repay him emotionally. Maybe David was trying to do the same. Perhaps David was staying late at work to take the edge off whatever he was feeling as well.

Anton stopped at the top of the hill and looked down at the city. Despite the tension of the evening, the thought of Rebecca made him smile. She'd said, *The birds, it's like they're trying so hard to be heard.* He wished she were with him now to see how different everything appeared in the moonlight. He would put his arms around her, whisper something in her ear, press his lips to hers.

When he came down the mountain, David had gone and Anton went into the lab. He sat in his office studying the data sheets as they inched out of the printer. When he'd first begun to work on birdsong he'd only seen squiggles and stacks of lines, shades of gray scratched onto paper, but with David's help, he'd learned to read the print-outs. He looked at the three traces of lines. The top trace corresponded with the normal song, before the bird was muted, showing the undulating lines of the bird's respiration. Inhalations circled down and were silent, exhalations went up and made song. It was true, as David said, the digitized tracings let you *see* sound. He labeled the syllables: 1, 2, 3 for the different notes in the zebra finch's song. His face still felt hot from too much sun during the outing the day before. He often forgot how water and snow reflected sunlight, how susceptible pale skin could be at the end of winter. He got up to splash cool water on his face.

When he sat back down, he lined up the sheets of paper, comparing the breathing patterns of the muted and unmuted birds, only they didn't quite match up. At first, he thought it was a problem of perspective and turned the paper toward himself. He reached for a ruler, set it on the two traces and convinced himself there was a problem. He called up the file on the screen and looked at the monitor. He scrolled forward and backward in time and began to see a pattern. The muted birds were adding strange, albeit silent, syllables to their attempted songs. By sunrise, he'd reviewed enough files to be sure of what he'd found.

As he left the building, the sky was mauve and the air fresh. The days were lengthening. Excited by his strange discovery, he stopped by Rebecca's apartment to tell her the good news, but even though there was a light on in a back room, she didn't come to the door. He stood for a few moments waiting and listening, thinking he could hear voices inside. He rang the bell once more before continuing home and crawling, elated, into bed.

As soon as Anton arrived at the lab later that day, he told David about the muting experiment.

"Keeping secrets, huh?" David said.

"I wanted to be certain."

"Still trying to find the keys to memory?"

"I will figure out how to show you an engram."

"How did you?"

"Mute the bird?"

David nodded.

"Pins through the labia. Keeps them from vibrating."

David was quiet for a moment. "What is it, Anton, that you're trying so hard to remember?"

Anton ignored the question and spread out the sheets of paper with the traces on the conference room table. "But there's more, David. The muted birds are behaving strangely, adding syllables to their silent songs."

Even stranger was the repetition of these syllables over and over, like a scratched record in the middle of a song. In their silence, the birds had begun to stutter.

"Look at syllables one, four and five," Anton said.

"How old are these birds when you mute them?"

"120-150 days."

"Past crystallization," David said.

"The song is supposed to be set at 90 days, and to not change after that," Anton said, "but eighty percent of them do it."

David studied the sheets of paper, shifting them left and right, getting

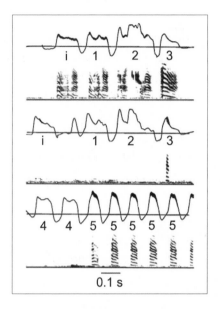

0.1 s

perspective, flipping from one to another. "Then it's disrupted auditory feedback." His voice was just louder than a whisper. "And that, it would seem, can disrupt song."

"And I can reverse them. I can take out the pins and un-mute them. It's a way to test the engram idea. With a big sample of birds, we can study their brains before and...."

"Forget engrams, Anton. This could be really important without dissecting bird brains. No one's ever muted and un-muted a bird before. No one's been able to *make* a bird stutter."

Rebecca, who had been listening, spoke up. "Why would you want to *make* an animal stutter?"

"Think about it," David said. "What do canaries do when they sing? They repeat over and over. First one syllable a bunch of times and then they switch to another syllable and repeat that one over and over before switching to another syllable."

"But they do that naturally," Anton said.

"Right, we could say they stutter normally. Repetition of syllables is the feedback they need to sound normal to themselves."

"You think we can stop their stuttering?"

"Yes. And then we can compare the zebra finch, who *begins* to stutter when he can't hear himself, with the canary who *stops* stuttering when he can't hear himself." David was excited. "And then, we're going to find out why some humans stutter, why some people struggle to express themselves, and then we'll figure out...".

Rebecca interrupted him. "Birds shouldn't have to pay the price for human problems, for the inability of men to express themselves."

David laughed.

"Rebecca, please," Anton said. "That's not respectful. It's David's lab." Couldn't she see that this was the best thing that had happened? He'd finally had a break-through in the work.

"Respectful? I work here too. I get to ask why we're doing this."

"That's true," David said. "You can ask, but why don't you ask Anton? He devised the muting technique. Anton, why would we mute a bird?"

"Because we can," he said, looking straight at Rebecca, incensed that she would be so brazen.

"That's not good enough," Rebecca said. "We can do lots of things but we don't because it's not right."

"I agree with Rebecca," David said. "That's not a good enough reason."

"Come on. They're animals," Anton said.

"They're more than animals," David said. "They're collaborators."

"Collaborators? What?" Anton said. "That's ridiculous."

"Or victims," Rebecca said.

"No, I don't believe that," David said. "They're not victims. We're collaborators. We're in this together."

"Unfortunately, we are." She wiped her hands on her jeans and looked at David.

David laughed again, an uncomfortable nervous laugh.

It seemed to Anton that David and Rebecca had shared an inside conversation, and the fact that he hadn't been able to keep up angered him. "You're both so American," he told them and went back to work.

The conversation was never finished, but in the days that followed the discovery of stuttering, the lab buzzed with communal energy. David hired four new students and asked Rebecca to train them. He set up the cot in his office and it became clear to everyone that he was living in the laboratory. Anton might as well have been doing the same, returning home later each night and then leaving again first thing in the morning. Only Rebecca kept regular hours. The sudden discovery of stuttering birds had changed their schedules and now that Anton didn't have time to cook or tell her stories, she began to sleep at her own apartment.

Anton began to mute the canaries and set up learning experiments to determine whether it mattered if birds were muted early in life or later in life. He believed that either way, when he looked at their brains, he'd see evidence of song memory patterned on their nerves. He'd see an engram form and disappear and form again. He didn't care whether David believed in memory engrams. He would refine the technique, find the engram, and become the first to know how lived moments become memory.

Late at night David stared at the scribbles, wavy diagrams and numbers, a poorly rendered sketch of the syrinx that he and Anton had drawn earlier in the day, and contemplated the phenomenon of stuttering birds. If they could figure out the reason zebra finches began to stutter when they couldn't hear themselves sing, could he also figure out why a person stuttered? If he could make a canary stop stuttering, could they do the same for a human being? Was it a processing problem in the brain? The inability to hear oneself correctly?

A tiny zebra finch feather, striped black and white, floated slowly downward in front of him. He caught it in his palm and then opened his hand and let it float down again along the invisible air eddies. The birds in the laboratory were still singing even though he'd turned out the lights. With the longer days, they were calling late into the evening, singing morning, night, anytime they sensed that a female was near. He could relate to them. His energy had increased as well. He stood and walked to bookshelves along the far wall and took down a small volume, *Migration,* by Edward Matheson. He looked at the author photograph. Ed was tan and fit. Behind his three-day beard, his eyes twinkled at the photographer as if they were sharing a secret. As always, binoculars hung from his neck. David missed Ed enormously. He'd been like a brother or perhaps better than a brother. A bond that David had believed could never be broken. He opened the book randomly to the middle.

Ruby throat

Every April, the three-inch, three-gram Archilochus colubris, *Ruby-throated hummingbird, migrates over six hundred miles from Mexico to eastern North America. In September, it travels back again. Early one spring morning in the late 1960s, as a teenage bird enthusiast, I caught a ruby-throat in a mist net on my family's farm in Indiana. I untangled the bird from the net and in my hand the tiny, static bird seemed wrong, no longer the bird I had always known it to be. Not a hyperactive, buzzing, nectar-sipping animal, but a tiny, quiet almost weightless, iridescent being. In the proximity of flesh and feather, the bird became something new and different. I snapped a tiny, numbered band around its leg, and let it go. The next spring, I caught the exact same bird in the same net in the same place on the farm. Again, I held the bird, and again, I let it go. The ruby-throat was once again a ruby-throat, dashing off on its migration and I was left to wonder, wait, and hope for next year.*

David quickly shut the book. *Proximity of flesh and feather.* Had Sarah also become something new and different for Ed in Peru? Had there been proximity of flesh and feather? In many ways, he and Ed had lived parallel adolescences. Both rural, alone, obsessed by birds, but despite this, Ed had managed to develop an easiness with people that David had not. Ed and Sarah had always bantered and laughed together. Had that been all they'd had?

He heard a quick call from a male zebra finch and listened as the rest of the birds in the laboratory took up the cue, singing "tiah tiah tiah" in sync.

Unlike the white-crowned sparrows and the robins, zebra finches did not exhibit *zugunruhe* behaviors. Zebra finches did not migrate, and in the laboratory, they didn't have specific seasons for mating. He returned Ed's book to the shelf. He gathered his things, folded up the cot and leaned it against the wall of his office. Tonight he would go home. He needed to let go. The past was just that and he wasn't helping himself by this constant remembering.

Halfway up the canyon, he slowed down, lowered the window and listened for owl calls. He pulled onto the side of the road and got out of the car. Cupping his hands around his mouth he mimicked the hooting call of a Western screech owl, the hoo hoo hoo sounds that sped up toward the end of the call like a small rubber ball bouncing on the ground. He listened. He called again and waited, but nothing called back. Once home he was struck by the silence and immediately regretted having come back. The laboratory, it seemed, was now the only place he felt at ease, science the dam that held back his loneliness.

On his way to work the next morning, David glimpsed an injured magpie, jouncing and fluttering at the side of the road. He eased up on the gas and rolled to a stop along the shoulder, turned off the car and walked the tarmac back towards the animal, a fledgling magpie. The bird, one leg bent in half, flapped its wings and hopped with difficulty on its good leg. Confused by its injury and not yet sure of flight, David was able to catch it easily. Without exploratory surgery he couldn't know whether it was a male or female because all magpies had the same white breast, iridescent purple-black feathers, long bobbing tails and black eyes. He studied the damaged leg and saw that it had been severely pinched. In his hand he could feel the bird's thinness, its breast bone jutting out under his index finger. Except for the madly beating heart, the animal seemed frail. He lessened his grip. There was a sudden flapping and flailing as the bird jumped back to the ground. He reached down and grabbed it again, this time stretching his hand wide over the lean breast, holding more firmly. The bird turned its head, opened its long beak and bit onto the skin on the top of his hand.

"Ah, mad are you? Lucky, I'd say."

He looked into the bird's black eyes and saw panic, but he also thought he saw curiosity. He liked magpies. They were intelligent, related to ravens and crows. An idea began to form in his mind. Perhaps this magpie could be trained. The time for imprinting had passed. He'd never have it following him around like Konrad Lorenz's ducklings, but the bird might be useful. Perhaps he could test ideas about hearing, do some sort of experiment on sound perception and memory. He might become a behaviorist after all. Sarah, if she knew, would be pleasantly surprised.

He returned to his car and transferred the bird to his left hand. With his right, he opened the trunk, found an old towel, shook it out and laid it across the driver's seat. He got in, sat on the towel and drove one-handed the rest of the way to the laboratory, the bird on his lap held steady with his free hand.

When Anton and Rebecca arrived, David introduced them to the magpie.

Anton eyed the bird skeptically as it beat its purple wings once against the metal bars, lose its balance, topple and then right itself again.

Rebecca stepped in close to the cage on the countertop. "What's wrong with him?"

"Injured leg, looks like it's been pinched but hard to know how it happened."

Anton stepped away and began to make coffee. "Getting soft, David? Rescuing wounded birds?"

"I've found my Munin," David said.

"Munin?" Rebecca asked.

"Norse mythology. Odin, the one-eyed god of poetry and war, had two ravens: Hugin and Munin. Hugin means thought and Munin means memory. Each morning at sunrise, Odin would open the shutters of his house, let the ravens out and the birds would fly around the world like spies. When they returned to the house in the evening, they perched, one on each shoulder, and whispered the news into his ears."

"So now you have memory and cannot forget anything," Anton said. "Sounds like a curse, David."

David laughed. Even though Anton always had something quick to say, David suspected that his true thoughts, reserved only for himself, happened simultaneously on another track, in Italian or German, one translation away.

"Isn't that what *you* want, Anton?" Rebecca asked. "To understand memory?"

David noticed that Anton ignored her question, opened the canister of coffee beans and tipped it to fill the grinder.

"I thought you said, David, that memory is not interesting to you. What did you say, it's all faulty?"

"*Engrams* don't interest me. Thinking you can locate memory in one place is futile, but figuring out how memories, even faulty memories, affect behaviors is interesting."

Anton nodded his head.

"What will you do with this memory-magpie?" Rebecca asked.

"Put her in a Skinner box, see what she tells me about hearing." A sense of regret passed through him as he said this, knowing that this would be a project without Sarah.

"How do you know your memory is a she?" Rebecca asked.

Anton pressed the button to pulverize the beans. Over the grinding whirr, neither of them could hear David's answer.

Rebecca and Anton drove to the mountains to spend the day together. There had been a distance between them ever since the stuttering was discovered and the conversation with David in the laboratory. Before Anton had been focused on her but now he was thinking more about the birds and their stuttering. He had no idea what it might mean but as he maneuvered the curves of the mountain, he realized he hadn't felt this good in years.

He parked the car and they got out, zipping up their windbreakers against the wind. It was late April but at the higher altitudes the snow had not yet begun to melt and the sky was a deep blue, the light blinding as it bounced off the white world. Rebecca squinted against the glare. She never seemed prepared for the elements. No hat and scarf in the winter, no sunhat in the spring. He dug into his backpack and tossed her a baseball hat. They began to climb, the snow below their boots giving a firm footing. He ascended more quickly than she did. The mountain was quiet. The white-crowned sparrows, tanagers and towhees, the few birds he'd learned to recognize, had not yet completed their migration back. He heard the rattle of a chipmunk or maybe it was a squirrel. Higher up he stopped at an exposed rock, removed his backpack and leaned it against a small conifer tree. He stretched his arms above his head and peered out at the steep white peaks. From here, the world was mostly frozen mountains and in the distance only a tiny triangle of the valley and city below. With snow these mountains reminded him of the Alps and the new research made him feel that much closer to home.

He sat down on the sun-heated rock and inspected the gray and green lichens covering its surface. He removed his orange cap and waited for Rebecca to finish the ascent. They ate lunch in silence and when they were finished he lay back on the rock and pulled her over to kiss. Just above there was a pair of birds in the tree, their tiny feet clasping and releasing the branches, their wings flicking with each high pitched call.

"Two birds, very close," he whispered. He watched their hyper movements, the pale undersides of their yellow-gray bodies, the green and brown of the tree and above that, deep blue sky. Rebecca buried her head in his neck, and he felt her lips on his collarbone. He shut his eyes for an instant, listening to the rustling of their tiny bodies, the high repetitive *see-see-see* notes of their song. Whatever they were, they seemed to stutter too. When he opened his eyes again, they were gone.

"What's the real reason you want to keep this relationship a secret?" she asked, her head resting on his shoulder.

"I told you. Jealousy and dynamics in the lab."

"There must be something more. It just doesn't make sense."

"More? No." He didn't know how to tell her his truest feelings. The thoughts, formed effortlessly in his mind, the sounds so easy to make in Italian or German, did not materialize in English.

"There's something different about you," she said. "You've been acting distant."

He rubbed his hand over her breast. "I am very close."

"I don't mean physically."

"Rebecca, there has never been anyone else in my life like you." Even so, he realized she might be right. Much like a male bird late in the season, having little reason to sing for a female or defend his territory, maybe he was disconnecting from her, reserving his energy for the upcoming migration home.

He looked out across the valley. In the winter, the mountains in Utah reminded him a bit of home but the parched desert summer that he knew was coming was nothing like summer there. At home, he would get up at sunrise and go up into the mountains to hike. Next to his grandfather's village was another, even smaller village perched higher up on the mountain with only eight or nine houses, all made of stone, the roofs gray slate.

Walking through this village one day and on the way back from a hike he passed an old man, white hair, the grey stubble of a two-day beard, standing in the small doorway of his house. Usually, the local people were distant, never offering more than a curt hello, naturally suspicious of strangers, but this man motioned Anton over with a hand gesture. He saw the man's half-sagging face and dangling arm and understood immediately that he couldn't speak and assumed he'd suffered a stroke. With his good arm, the man bid Anton to come in, stooped below the low doorframe and disappeared into the darkness of the house. Anton ducked his head as well and followed the man inside. The house was cool, the thick stone walls and slate roof keeping out the heat. Along the long wall of the room there was a large table decorated with a Christmas village scene of little wooden figurines, hills, animals, a manger, Joseph, Mary and baby Jesus. The man leaned over, flipped a switch and the figures came to life. Anton saw women combing wool. Men milking cows. Sheep with bells. Mary's hand rocking Jesus' cradle, the three kings continuously approaching with their gifts, never getting to give them up. It was a whole village clinking and clanking, so well-imagined and engineered, it must have taken years to carve and dress the people and animals, wire up the electricity, make it all work.

Anton had the sense that in the future he was going to be like that man, tucked away in a stone house in the Alps, one bookshelf full of books and another with classical music, weeding a small garden, turning the soil over on itself, harvesting lettuce and basil in the summer, potatoes in the fall. Rebecca was right. He had become distant.

"I don't understand how you can think it's right to mute the birds," she said.

Her voice brought him back to the moment. "Rebecca, we talked about this before."

"And you didn't answer well."

"I didn't answer what you wanted me to answer. I'm not sure we'll find a cure for human stuttering."

"That's not what I mean and you know it."

"You mean morally correct?"

She nodded.

"I don't think it makes a difference. I think moral is a human creation. It doesn't exist in the animal world."

"But you live in the human world."

"True, but I work with animals and only have to follow their rules."

"*Their* rules? How can you possibly know what their rules are?"

The look on her face was something new, a look of disgust.

"You don't have any guilt about subjecting them to experiments?"

"I think about it, of course. I am human, but guilt? No." He propped himself up on his elbow. "Zebra finches have been bred for many, many generations. They are accustomed to captivity, and they are taken care of very well. You know this because you feed them. Food and water *ad libitum*."

"But that's not the point. There's a difference between keeping a bird and playing Frankenstein with it."

"Is there?"

"Of course there is!" she said.

"I don't know," he said. "The surgeries are done with anesthetic. Plus, pain is relative. You Americans have low tolerance to pain."

"We Americans? What do you mean by that? Pain is pain."

"Definitely not," he said. "Some people hardly feel it."

She didn't say anything. He could tell he was making her mad, which he didn't want to do, so he tried to explain what he meant.

"In Europe, you go to the dentist and they don't inject anesthesia when they work on your teeth."

She looked at him with the look of disgust again. "I wasn't only talking about physical pain."

He waited for her to continue.

"Emotional pain. Spiritual pain, but I guess some people don't feel that either."

He sat up. "What? You think the birds feel emotional pain?"

"David knows they do. I can tell by the way he holds them and the way he talks to Munin. He and I talk about it."

"David is a scientist. He just wants to get another *Science* paper and another grant. Don't let him, or the attention he gives you, fool you."

"What do you mean by that?"

"I mean I've seen the two of you having those conversations and I'd just say this: you shouldn't trust him."

She stood abruptly and started to walk. "I'm going back to the car."

Anton sat back on the rock and watched her moving away in large, quick steps. Her sudden departure surprised him and these repeated discussions about the birds frustrated him. Only privileged Americans had leisure time to spend on these thoughts. He looked up at the white mountains beyond. He closed his eyes and turned his head to face the sun, listening to the chirp of a chipmunk, the faint whoosh of the breeze through the pine trees, the drop of a pine cone. The muting work was going to change everything. He just needed to put in some long days and long weeks and they would produce the *Science* paper he was hoping for. He was homeward bound, intent on returning to the Alps. He stood and followed her down the mountain. They didn't speak on the drive back to the city. When he pulled up in front of her house, she grabbed her bag, and gave the door a heavy slam. He put the car in drive and drove downtown to visit Francesco at the Italian deli.

They're trying so hard to be heard. It was obvious to her. Why wasn't it obvious to them? It was clear, as she leaned into the toilet that night, vomiting up the four gin and tonics she'd had. They only valued that which they could understand in words. Look at how much was happening because they couldn't understand each other or maybe even themselves?

David had taken her seriously when she presented him with the question, and had surprised her in not answering as Anton had, but then their conversation had been interrupted. Still, she'd seen it in his eyes, hadn't she? He didn't want to harm the birds. David cared for them as Anton did not.

She waited for another wave of nausea. Who knew how many pounds of birds were thrown into the freezer each year? Accumulated. Incinerated. Bodies given up for science. To what end? She gagged and felt the burn of food move up her esophagus, knowing she was complicit by caring for them the way she had.

If you don't speak, you won't be heard. In that, they were wrong.

David got out of his car, pressed the lock button and listened for the beep. Now with the semester finished, the campus was deserted and quiet at this early hour, the birds no longer singing courtship or territorial songs. He heard a robin call first, then the quick whistling of a starling. A magpie, hardly bothered by his presence, flapped across the sidewalk in front of him. The robin called again and was answered by another male down the hillside. He walked quickly toward the institute, counting their short calls as he went. Robin, starling, magpie, house sparrow, an easy one, two, three, four. House finch-five, Lazuli bunting-six. Warbling vireo-seven. Flicker-eight. Downy woodpecker-nine. Sometimes, at this time of the year, he could make it to ten before arriving at the entrance. He slid his ID card through the box and opened the door.

Upstairs he unlocked the laboratory. The birds were awake, hopping and calling in their cages. He passed through the lab and conference room to his office to set his backpack on the desk. Back in the laboratory at Munin's box, he unlatched the door. The bird cawed. David smiled.

"Hungry, are you? Come on, let's get you some juicy worms." Removing her from the box wasn't exactly the right way to train her, but he liked the bird's company. He reached in and took her in his hand. She turned her head and tried to bite his wrist. He lessened his grip. He no longer could feel her breastbone.

Using his left hand, he opened the refrigerator and removed a plastic container of worms, shook a few out onto a tray and replaced the container, kneeing the door shut. As they began to wiggle, Munin fixed her gaze on the warming worms. Back in his office, he put the tray onto a side desk and set Munin on the back of a chair next to the worms. Instead, she flew up into the air and perched on the light fixture.

"Fine," he said, "but breakfast is down here."

She cocked her head right and left. Sunlight coming through the windows made her purple feathers gleam. He turned his back to her and booted up his computer to check his email. A few seconds later, there was the faint swoosh of the bird dropping down to eat.

In his inbox he found an announcement from *Science* and clicked over to review the newest issue. He wasn't surprised to see Stan's phase II work on memory drugs published, but he was surprised at his ungenerous feelings about Stan's success. He would have his own *Science* paper as soon as they finished the first round of stuttering experiments. In fact, he should put Munin back in her box and get to work.

"Come on now," he said. "I know you don't want to go in, but it's time."

The magpie fluttered her wings, but David was quicker and caught her in his hand.

"Here, bite my finger if it makes you feel better."

Silence and then she let out a grating caw sound.

"It's only for a while." He carried her into the lab and put her into the Skinner box. "A change of scenery, Munin." He closed the door.

Using the remote camera, he watched her inside. She hopped and pecked at the levers. When she pecked at the red lever, he played one tune. When she pecked green, a different tune. He'd done a scan of the literature. If Munin wasn't stressed, he could expect her to live ten years, maybe more because birds in captivity always lived longer than those in the wild. Good food. Good care. No predators. Not such a bad life, was it?

"How is the memory?" Anton asked as he entered the lab.

"She seems to like either red or the song that goes with the red button."

"You can switch them to find out."

"I will."

"Coffee?"

"Sure."

"Where's Rebecca?"

"She took some vacation days."

Anton stopped what he was doing. She'd said nothing about days off, but of course, their last conversation during the hike hadn't ended well. He would try to call her later. He poured water into the coffee pot. "I am thinking we can mute this memory of yours."

David looked at him trying to gauge whether Anton was serious. "No way."

"We are getting good ideas of finches and canaries when they sing without hearing themselves, but those birds all learn their songs after they're born. What happens when you mute birds, like a magpie, birds that never learn, birds that are born knowing their songs? I wonder. Do they stutter too?"

"Your ignorance of birds, Anton, is remarkable. Magpies do sing and they do learn. They're oscines but what you're hearing are their calls and you're right, those aren't learned. You don't hear their songs because they're soft, like whispers."

Anton pressed the button to grind the beans.

"Besides," David said, louder now, to be heard over the grind, "it would be useless. A sample size of one."

During the day Munin listened to sounds and pressed levers when she was asked, but mostly she flew around the laboratory. David set out flashy items, coins, pieces of tin foil, candy wrappers around the laboratory and waited for her to bring them back to her cache in his office.

"The animal care guy came by yesterday," Anton said. "He wasn't happy to see Munin out of her cage again."

"What time?"

"Noon. He said he is going to write a report."

"Okay," David said. He whistled, held out a shiny quarter and Munin flew to his arm. He placed her back in the cage and gave her a mealworm.

That evening David repaired the old aviary that Sarah had built. He stretched new heavy wire cloth across the wooden frame and stapled it to the wood. He carried Munin's cage to the aviary, pulled open the screen door, went in and let the door swing shut behind him. He undid the latch and opened the door. She didn't come out. He opened a small plastic container and spilled some worms into the damp leaves in front of her opened door. From his pocket he took a quarter-sized piece of foil and wedged it into the wire of the cage. In the morning, sunlight would hit the foil and Munin would collect it for her stash of shiny treasures.

David left the aviary and mounted the twenty stairs to their house, his house now, which was quietly tucked among trees on the mountain without a view of any neighbors. Once inside, the first thing he always did was to go to the stereo and turn on music. Shaded by oaks and firs, the house was dark and so he moved around the room, switching on lights. At sunset, there was often a rush of emotion, a sensation of panic. It was a feeling that had increased lately.

"Science is like this," he'd told Anton. "You only have the potential to be doing good stuff if you're not sure, if you're afraid. Whenever I've felt like my idea is a bit crazy or very stupid, those have been the moments when something exciting has happened. It's like being on the edge of a precipice, and then for an instant, saying to hell with it all, and being brave enough to look down."

David recognized the gleam in Anton's eyes when he revealed the muting experiments, a look that had been so well fictionalized in movies. In real life, the look meant not a crazy scientist, but someone of vision and passion. If it was the difference between a magpie and a white-crowned sparrow, Anton, he knew, was a magpie.

A memory of Sarah came to David as he sat on the porch watching Munin in her aviary, the rippling sounds of Count Basie's piano coming from the living room, from a time just after he'd started working on birds. He had been sitting at the kitchen table in the house they'd rented in Pennsylvania. It was their first winter and all the birds were inside. Sarah was in the living room, collecting seed containers, a water dish, talking to the parrot and to him at the same time, telling him the ups and downs of her work. She came back into the kitchen with the tray of containers.

"I love your voice," he said.

His sudden declaration caused her to stop and turn mid-kitchen.

"When you speak, I feel the waves of energy." Then he had continued. "I'm not sure where some of the sounds are generated. Definitely not a sinusoidal vibration because that produces a single, pure tone. You have all of these overlying harmonics. Sometimes, it's hard to pick out the pattern."

"Well," she said. "I guess you'll just have to learn how to calibrate."

He realized that he had never learned. When she returned from the trip to Peru she surprised him by moving the birds out of the house.

"I'm a bit tired of it, birdsong in the morning, escaped crickets singing at night. Maybe they should go to the laboratory." Except for Skinner who was given away to one of her patients. Now he saw it clearly. Calibrated perfectly. If their life together was a series of sounds, the trip to Peru was the oscillator, the thing that set forth the sound waves. The moving of the birds was meant to be those waves hitting his ears, his perception of a problem but at the time, he didn't see, or hear, any of it. He joked as he filled the university van with the cages of zebra finches, conures and doves.

"I almost feel like part of me is moving out. Are you bidding me to go?"

She didn't respond, but went back into the house for the heavy bag of seeds, and after that, she fetched the plastic containers of peas, corn and broccoli. Sarah began to take patients in the evenings. "People are busy during the day." she explained. "They need me after work hours."

Evenings without the birds were quiet. The mornings, painfully so.

They were left with only the sounds of each other. David quickly learned that there were many kinds of silences.

Silence made up of not speaking.

Silence from not hearing.

Silence of not knowing.

A nton sat in a cubicle in front of the computer, humming, swiveling his chair left and right. These hours spent analyzing second after second of birdsong were exhilarating. He was separating those birds that stuttered after muting from those that didn't. Rebecca was supposed to have returned from vacation, but she hadn't shown up yet and so he had fed the birds and done the cleaning himself, which he didn't mind, but she hadn't answered his phone calls for the past four days, which he did mind. Clearly she was upset about their conversation on the mountain but he couldn't understand why this had become such an issue. For all the past months, they'd navigated around their differences. Or at least, he'd thought they had. He no longer knew, and not knowing bothered him.

David had hired a small army of undergraduate students and the lab had gone from a quiet place to a crowded, drumming space that worked around the clock. The lights were on most of the time and the birds sang day and night. David forgot to cut his hair and kept brushing the long curls from his eyes, tucking the strands behind his ears. Anton went home only to shower and often forgot to shave, the stubble on his chin now matched his closely shorn, balding head. They ate most of their meals, order-in pizza and sandwiches, in the conference room, the garbage cans full of greasy cardboard boxes. "The tides have turned," David said between bites. "We're going to get a *Science* paper."

Colleagues stopped by to inquire about the work. Anton heard David speaking to them.

"I'm incredibly excited by this. We can make non-stutterers, like the zebra finch, begin to stutter, and stutterers, like canaries, stop stuttering."

"Is it genetic?" they asked.

There was the clicking sound of David's heels as he paced across the floor. "Likely. Partly. Only certain birds do it."

"Environmental?"

"That's the interesting part," David said. "These birds have only had computer parents. For the first time, stuttering can't be blamed on the mother."

The men laughed.

"Really," David said. "Forget Stan Sommers and all his drugs for aging baby boomers. Who cares about an old person's memory?"

"A lot of people care about memory," a colleague said. "Especially the funding agencies."

"But we can help people who are stuck say what they want to say right now."

Anton smiled to himself. David did care about memory. Why else would he have named his pet magpie Munin, for memory? David's mood had improved greatly in the last month. At first Anton thought it was the discovery of stuttering but now he suspected it also had something to do with the magpie, a sort of surrogate companion, traveling with him to work and home each day. He also knew that David wasn't telling his colleagues everything. They had begun experimenting with delayed auditory feedback and were testing the idea that if stutterers couldn't hear themselves singing, they stuttered less. It was another way into understanding the need for auditory feedback. He suspected that David felt the same way as he felt. Being involved in this new research project felt as if they'd both been given shots of adrenaline. As if they'd trained for a marathon and now were rewarded by the benefits of being close to its completion. Anton programmed the second analysis into the computer, checked the commands and then pressed start.

He turned from the screen and looked out the window. Outside the campus was green and alive, but that was only because the sprinklers came to life at all hours of the day, although in the late afternoon, much of the water misted upwards and disappeared into the dry air. Beyond the campus and the city, the desert was dry and brown, the summer heat having settled over the valley like a brittle shroud. Fires were burning over large parts of the state. There were house evacuations, fire fighters jumping into flames, helicopters dropping pink clouds of retardant. Some days, when the winds shifted and the air whitened with ash, he couldn't get the burnt taste out of his mouth.

He noticed a black and yellow swallowtail butterfly move past the window, two slow wing beats followed by a long glide. Unlike birds, butterflies made no noise. Silent in both takeoff and flight. Rather than song, they communicated by smell, micromoles of scent released by one butterfly and captured miles away by the tiny brushes of another butterfly's antennae. A quiet experience. A deaf person would miss nothing watching a butterfly. A deaf person would see a butterfly exactly as it was.

He heard Rebecca's voice and swiveled away from the window to turn toward her. The change was abrupt. No more red nest piled on her head with sticks, she'd cut her hair very short. The tiny diamond in her nose had been replaced with a blue gem. She didn't make eye contact with him but directly began the day's work recording information on the clipboard. She slipped the clipboard over a hook and let it go. There was the clank as it hit the wall, the pen dangling on a string. She moved on to the dove's cage, pulled the water and food dishes out in one quick movement. She looked pale, maybe ill. He saw the characteristic absentminded milling motion of her jaw. Lately, he'd seen her taking bits of birdseed into her mouth.

He wondered why she was feeding birds and cleaning cages when she could be, should be, taking pictures. That winter day, when she'd fallen ill and he'd gone to her house with flowers, he'd been impressed by the photographs. They were good. She had talent. When he'd asked her again about the pictures she'd said that she wasn't interested in photography anymore, but she hadn't told the truth. Recently, he'd seen her on campus with a camera, the strap looped around her neck, taking pictures of the buildings. She was holding the camera in her hands like you might hold a newborn puppy.

She finished with the dove and was starting on the pale canaries. He swiveled again on his chair, booted up the second computer on the desk. If she wasn't going to acknowledge him, he wasn't going to make the effort either. He began to work. He had not written to his mother about Rebecca. What would he write? That he'd fallen in love with an American who didn't speak a word of German or Italian, who had bright red hair, who was a photographer who fed birds? That for a few months he'd never felt as close to another person in his life but suddenly, for no apparent reason, they were moving around the lab like blind strangers?

He heard the caw of the magpie and saw the bird flying directly toward him. He ducked. David followed the bird into the laboratory.

"David, you're going to get a citation for having free flying birds in here."

David ignored Anton. "Rebecca, you're back."

"Yes."

"How was your vacation?"

"Fine."

"You cut your hair, very stylish. It's nice," he said.

"Do you know what happened to the temperature and humidity meter in this room?" she asked.

"Haven't seen it. You Anton?"

"No, I haven't seen it for a while either."

"Anton," David said, "I'm going to the seminar. Want to come?"

Anton shook his head. "No, I want to finish the analysis."

David left the lab. Rebecca flipped noisily through the record sheets. "Then, if you haven't had a temperature or humidity meter, how come you knew what to write for all these days that I was gone?"

"I made it up."

The weather inside the buildings was pretty much unchanging and the truth was that humidity and temperature, which fluctuated little in these rooms, didn't factor into their work. Recording it was merely part of animal care protocol. What mattered most, the light schedule, was on a timer. Twelve hours of light, twelve of dark.

"I thought scientists kept good records," she said.

"What is bothering you, Rebecca?"

She looked at him, held his gaze. He could see her jaws grinding around a seed. "That you're dishonest."

He didn't know how to respond and so he forced his attention back to the screen, to the paper he was writing. Rebecca turned and left the room.

The next day David called out from the conference room where he was mapping out new experiments on the white board. "Rebecca, we need more birds." When she didn't answer, he came into the laboratory, the magpie perched on his wrist, talking more quietly now. "From as many distributors as you can find."

"How many victims do you want?" she asked.

David ignored the comment. "Thirty of everything. Zebra finches, Bengalese finches. The rest I will have to collect in the wild."

The magpie let out a caw as it flew from David's hand to the light fixture. From that perch, the bird shifted its head, as if taking in the laboratory, the cages, the black countertops, the surgical table, cubicles and computers. David went back to the conference room. Rebecca dialed the phone number and when the customer service agent came on the line, she made the order: twenty male zebra finches, ten females. Thirty Bengalese finches because with Bengalese finches the feathers didn't tell you who was male and who was female; it was a matter of waiting to see which ones sang and then by elimination, the rest were females.

Some birds couldn't be bought. Every summer, David spent days in the mountains collecting baby birds, the robins, starlings and white-crowned sparrows that couldn't be bred in the lab or bought through a distributor. The undergraduates followed him like uncertain ducklings. He was pleased he could offer them this much at least, a window into the world of science. For many, even the bright undergraduates, this would be the last time they looked. Of course, he knew why they followed him so intently, coming to him more for the letter of recommendation they needed for medical school than any great interest in birdsong or scientific research, and he wondered why a letter from him should matter. What could he really say about any of them? *Student Y, attentive and confident, arrived to work on time. Let him into medical school and he'll master the techniques, show up for scheduled surgeries. Student X showed initiative and turned in well-written reports. She also listens well, smiles pretty. Patients will feel some comfort before they die.*

As they proceeded up the mountain trail, he listened and pointed out the songs he heard, always trying for the softest, most far-away caller. "Hear that?" He imitated the song. "A ruby-crowned kinglet singing off to our left." Of course, they hadn't heard. He waited and then pointed with his finger as the bird sang again. This time, the two women heard, but the young man still did not. Probably deaf from years of sound abuse, music turned up too high, but he kept this thought to himself. Once he'd actually said it jokingly to a student and he'd been politely corrected, told that no, it wasn't a problem of loud music, but the hearing loss was due to an untreated infection shortly after birth. Since then, David had become more careful with what he said.

The day was warm, the snow at this elevation gone, and ten or twelve species of birds singing loudly. He turned and continued hiking with long strides along the trail. If he moved quickly, he could be back in the laboratory by early afternoon. As he began to move uphill again with the student ducklings behind him, he thought of Aisha, the Lebanese-American interpreter, who yearned for a world without sounds. He wondered where she was. He'd asked for her email and had thought about contacting her many times, but the discovery of stuttering had distracted him.

"As far as I'm concerned," Aisha had said to him, "there's too much noise in the world."

They had just made love and were lying in the bed together. "I hate it. It's impossible to get away from noise. You can hear it right now, the hum of the refrigerator, the air conditioner, the sounds from people in the hallway. It's just impossible to create soundlessness. You can put on a mask and stumble around in order to imagine blindness, but it's impossible to mimic deafness."

He thought to ask her whether she'd ever been tested for Lyme disease. He'd once read that it could cause a debilitating sensitivity to sound, but he didn't say this. He ran his hand up and down her thigh. He had not touched another woman besides Sarah in over fifteen years and he'd always assumed that any other woman wouldn't seem right. He was surprised to find how fine it felt to be with her.

"You know," Aisha told him, "one time I was in Shanghai for a conference and I went out for a walk. You can't imagine the noise. Motorcars, horns, stereos, squeals of bus brakes, bicycle bells. Decibels reaching at least one hundred but I made myself walk on because I didn't want to have been in China and only seen the inside of a hotel. It was like being physically accosted by sound." She paused to prop herself up on her bent arm. "Then I saw a park across the street and there was a huge group of people, a hundred, maybe more. They were wearing light clothing, white or pale yellow and moving simultaneously through these slow complicated gestures as if they were speaking to one another, miming in a language I'd never seen. Their heads were bowed and like a school of swimming fish, it was as if they were sensing direction and pace without having to see or hear. I stood watching them and suddenly, as if someone had turned down a dimmer, the blaring of the horns, the terrible, violent sounds of the city, became white noise and then completely disappeared. For a moment, there was perfect silence."

David stopped hiking abruptly and the students stopped as well, standing quietly a few paces behind him. In his mind, he saw people, hundreds of them, going through their tai chi motions, their loose white clothing rumpled, sleeves slipping up and down their arms. He tried to imagine the soundlessness Aisha had spoken about. Then he heard the shrill alarm call of a female white-crowned sparrow.

"This way," he said to the students behind him.

He stepped off the trail and into a small grove of conifers. The students hurried after him, impressed with his ability, the fact that he could recognize the squawk of a white-crowned sparrow defending her nest. They had never been in the field, trotting after a man who heard birds. They didn't know that he was both common and special. There were thousands of bird watchers who listened and recognized songs, but few in the world were as good as he. They had no way to judge his ability, no scale on which to put him.

Once he found the sparrow's nest with the chicks, no more than pale gaping beaks revealing hungry red insides, he reached in and in one handful, took the entire lot. He placed the three monstrously ugly chicks, pink, wrinkled and featherless, into a canvas sack and handed it to one of the students to carry. During the next two hours, he hiked up and down the mountain, pointing out different songs and telling anecdotes about birds until he had succeeded in raiding two more nests. When each undergraduate carried a white canvas sack of birds, he nodded his satisfaction to them and began the descent toward the van. "Careful now," he called back. "Try not to swing them around too much. We don't want dizzy chicks." The students giggled as expected.

Back at the lab, he left the nestlings on the countertop for Rebecca. She placed them in small plastic containers lined with industrial white paper towel and over the next few days, she fed them every thirty minutes. The insides of their mouths, cartilaginous red arrows, directed where to put the food. Using a toothpick, she would stuff globs of runny puppy chow down their throats, and afterwards, they would briefly stop their faint, high-pitched squeaks, hunker down to digest before opening their beaks wide again and stretching their featherless necks into the air, trying once again to out-beg their nest mates. Miraculously, these bald, wrinkled nestlings doubled in size every day, eventually growing feathers, turning fluffy and cute, hopping and pecking about. When they finally tried out their wings, it would be time to put them in cages.

Zebra finches, on the other hand, the standard lab rat of the neuro-scientist, could be bred. David sent Rebecca to the aviary with a net to catch a showy male and a drab female and put them together in a breeding cage. In the notebook in the conference room she marked down the color and number of each bird's ankle band and the date when she put them together. The birds mated and the female would lay eggs.

When David wanted isolated birds, those that hadn't learned their father's song, he told her to remove the father bird as soon as the eggs hatched. Sometimes, the mother bird, disturbed by the sudden absence of the male, responded by knocking the brood out of the nest, killing her flock. When that happened, Rebecca tipped the entire contents of the cage—broken eggs shells, scattered seeds, soiled newspaper, and dead chicks—into the trashcan and began the breeding protocol over again.

Whatever way David got the birds, by stealing or breeding, only the males interested him because only males sang. Once the wild-caught fledg-lings were big enough, he would put them under anesthesia, turn them over on their backs, make a small slit in their lower bodies and check for ovaries. The ones without, the males, were put back into cages. The others, the females, he popped head-first into small glass jars with chloroform-soaked towels, a quick sleepy death.

He glanced over at Rebecca, his face pained, and explained. "It's humane. In the wild, half of them would die of starvation or predation anyway." The insertion of female birds into glass jars was a seemingly sim-ple motion. Those who didn't know him would say that it appeared to be done without emotion or fanfare, much quieter than say, a person might swat at and kill a housefly.

Anton wasn't expecting Rebecca when she arrived at his apartment very late. They hadn't talked in two weeks, and he didn't want to continue the conversation about birds, but when she stepped inside, he realized she hadn't come to argue. Her fingers wrapped around his wrists. She lifted his arms, pulled his shirt up over his head and tossed it on the couch. She unzipped her dress, let it fall to the floor and took off his pants. She looked younger without her long hair. She said nothing and led him into the bedroom where he measured the space of her mouth with his tongue, the size of her breasts, the shape of her hips, the softness of her inner thighs. He wanted to make a map of her body so that later he could find his way back to her in his mind.

After she had fallen asleep Anton thought he could see traces of a smile on her face. He watched the rhythm of her breasts and stomach moving faintly with every inhalation and exhalation. The windows were open, and there was a breeze. Underneath her efficient exterior, her perfect skin, pale almost white against the dark blue sheets, there must be a bruise that would explain why she'd given up photography, why she was feeding birds, why she was so angry. The warmth he had felt from the beginning had returned. If she was bruised, it wasn't because of his touch. Tomorrow he would invite her to lunch and they would talk and laugh and everything would be as it was before.

He rose carefully so as not to wake her and went into the living room. He switched on the light, sat down on the sofa and picked up the Sufi poem. As the birds journeyed across the seven valleys on their way to meet Simorgh, their god, they heard stories about kings and queens, dervishes and slaves. Many of the tales spoke of love between unequals, the transcendence across man-made boundaries as one moved toward Simorgh. The tales instructed how to let go of self, love, fortune and fame. He read about the Valley of Love and wondered, not for the first time, whether his mother's leaving had had something to do with *love's flame* and the *knowing of no prudence.* She'd never said what made her go off that first year to Africa. When he was a child he had always believed it was for her work. Now he imagined that there were other reasons as well. The clock said 3:00 a.m. He shut the book and slipped back into bed with Rebecca. It was true that he had wanted to keep the relationship from David, and not just out of fear of jealousy and the worry that it would change the dynamics in the laboratory. There was more. He didn't want to reveal the relationship to David, or to his mother, or Francesco because that would mean he would have to admit it in a new way to himself. He didn't want to think about the possibility that he could end up like Francesco, stuck in the U.S.A., resigned to no country at all.

When he woke the next morning, Rebecca had already gone. He looked on the dining room table, where she usually left a note, but there was nothing.

David drove his car into the institute's lot. As always, at this early hour he had his pick of spots. There was a stuffy breeze. It was the hottest, driest summer on record and this day would be exceedingly hot. He swiped his security card through the machine. Inside, the building was cool. Up the three flights of stairs, he pulled on another door and walked down the hallway toward his laboratory, slowing his gait as he neared. He felt the silence without comprehending it. In the seconds it took for him to reach into his pocket for his keys, he understood that something was wrong. Quickly, he turned the key and flung open the laboratory door. No zebra finch calls greeted him. No whistles from starlings, no canary trills. Where there should have been scarlet-beaked birds flitting on and off their perches, there were rows of cages with open doors, all empty. He dropped his briefcase on the floor and ran to each cage, afraid to touch anything, but still not believing the birds were gone. He looked toward the light fixtures, where the zebra finches normally flew when they escaped. Nothing. He rushed to his office to call campus police, but stopped short when he saw what they had done.

On the conference room floor outside his office door they had left a cemetery for birds by fashioning hundreds of crosses out of white pipe cleaners and fastened tiny black and white zebra feathers to the ends. The crosses were lined up in neat rows, inserted in Styrofoam and together they resembled a miniature Arlington.

He turned away from his office, went back through the quiet laboratory and ran down the hallway toward the aviary. A swipe of his security card allowed him to open the door. Birds exploded out, careening in wild flight into the hallway. He quickly pulled the door shut behind him. The sound deafened, two hundred birds calling, flapping, swooshing in a mad panic around his head. After a moment, the birds that hadn't flown out organized themselves somewhat naturally into the cramped space. The zebra finches, huddled on one side so as to avoid the more aggressive starlings and cowbirds on the other. The white-crowned sparrows were clustered, dehydrated and panting in a corner on the tiled floor. David felt his hair beginning to wet with perspiration. He needed to get out of the aviary, away from the chaos and noise to a place where he could think. He stepped backward, still not understanding, and then he found the door handle, pressed it down, leaned with his shoulder and fled through the crack in the door.

When Rebecca arrived at the laboratory, he was waiting for her, Munin perched on his arm. She looked at the empty cages and then at David. The two of them stood staring at one another in complete stillness. No words or movement. No birds. Just the hum of the refrigerator, the soft, usually imperceptible buzz of the computers, the muffled sounds of people scooting chairs, emptying trays, washing beakers in the mouse laboratory next door.

"I called animal care. They'll call the police."

And then there was a coo from the dove. David turned. Sarah's old dove was still alive and in its cage. He'd entirely forgotten it. Oddly, it had been left alone.

They hadn't killed the birds; they'd killed the research. They had understood that the birds had already been sacrificed, and there were more birds where those had come from. Instead of killing them, they'd removed the ankle bands from each bird and put the white-crowns, robins, starlings, zebra finches and cowbirds together in the aviary. The zebra finches became not "Blue 17" or "Red 39," but male or female. The Bengalese finches, whose coloration didn't change with sex, were just finches. But that wasn't all. The computers had been cleared, the files erased. The two shelves in the laboratory that had held the binders with the back-up cds of files were empty.

The police agent who was called in to investigate asked for the names of everyone who had access to the lab. David listed himself, Anton, Rebecca, and stammered through the rest of the names, the students he'd recently hired: John, Valery, Amanda, Stefanie. They'd all had keys to the door.

"Do you think it could have been someone in your lab?"

David looked from the police officer to Rebecca, out the window and then back at the police officer. "No, it wasn't anyone here."

"We'll dust for prints," the officer said, "but I can already tell you, I won't find any but yours and those of the people in your lab. There are two kinds who do this: those who want you to know who they are, and we would have heard from them by now, and those who think they are god, passing judgment. This is the way they get their message across. No words, no names."

Three mornings after the sabotage, Anton found David at the counter near the surgical desk, his head bent over his work holding a glass jar on its side. An overcrowded cage with zebra finches, Bengalese finches, robins and starlings rattled at his side. Munin, perched on the light fixture above him, rustled her wings and peered down. With his free hand, he slid up the door of the cage, reached inside, and almost without looking, grabbed hold of a brown and white mottled Bengalese finch from the cage. He slipped the bird into the glass jar and held it firmly. Before him on the counter lay a row of dead birds. Robins, starlings, zebra finches, lined up from largest to smallest on sheets of industrial paper towel. The previous bird he'd put to sleep had been a female zebra finch.

Rebecca came into the laboratory with a tray of food dishes and then stopped a few feet away from Anton. "What are you doing?"

David's lips were drawn back and there was the rhythmic bulging and pulsing of jaw muscles being clenched. He barely opened his mouth to speak. "Finishing what was started." The words came out like a whisper.

"Stop! I'll take them," she said.

David looked up, the bird steady in his hand, and fixed her with a blank gaze. Just then, as he opened his mouth to speak, the female zebra finch, the last bird he'd put to sleep, began to tremble. Its thin right leg stabbed at the air and there was a quiver in the shoulders, the beginning of a flutter.

"Shit," David whispered. His eyes were on the jerking bird, but his hand held the Bengal in the jar steady. He reached out with his other hand and covered the trembling zebra finch with his palm.

Anton also wanted to tell David to stop, but he didn't know how to say it.

"Stop," Rebecca said again. "I've cared for these birds. You have no right....". She slammed the tray on the black countertop. The empty food dishes bounced and rattled onto the floor.

David looked up again, his voice calm, his cheeks now relaxed. "The lab won't be needing any more animal care. I've already filed the paperwork. You'll be paid for another two weeks. You're free to go."

The two of them stared at each other for a few moments, and then Rebecca, without a look in Anton's direction, backed up a few steps, turned, and left the laboratory.

ater, what Anton would remember most about that day was a single image: David bent over the laboratory bench fighting against the jerky shakes coming from his body. David's furtive gesture, the back of his hand wiping away a tear. David's twisted face of grief. Anton had gone to David and put his hand on his shoulder. In his memory, though it hadn't happened this way, he had looked out the window then, and seen Rebecca standing on the hillside outside the institute, looking in.

That night Rebecca came to his apartment. The sky was blackening and there was wind and lightning, but no thunder. The room went dark. There had not been rain for almost three months and there would be no rain tonight, only heat and muted breezes. They were sitting on the sofa. The Ferris wheel had indeed come full swing, settled abruptly at the bottom with a violent jerk. It was time to get off and go home.

"I know you want to know if I did it," she said.

Anton didn't answer her, fearing words would betray his suspicion.

"You believe him?"

He shook his head no, but shifted his eyes away from hers. He heard the things she'd said in the past, the questions she'd asked. *Does it bother you to work on them? Have you ever thought of letting them go?*

"You think I did it, don't you?" she said, raising her voice.

An issue of morality. Spiritual pain.

He lowered his voice. "Did you?"

"It's your fault." Suddenly, she was yelling.

"My fault?"

"And cruel. You know? You can't face me. You can't say anything and it's not only because you're a half-fluent foreigner. It's because you're a coward. He wouldn't have done it if it hadn't been for your stupid muting experiments."

"What are you talking about?" Her explosion surprised Anton and he struggled to both hear and understand her words. Cruel. Coward. His fault? And who was *he*?

"You prayed for them."

"What?"

"You did, or have you forgotten? That day just after your bird died and I found you in your office. Your head was bent and you said you were praying. You said you didn't like to work on them, but that wasn't true, was it?"

"I don't know what you're talking about. It's true I don't like to work on them but it's not because I think they're holy or special. I just don't like them." Her face was contorted, as if she was trying not to laugh. Anton didn't like her in this moment. "What I remember," he said. "Is that your hair was long, and I preferred it long."

She stood. "You're incapable of real love." She turned and left, walking out the door, not bothering to pull it shut behind her.

He stared at the open front door, felt the hot air come in, and then got up to close it. He could see her walking down the sidewalk, getting smaller and smaller with each step until she crested the hill and went over the other side. He saw a group of birds, city pigeons, black against the evening sky, banking and turning and waving as one perfectly coordinated being, appearing and then disappearing as they swooped. Likely they were looking for a place to roost, and then suddenly, having found one, they were gone, swallowed by the dark.

That night he showered under cold water, and while still wet and naked, lay down on the bed, his arms and legs stretched out without any covers, too hot to have anything touching his skin. What had she said? That he was a coward. Did she really say that? Had he heard wrong? Incapable? What could she have meant? He felt the beads of perspiration forming on his skin. It wasn't true that he was cold. And he did love. Intensely.

Outside, another lightning storm was approaching. He thought of the laboratory, the years of work and the only thing he'd accomplished was a single, three-page paper. What would David do now? No Sarah, no research, no post-doc. Only the magpie, whose name meant memory. He decided that he would write to Gianetti in the morning and see if there was a place in the laboratory in Turino. He'd work on any project. He didn't care anymore. He just wanted to go home.

Anton had read once about a writer whose novel had burned in a fire, and afterwards, the novelist had never written another word. He hadn't been able to understand that. The book must still have been in the author's head. Couldn't he have written it down again? It wasn't like a photograph that you only got to take once. His mother, he knew, always kept her negatives in fire-proofed boxes buried in the backyard for just that reason. Now, given everything that had happened in the lab, Anton thought he did understand. It was possible to lose the urge to begin again.

He closed his eyes and tried to sleep, but the lightning flashed into the darkness of the night, keeping him awake. What was the truth? It seemed to always come down to questions of perception. The one impossible and unquantifiable variable. His perception and Rebecca's were completely at odds.

Even back in 400 B.C., people knew about vulnerabilities and the vagaries of personal state, that every sense could be subjective, that every truth was suspect. *Eyes and ears are bad witnesses for men*, Heraclitus said. They knew first-hand the problems that arose when sound and meaning were disconnected. They grew tired of misperceptions. And so had Anton.

The clouds moved off into the distance, but the lightning continued, silent and unrelenting. At every bright flash he imagined another wildfire sparked in the dry desert. Sagebrush went up in flames, a jack rabbit sprinted off, insects popped and crackled in the heat. From far off the sirens of firetrucks had begun and now they would scream all night.

For months, humiliation consumed her. She did not know whether she was to blame. The day of the sabotage she had rushed to her friend Marla's house. "Marla, I think I said something crazy at that party we went to."

"At the restaurant?"

"Yes, at the restaurant." The whole evening was foggy. The place had been packed. She had sat at the bar with Marla and a group of out-of-towners, ordering mojitos. She drank gin and tonics instead, the effect of the cold, bitter drinks changing her sullenness to anger and then to giddiness. Everyone talked louder and louder making it harder and harder to hear.

"I can't remember, but I think I made a mistake, a big mistake. I told this guy about the bird research." Up close his skin was pale, the color of a cheap supermarket egg. His wrists were remarkably thin. Even in the flickering candlelight, she could make out all the bones of his hands.

"And what? He wasn't interested in the birds?" Marla asked.

"No. I think they sabotaged the research." She was frantic now.

"Whoa, slow down, Rebecca. Who's they?"

"I don't know."

His clothing had been too big for his frame, as if puberty had skipped his body. He was young, maybe just turned twenty-one, and she remembered that there was a mixture of intelligence and curiosity about him. She had described the birds and how they sang. How the females didn't sing. He leaned closer. He was interested.

"Where do they get them?" he asked.

"Oh, we breed them or order them or steal them from nests outside. That's the easy part."

"And you keep them?"

"Yes, that's my job. My friend, Marla, says I'm a bird waitress and I guess it's true. I feed, serve, and clean up the mess."

"Where are they kept?"

"In the lab and different experimental rooms. I don't know, maybe they don't mind it. They do get regular food and all kinds of supplements that they have a hard time finding in nature."

He ordered two more drinks. She was keenly aware of being drunk and yet she drank more.

"They tell me I'm anthropomorphizing, that I'm just sensitive because I'm a vegetarian. Of course, I don't think we should eat animals, but should we be studying them like this?"

She shifted her voice to mimic a male's voice.

"Where do you think new drugs are developed? That's what they always say, and I get it, and I take medicine but still, something... When you look at them in their eyes, really see them up close."

He moved closer to her.

"They just developed this technique where they can temporarily mute a bird and then use that to study, I don't know what, hearing, auditory feedback, stuttering and maybe even memory."

"Mute a bird?" He was appalled.

"That's what I said too but you can reverse it, and then they start singing again, but at first when they do, it sounds like croaking." The music got louder, the bass so loud that she could feel it through the bar stool. She leaned up and yelled in his ear. "I like robins the best. I have these fantasies of letting them go."

They sat together, drinking, the music too loud for them to talk. She wondered whether he was trying to pick her up, wondered whether she wanted to be picked up, felt a weariness come on and excused herself to go to the restroom. When she returned, her purse was on the barstool and the young man was gone.

She thought of the day David euthanized the birds. Anton's confused, inquisitive look. She had wanted him to say something to stop David but he'd stood mute and she was furious at his refusal to speak up and support her, his unwillingness to make David stop. She remembered the last time they were together, him naked and shuddering in her arms, his quivering scar. She doubted he was aware of how he held on to her like a pillow at night, as if afraid to let go. She could not have explained how she embraced him, murmuring and dreaming like a boy, as if she were a mother.

Now everything was over. She'd had two relationships in her life and both had ended in drama, disgust, dread.

MEMORY

David sat at the desk in his office and stared at the armadillo fetuses in the jar. The lab was quiet. He looked outside beyond the manicured lawns of the campus and noticed that the hue of the valley had turned, seemingly overnight, from summer to fall. Tinges of brown, red and yellow had crept into the green plants. Soon they'd be pulling back their chlorophyll, shutting down their veins, letting go of this year's leaves.

David had been sitting in this same place when he received the news of Ed's death. No phone call. No voice. Email, the quiet messenger, nothing more than a click on his mouse. Words typed and transmitted to a long list of recipients from the Rapid Assessment Program headquarters.

The accident happened a few months after Sarah's trip to Peru. Ed's six-person airplane had gone down in eastern Ecuador, and in a single stupid accident, the entire RAP team, the most gifted tropical surveyors in the world, were killed. David read the statement again. He saw Ed, tall and bearded, his smile sly as he handed over his list after a morning of birding together. David closed the email and opened it again. Minutes went by in blurry disbelief until finally, he picked up the phone to call Sarah at work.

"It can't be true," she said. David heard the click of the phone. Thirty seconds later, it was ringing again. He heard a gasp on her end.

"I'll pick you up," he said. "We'll go home."

For the next month they lived in a state of shock, Sarah bursting into tears several times a day. At first, they spoke of nothing but Ed and after that, they spoke little at all. Sarah became angry in a way that was completely new. David thought that it was just a passing stage of grief, but instead of lessening with time, it deepened. He became suspicious, countering her anger with silence and longer work hours.

David knew that one woman had survived the crash and that despite a broken leg, had miraculously crawled her way out of the forest. He knew he could call her to find out the details of Ed's death, but he never did. He preferred to believe that Ed didn't die on impact. He imagined that when the noise of the crash was over, after the alarmed birds had flown up in a loud cackle of calls, after the last tree had cracked and split, there was a moment of silence. He wanted to think that in that moment, before bleeding and shock set in, before the neurons exploded in one last desperate spasm, that the final sound to hit Ed's ears was the song of an unknown species of bird.

In the weeks and months after Ed's death, he learned about the loneliness of an increasingly quiet marriage, the sadness of slipping into bed, Sarah's back to his side, and then rolling out of the same bed the next morning, barely a word or a touch, only misgivings and Ed's death between them. He'd longed for their graduate school days when the two of them, and if Ed was home, the three of them, would stay up all night drinking and arguing about behavior, psychology and the nature of their work. Now sitting in his empty lab, he remembered a conversation they'd had all back in Louisiana.

"You're more comfortable in the lab, David, because you can control things and you *need* to control things, or at least you need to *think* you are controlling them," Sarah said.

"Of course," he said. "If we're not controlling the right variables, then we are just being natural historians."

"I disagree," Ed said.

"With what? That David likes to control variables?" Sarah asked.

"With the idea that you need to control variables to be a modern scientist."

"I didn't say modern scientist," she said. "What kind of label is that anyway?"

"That's absurd, Ed," David said. "Of course you need to control variables to be a scientist. Otherwise, we're just observing and making assumptions based on our perceptions. There's no objectivity if you don't control."

"So, in your eyes, I'm not a scientist," Ed said.

"I'm just saying that without controlled experiments, we can't know what we're learning with certainty."

He had believed the words at the time.

Ed laughed. "You're just upset, David. My bird list has gotten so long you'll never catch up."

"Ah," Sarah said. "Now we've slipped into male-male competition."

David laughed then too. "Especially if you keep discovering new species every time you go to the tropics."

He missed those days with even more intensity now. Ed dead. Sarah gone. The birds destroyed. Sarah's questions had always helped him hone his ideas, but their conversations had suffered with Ed's death. As he'd gone deeper into mapping the bird's brain, into understanding how a syrinx vibrated, and how air moved through the body, she had said she was stepping back, becoming more interested in the "unknowable" that guided a life.

"Sounds like mumbo jumbo to me," he said.

"And what you do is less mumbo? You've got a bird in a cage and you can see what neurons fire for different behaviors, but what does that have to do with that bird's life?"

"Everything," he said.

She began to cry then, just softly at first and then in loud sobs, and although he wanted to go to her, something had held him back.

He wished now that he'd been more generous in that moment. He remembered a dinner party, also after Ed's death, when a colleague's daughter asked him about his work and Sarah had answered for him. The memory still pained him.

"He steals baby birds from nests, raises them up, and then sticks wires into the males' brains to measure how they sing."

He had laughed nervously, shocked at her glib response. She'd had too much to drink.

"But you can't really know which ones are male when you collect them, can you?" Sarah continued. "I mean a baby bird, male or female, isn't more than just a bit of pink chicken skin, is it?"

"So how do you know?" the young woman asked David.

"When they get bigger," he explained, "you put them under anesthesia, open them up and look for ovaries. It's a simple surgery."

"And what do you do if they're female?" Sarah asked.

He was embarrassed by her. She was talking too loudly. He leaned over to the young woman and whispered in her ear. "I set them free."

The conversation hung between them, a swelling silence that grew. He despised the quiet evenings at the house and so he bought a folding cot, called home and left a message that he'd be working late.

A few months later, she'd spoken across the silence of the living room. "I guess I'm just not that interested in birds in cages anymore." This time there was no anger in her voice. He remembered standing up and walking out of the room. He remembered the drive back down the winding canyon to the university. The night, turning and turning on his cot. The

next morning, he drove back to their house, spoke to her even before she
got out of bed.

"It's because of you and Ed, isn't it?"

She fixed him with a look, and he immediately felt shame. A violation
of his friendship with Ed, a violation of his memory.

"I suppose so." She sat up and stretched, her eyes blinking at him and
the sunlight of the morning.

He waited. She offered nothing more.

"And?"

She pushed back the covers, as if brushing him away, and stood.

"Come on Sarah. That's all you're going to say?"

Her back to him, she took off her nightgown and began to dress. "It's
not what you think. Besides, Ed's dead."

"Damn it, Sarah! You're so bloody verbal, so good at getting all your
thoughts and emotions into neat little packages, everything described perfectly with just the right amount of emphasis on each word, and now I'm
getting the silent treatment?"

She buttoned her blouse. She still hadn't turned around. She spoke in a
quiet, controlled voice. "I need some space."

Afraid of learning more, he hadn't challenged her.

He rummaged on his desk now for the letter she'd sent most recently and
ripped it open.

> *I was trying to open a space for us. All you ever spoke about was the
> neuroscience of birdsong, not even the birds themselves, just the
> nerves and muscles that made a bird sing. You became stingy, told
> nothing of yourself or your feelings.*

"Maybe I had nothing to tell?" he said out loud.

> *You even quit going out to watch birds. You were only interested in*

what you could do in the lab. And then you wouldn't agree to visit Ed and I was so disappointed that you didn't come. I thought you'd realize it when the birds left. Without the birds, I thought the living room might fill with new sounds.

What bothered him most as he read this letter was that he only had her words on paper. He couldn't hear her saying any of this. He couldn't tell if there was regret or relief in her voice.

A kind of fog had settled over his thinking. Certainty. He'd always wanted it and he'd relied on the ability of science to show him what was certain in the world. Of course, at some level he knew science was just one way of knowing. There were truths to be found, but also mysteries he'd never be able to answer. Ed's absence meant he'd never have the chance to have another conversation about certainty or experimentation or a million other things he thought they'd have time for. The sabotage and death of the birds meant that the muting experiments were over. And he would never be able to ask Ed about Sarah's trip to Peru, though he guessed he wouldn't have had the guts to do that anyway. He suspected they had come closer, recognized a long-standing attraction and acted on it, and that Sarah had realized what she'd been missing all the years.

He folded the letter, picked up his bag and drove home. From inside the house, tucked within the spruce trees, he could hear the grumbling of an approaching thunderstorm as it worked its way up the valley and he knew that if he drove out to the ridge he would see the dark clouds, rain already coming down like a shroud being pulled across the sky. One of the few summer storms this year. He heard Munin squawk in her aviary and decided to bring her in so that she could wait out the storm in the house. Outside the moist wind whipped against his face as he descended the wooden steps toward the aviary. Munin spied him, jumped from one perch to another and squawked again. She opened her wings, black in this light and flew toward the door when he approached.

"Back now."

She flew to the other side of the aviary, perched with her good foot, using her bad leg for balance, and waited. He unfastened the latch and entered the aviary, pulling the door shut behind him. He took a piece of foil from his pocket and held it in his left hand for her to see. Munin cocked her head. He held his other arm straight out so that she could land on his forearm. He flicked his left wrist, but in the dark light, the foil barely shimmered. Munin opened her wings and began to fly toward him, but in the last second there was a gust of wind. The door to the aviary banged opened and with a quick change in angle, she flew out, perching tentatively on the branch of a nearby spruce tree.

David hurried outside after her. "Munin, the shiny stuff's down here." He extended his left arm, gently rocking his wrist with the foil. It had gotten darker and the bird oriented toward his voice, studying him, as if she had just realized that she was not within the confines of the aviary. Strong gusts of wind blew his hair into his eyes. He twirled the foil and held his right arm stiff. The bird ruffled and opened her wings slightly before closing them again. He felt a first and then a second drop of water. A gust of wind slapped across his face. The bird puffed up again, this time opening her wings wide, and then she was gone.

How does a relationship end? Beginnings are easy. There are always fixed points. An irresistible voice, a smile, shared interests. An inexplicable tingling on the skin, a wrist taken abruptly, bread bitten straight from another's hand. The channels of communication open, neurons sensitized, sensory organs available. There is a burst of energy, a frenzy of activity, something like a bird's *zugunruhe* before migration. The beginning is fattening, restlessness, take-off, flight. A setting out for destinations unknown, a movement north or south, no questioning of why. The end is less exact. Weariness, suspicion, nostalgia, thoughts and sensations existing without a past or a future. In the end, there is the absence of sound, a cessation of neurons, a magpie's quiet escape through an open door.

At first Anton didn't discuss Rebecca with David, but her absence, like that of the birds, was palpable. In the weeks following their last conversation, Anton kept returning to the one thing he didn't want to think about: Rebecca's outrage. He had gone once more to her apartment, but when he knocked on the door, she didn't come out. He cupped his hands and peered in through the dark window. He tried the doorknob and realized the door was unlocked. The place, which had been sparse when Rebecca lived there, was now bare. She had left a futon mattress, complete with sheets, and the bed light, but when he opened the closet door he saw an empty rack that before had been crammed with her clothes. Even the air smelled of something else, not lemon, something other than her, a musty smell as if the apartment had been closed for a long time. All traces of Rebecca were gone, as if she had never lived in that place.

He heard her asking: *Doesn't it bother you to work on them?*

His answer: *Of course.*

"You think she did it?" Anton asked David in one of their last conversations. "Is that why you fired her?"

"I didn't fire her, Anton. The market went south. I downsized."

Unsure what he meant, Anton didn't respond.

"Look, Anton, I don't know if she did it. There were, how many, eight, ten people working in this lab the last couple of months? Plus, the weekend animal care folks. Do I suspect her? Yes."

"She didn't do it," Anton said.

David raised his eyebrows.

"I know her."

David looked out the window for a moment and then he turned back to Anton. "Just because you're sleeping with someone doesn't mean you know them."

Anton shook his head.

"I'm sorry," David said.

Right after the sabotage, Anton had wanted to tell David that he had suspected her too and then to confess how bad this thought made him feel, but to do so, he would have had to reveal their relationship and he hadn't wanted to do that. Now it was clear that David had known about it all along. Perhaps Rebecca was right. He was a coward.

"You don't have to leave," David said. "We can order more birds, begin again."

Again, David seemed to already know Anton's plans.

"How do you know?"

"I got a call from Gianetti. He wanted a reference. He asked about new technical skills, the neuronal work. I told him you were a master, had figured out the muting technique."

"Gianetti needed a reference? Has he got early dementia? He's the reason I came here. He knows my work."

"Anton, I hope you find the memory traces. I really do."

The rest of September was hot as usual in the valley, but cool at David's house. Below the conifer trees, night came earlier than in the valley. David sat on the deck at dusk, a whisky in hand and stared at the empty aviary, the door propped open. Every couple of days he still went down to put food inside in case Munin returned, but so far, he'd only been feeding raccoons. He swirled the glass. The two ice cubes clinked together, melting, and the water formed little eddies in the whiskey. He thought about the part of the poem in which Odin, the half-blind Norse god, worries about his two ravens: Hugin and Munin. Thought and Memory.

> *I fear for Hugin*
> *That he may not return,*
> *Yet more am I anxious for Munin.*

One would always have new thoughts. It was the memories that went astray. He took another sip of the whiskey and felt the burn at the back of his throat. He didn't have much of a taste for the drink, but lately, he'd been thinking about Ed and that had been Ed's nightly ritual.

"After a day in the forest, you feel invincible," Ed had said. "You sit at the lodge, feet up on the railing, a cold whiskey in hand, and watch the day go dark. You listen. Half the world goes to sleep. The other half wakes up."

David heard a hermit thrush, its melancholy song clear and piercing, as fitting as any this night. He thought about the time in Louisiana when he had accompanied Ed to a fundraiser for a local conservation organization. As a challenge Ed had offered his ears and bet a thousand dollars that he could identify the birds on any tape brought to him from any place in the world. His only requirement was that he be given the name of the country where the recording was made. The challenge was put up for auction. A local businessman and avid birdwatcher bet ten thousand dollars that he could stump the bird man. Ed accepted the bet. On the agreed evening, in front of an audience of fifty, Ed sat alone on stage, smiling sheepishly at the murmuring crowd of bird fanatics gathered to watch him. The businessman walked up and ceremoniously placed a cassette player onto the table and said "Bolivia."

Ed sat down and pressed the play button. The recording was low-quality and scratchy. Ed listened, cocked his head, finished listening to the tape, re-wound and listened again, this time taking notes. After the second re-wind, when he again pushed the play button, he began to name each species of bird as it sounded on the tape, skipping just one. Everyone was impressed. He'd just earned the conservation organization ten thousand dollars, but David could tell that Ed was disturbed. After the clapping ended, Ed went back to the one bird he hadn't named. He played it over and over.

"That," he said, leaning into the microphone, "sounds like an antwren in the *Herpsilochmus* genus, but I know all those wrens. It's not one I know."

Two years later, in Pennsylvania, David received a reprint of a paper reporting the existence of a new species of antwren, which lived only in remote tropical forests of Bolivia. David looked at the drawing of the small, brown bird. Across the top, Ed's scribble. *The one I heard on that Bolivian tape.* Ed had identified, by sound alone, a species new to science.

It was dark on the porch now. The whiskey had warmed. There was no burning, just the heat of the drink going down. Unlike Odin, Ed had never worried over memory. Ed was a man who had never forgotten a song, not even the song of a bird he'd not yet heard.

David called Ed to congratulate him. "Once I get going on this neuro-science research I'm going to put you in a box, stick electrodes in you and take some scans while you're identifying birdsong. I'm going to figure out how you do it."

Ed laughed. "Sure, I'll be up the Tambopata River. Just give me a call."

As David took the last sip of whiskey he heard Ed's voice, the sound clear. Ed was saying, *You forget yourself. You could walk out into the forest, listen for as long as you want. You could keep going, and no one would ever find you.*

Before he left the States, Anton went to the deli. Reading his face in an instant, Francesco came around the stainless steel counter, his apron dusted white and crisp with flour. The balls of soft dough and strips of pasta waiting to be cranked through the machine were left without a thought, even though they would be ruined from too much time in the dry air.

As soon as Anton sat down, he began talking. He told Francesco about Rebecca and David, about how he'd remained silent, kept the relationship a secret, about the muting and stuttering and sabotage.

"I think she is responsible," he said. "She asked so many questions about the birds, morals, right and wrong, and her behavior lately was either incredibly sweet or angry."

Francesco listened. When Anton was done, Francesco brushed the flour off his hands with a dry towel, went to a cupboard, took out two small glasses and a bottle of port.

"I lied to David. I denied that she could have been involved even when I think she was. I saw her a few times on campus with her camera, but she told me she wasn't taking pictures anymore."

A quick pull on the old cork and Francesco filled the glasses half way up.

"I didn't ask her about having seen her with the camera."

Francesco wrapped two fingers around his glass and raised it. "There is always risk in speaking."

They tapped glasses ceremoniously, making little sound.

"And when I went back to her house, she was gone. Why wouldn't she tell me?"

Francesco waited for Anton to continue.

"I feel like I betrayed David."

They drank, emptying the small glasses.

"I also feel like I betrayed her," he said. "Why do I feel this way?"

"Because you loved."

Anton shook his head. "I don't know if I did, really. There is so much I didn't share with her. Couldn't share."

Francesco reached for the bottle and filled their glasses again. "We are rarely brave."

Anton left the States, returned to Europe, and established himself in Gianetti's laboratory in Turino where he was free to work on memory, which continued to be elusive and slippery. He felt confused by what had happened with Rebecca and disappointed that he and David had never accomplished much with the birds. He was back to mice, horribly passive creatures, but better suited to finding the keys to memory. He reacquainted himself with the work culture of Italy, to the regular lunch hour when everyone left the lab instead of eating over their desks. He drank espresso after lunch and chatted with his new colleagues. There was a hollow feeling whenever he thought of her and so he tried not to. He waited for his mother's letters from Africa, for her upcoming return.

Fall was short that year and snow fell early in the Alps. The first chance he had, he went to his grandfather's house in the mountain village in

Südtirol where he'd spent summers as a child. He bought snowshoes and hiked for hours over the wet snow and then he ventured higher into the silent mountains, the snow deeper and harder, layers of crystallized water packed upon layers of crystallized water. Come spring there would be the sounds of bells on sheep, bleating goats, barking dogs. The migrant birds would return and nightingales would sing from early morning through most of the night. He was happy to be back in Europe but not as happy as he thought he would be. There was a sense of relief but also some disappointment that he couldn't precisely understand.

He mentioned his depressed state to David. *Time,* David had written back, *give yourself time. You'll find the excitement again. It always comes back. Science is part of you. You can't stop it.* But he hadn't expressed himself well to David. It wasn't only a problem with science. He listened to the crunch of his shoes on the snow and remembered a conversation he'd had with Rebecca.

"So how does this bird-poem end?" she asked.

She was standing next to the open window, her hair still long, hanging over her back, the air coming in, the sweat of love-making evaporating off his skin. She lay down next to him and rested her head on his shoulder, her arm over his chest, her fingers massaging him.

"After the long trip through seven valleys," he told her, "the birds arrive at the holy land. Only thirty remain. They are broken, their feathers ripped. They are hungry and very, very tired, but the door keeper tells them they cannot come in. They should turn around and go back. The birds say no. They feel tricked, disillusioned. They have traveled a long way. They want to see their king. They insist."

"Finally, the keeper opens the door. Inside it's bright, so bright that they cannot see. He hands each bird a piece of paper and tells them that once they read it, the real reasons for their journey will be revealed. The birds grab the papers and read."

"What do the papers say?" she asked.

"Lists of sins, their sins. The birds feel shame and then they are angry because they feel like they flew the long journey for nothing. Then a big light comes toward them and at that moment, they see their god, and you know what god is?"

She shook her head.

"Themselves. A mirror. Apparently, in Persian, the two words have the same meaning. The Simorgh, which means thirty birds, see the Simorgh, which is the name of their god."

The substance of their being was undone,
And they were lost like shade before the sun;
Neither the pilgrims nor their guide remained.
The Simorgh ceased to speak, and silence reigned.

"They reach silence, but I don't think it is death," he said. "More like understanding."

"And that's it? The end of the book?" she asked.

"No. It's a strange book because after that scene, Attar, the poet, keeps writing for many more pages and tells another story, this story about a king who falls in love with a beautiful, lovely boy and he won't let the boy out of his sight. The boy gets tired of being around the king, so one night, while the king sleeps, he runs away. When the king finds him, he gets very drunk and angry and orders the boy to be beaten, carried into the square, hung and left to die. Only the boy's father saves him and hangs up another guy, a murderer who is going to die anyway. When the king wakes, he believes the boy is dead and he regrets his orders. *And as his anger went his sorrow grew.* He is very upset. He cannot eat. He loses weight. He understands that in killing the boy he loved, he killed himself." He paused. "It's a mirror, everything we do and say, what we love."

She waited and then lifted her head. "That's it?"

"No, no," he said, "eventually the boy goes back to the king. He loved the king, too. The last thing Attar writes is that the king and the boy put their heads together, they whisper, and go off as one. No one ever hears what they say."

"Hmm," she said.

"What?"

"The boy shouldn't have gone back."

"Why not?"

"The king betrayed him."

"It was a mistake. He learned that and besides, the boy betrayed the king too. He ran away."

"Maybe he was afraid to stay."

"I don't know. I think the king deserved a second chance."

Anton came out of the trees into a small clearing and stopped for a moment. He remembered her adamant response.

"I don't agree. There aren't any second chances. We do what we do and we deal with the consequences. You don't get to go back and do it again."

What had she meant? Afraid to stay? No second chances. Without second chances, new trials, experiments, nothing was possible. Without second chances, people would never progress. The statement reminded him of his mother, almost seemed to be something she might say about photography. You only had one shot to get the picture.

The snow crunched under his snowshoes as he trudged on across the open space. He heard the call of a jay, and then the reply from another further off. He stopped, removed his gloves and bent to scoop up a small handful of snow, wanting to taste freshness, but below the night's dusting, the snow was hard and hurt his fingers. He pulled his hand back and sucked on his fingers to warm them. He replaced his gloves, repositioned his backpack and walked on. He didn't realize he'd forgotten sunscreen. Later, he would feel how the sunlight, reflecting off the frozen snow, had burned his face just like it had in Utah.

What the sabotage really did was set David free, although it took him some time to realize this. After disposing of the birds in the lab and letting Rebecca go, after Anton's departure and Munin's escape, he passed weeks in a confused, depressed stupor. In the mornings he came into the laboratory, pulled the door closed behind him and sat in the conference room. He had felt crushed the day he put the birds to sleep, angry at the person who had rendered them useless by removing their bands. They had been made victims and he wouldn't tolerate that. He suspected Rebecca, of course, but it didn't add up, and he hadn't wanted to think it was her, both for himself and for Anton, and maybe even for her.

Now, he no longer felt anger, only loneliness. The lack of birdsong drove him crazy, but he made himself persevere, waiting longer and longer each day before he turned on a radio, until he could sit in the silence of the empty laboratory for hours, looking at his library of books, or out the window at the desert, or at his collection of bottles, bits of bird parts lined across the windowsill.

The day before he'd found Sarah's journal at home. He opened and closed it a few times but hadn't had the courage to read it. Now he sat with the book on his lap. They had always shared their journals. Would she want him to read this one or not? When he opened and flipped through the pages, a set of folded sheets fell out. He picked them up from the floor and realized they were a letter intended for him. She'd never sent it or given it to him.

October 20th Tambopata, Peru.

Dear David:

First day: this morning I got up and dressed quickly, slung a small bag over my shoulder and went onto the verandah. I was the only one up. I stepped into a pair of cold rubber boots and began to make my way along the muddy path toward the forest. A few stars were blinking against the blue-black sky. The palm shrubs I passed, dark and huge in the budding light made me think of black-laced Spanish fans. Below the trees it was still dark. Water dripped from the leaves. At first light there was an explosion of sounds, the world going from nighttime to morning in one split second. How could any animal hear another? The line from sender to receiver, singer to listener, hopelessly confounded by crowd, defying everything I know about the importance of song for communication. The thought that came to me unexpectedly and unpleasantly was that everything in the laboratory is misguided.

Then just above me, there was a roar of a howler monkey. I jumped, looked up and saw a male, his mouth wide open and red, canine teeth exposed. His forehead, chin and neck grotesquely swollen with worms. When he called again it felt as if he was yelling in my ear. His ugliness, repulsive and fascinating. Another howler answered him and they began a loud dual. At least for these two, sender and receiver seemed to be working.

At mid-morning, I came out of the forest onto the path back to the lodge. I picked up my pace and then suddenly stopped at the sight of a quiet dark green hummingbird perched on a branch, perfectly still, so close I didn't need to bother with binoculars. The bird turned its head and looked at me. Neither of us moved. I became conscious of a change in my mood. The binoculars hanging at my chest pulled on my neck. There was a faint burn when I blinked my eyes. Back behind me in the forest, the howler monkeys bellowed. I turned away from the hummingbird wanting to distance myself from its stare, and now as I write you, I think I'm finally acknowledging to myself how lonely I am.

He continued to read.

October 21ˢᵗ, Tambopata Lodge

Today after lunch Ed led our group on a walk and talked about the forest, ants, monkeys and jaguar. When we came to a clearing, a tree gap, he told us that tropical trees have shallow roots. The soil is spongy with water so sometimes, when the wind comes with force, it lifts all the trees up like a mini tornado. He showed us a giant ceiba, maybe the most beautiful tree I've ever seen. He said, the really, really big gaps are man-made and someone asked whether he meant slash and burn agriculture? In his typical witty fashion, which you would have appreciated, he shook his head and said: No, something much more efficient. Small airplane crashes.

David stopped reading and looked away from the letter. The irony was painful. He felt constriction in his throat. Why hadn't Sarah told him this after the crash? Had she forgotten that Ed had said it?

October 25th, Tambopata Lodge

Tonight, Ed said, "I have given myself over entirely to this world. It's like a marriage. A commitment I can't go back on; it's what I know you and David have; you're meant to be together." And then he said something really strange. He said, "This is the only place on earth where I can forget myself." He seems so alone. I miss you intensely.

The letter ended there. David folded it up and put it back in the journal. He read her final entry.

November 1, Flight from Lima to Los Angeles

Eight days in the forest and I'm on my way home. I have seen acres of bamboo, river otter, an ocelot and more species of parrot than I ever care to see again. I realize that I love two men whose principal love is not me, but birds and the sounds they make. They are men who pass through life listening. Men who only really understand the world with their ears. One lives in a wet forest and the other in a neat laboratory; it's as if they both come from a foreign world where ears are tuned with precision and every sound carries layers of meaning that only they can decipher. I once read that what most marked Count Basie's music is the silence, the space perfectly placed between the notes. They are two men who can hear such a difference. I am writing this as I land in Los Angeles. It is clear to me. The two men, who I love, share a language that I will never completely understand.

David shut the journal. He took a deep breath. He noticed a single zebra finch feather stuck between the corner of the wall and the carpet and he bent down to pick it up. He smoothed the tiny black and white striped feather between his finger and thumb and then put it on the table.

He stood and walked to the bookshelf along the wall and searched for the book that Ed once gave him on neotropical migrant birds. He couldn't remember having lent it to anyone. His eyes skipped back to the beginning of the shelf and then he saw an unfamiliar book. He pulled it from its place on the shelf. It was a small paperback, the binding stiff from never having been opened, and the cover showed a group of birds around a stream. *The Conference of the Birds*. It wasn't a book he'd ever bought. He heard Anton now. It was one of their last conversations.

"I am leaving you a book as a thank you."

"No need," David had told him.

"It's not wrapped. You'll find it later, I hope."

Until now David had forgotten about the book. He flipped to the back cover and read the blurb. A long poem written in the 12th century. Birds as the main characters. An odyssey to find God. A hoopoe bird as guide. He returned to his chair, sat down and opened the book and flipped through a few pages, focusing here and there on the poem. Back at the beginning he started to read, but the fifth line of the book made him pause.

He knew your language and you knew his heart—

He closed his eyes and heard Ed. "Sometimes when I'm in the forest, wrapped in my hammock, I think of you and Sarah. I hear the two of you talking about some paper that's just come out, the value of one methodological approach over another. I hear your low voice, the staccato cadence to your sentences, and then her voice trilling the way it does when she gets excited about something new. And then I hear those muffled whimpers that always come after those discussions. Whimpers and laughter, and I know there are no two people more suited to each other."

There was a bareness whenever he thought of her, not unlike the empty cages in his laboratory, but he also realized that all these months she'd been gone, he'd been talking to her, continuing his conversations with her, silently to himself.

You stopped talking, she said in her letter explaining why she sent the birds away from their home aviary. Perhaps it was true. He'd said less and less out loud, but in his mind, he was always communicating with her. And she had stopped talking to him as well. The silence had gone both ways.

In his jealous state, his obsession with whether she'd had feelings for Ed in Peru, he had missed the cues, had not understood the magnitude of memories and emotions Ed's death must have brought to the surface for her, irrespective of whether they'd been intimate or not. What had she said? *If you suffer loss young, you learn a vocabulary for grief.* Of course that wasn't true. Ed's death must have been doubly difficult for Sarah, triggering memories of the losses she'd suffered when she was young. Because he struggled so much to understand and put words on his own emotions, David had always deferred to her explanations of herself. Her psychologist's vocabulary, her measured speech, her insistence that perception meant more than signal, and that the rational mind could mold perception to its will. Words, words, words. She talked. He listened and believed. Now, with Ed dead, and eight months of her absence, Munin gone, Anton gone, the research destroyed, he understood that grief was grief no matter how many times you experienced it. If you let yourself love, you felt grief when it was taken away. A true loss was, and always would be, irreplaceable. Sometimes, it was also unbearable.

She had called and written repeatedly, but in the last while, her correspondence had tapered off. He would write to her now. He went to his computer and whispered as he wrote, needing to try out the words before he committed them to email.

Dear Sarah,
You know that I'm not much good at writing, unless it's in small yellow notebooks. The birds are all gone—sabotage—some animal rights activist, they tell me. They also erased all the data files. Anton, the post-doc went home. No need for a technician or undergraduates, and so now I'm the only one in the laboratory. Me, the books, the

armadillo fetuses you gave me. What did you call them? The surro-gate children you'd never have, always neotenic and cute, never crying for attention. They're still here. Still floating. This is a silly thing to be writing you after so long, I know.

This summer I rescued an injured magpie. I named her Munin from the old Norse myth of two ravens. Munin for memory and Hugin for thought. She was beautiful. Purplish-black, sleek and smart, but she flew away in September. I consoled myself by thinking that at least I was left with thought. But you know what? Without you there aren't a whole lot of good thoughts either. I haven't put anything down in a notebook for months. Is it because I know you aren't here to read it? I want you to tell me where you've been and what you've done and who you've met. I'm sorry I asked you to leave. I'm sorry that I was starving you. You're still the only person I want to talk to. The only person I want to hear.

When he finished writing, he read it again. He missed her voice and her ideas, her feedback as important to the maintenance of himself as his own auditory feedback. He looked outside and saw two chickadees, white tail feathers flashing, flitting around in the dense green oak leaves.

He remembered the time they'd gone to the field when he'd first started studying auditory feedback. They'd found some lazuli buntings in the fresh green oaks behind the institute, and he'd recorded a male and then played his recording back to him. She'd asked, *What happens when sound producer and receiver are one?* Now he knew the answer to her question. There was a breakdown in the signaling. There was confusion, stuttering and then quiet. The mind needed more than recurring thoughts. He needed her, not memories of her.

One of the chickadees hopped to an outside branch on the tree, opened his beak and sang. David couldn't hear the bird's call from inside the build-ing, but he heard the bird singing in his mind. Long ago, he'd memorized a chickadee's sweet buzzy voice. No, he thought, there wasn't a word for love. Not really. And no sound could symbolize its loss. Maybe it was better defined as quality of feeling, a sound most notable when it was gone.

He hit the send button on his email and then went back into the laboratory with a sense of relief. Without obligation to employees and birds, and having finally written to Sarah, there was only himself to contend with.

AUDITORY FEEDBACK

Rebecca crossed the porch. She squinted up into the spotless blue sky. Every year, spring and summer seemed to begin earlier than the year before. She had promised to meet her housemate, Marla, for lunch, but she was reluctant to leave the shade of the porch. As she went down the wooden steps, she heard clomp-clomp-clomp and looked up in time to see a male California quail tumbling, head over foot, from the roof. He landed in a thud on the grass next to the walkway. She picked him up and studied his plump chestnut belly, streaked white on the sides. His legs and feet were dark gray and leathery, strong as they should be for a bird that lived his life on the ground. What was he doing on the roof anyway? Up close, the bird's markings were astonishingly beautiful. She ran a finger over the soft black feathers of his chin and then across the white stripe above his eyes. The curlicue feather rising from his forehead, bobbed over her sweaty palm like a large black teardrop. She went back inside the house. In the kitchen she slipped the quail into a plastic bag and pressed the seal shut. She opened the freezer, felt a blush of cold air, placed him inside, and then she left for her lunch.

Dead birds no longer surprised her. At first, it was the cat who delivered them. She had returned home one spring evening to find the black neighborhood cat skulking at her front door. When she mounted the stairs, he nodded his head and dropped a greenish-gray female hummingbird at her feet. She picked up the tiny, drab bird, almost weightless in her hand. The next week, the cat brought her another hummingbird, this time a male with metallic green feathers and red chin.

"There are dead birds in our freezer," Marla said when she noticed.

"I know," Rebecca said.

"Why?"

"Habit, I guess."

"Well, can you put them in Tupperware or something? I can't stand those black beady eyes staring at me every time I get a popsicle."

"I'll wrap them in foil."

Rebecca thought little about these first two, but dead birds kept coming. She found a starling in the driveway, then a mourning dove in the park, their bodies stiff, but substantial in her hand. Over the weeks, the count mounted to include a house finch, two sparrows and a robin. When a small kestrel slammed into the living room window, she raced outside to fetch it and held it while it died. The print of its feathers, head and beak on the mottled glass, appeared briefly each evening in the diminishing light of sunset.

Except for the kestrel and the hummingbirds, she could find no reason for the deaths. The birds were not sickly or starved. There was no obvious injury, no blood, no boys with sling-shots. When she opened them up, their stomachs did not wriggle with parasites. They were perfect. Only dead. In the dark, quiet hours of the night she began to cut them open and remove their organs of song.

She put the thawed quail onto the counter on his back. She screwed the portable light onto the table edge and focused it onto the bird. Quails, being large, were easy birds, but still she moved slowly. Using tweezers, she plucked out the bird's neck feathers. She clipped open the bulging crop with scissors. Pale round seeds tumbled out. Commercial bird feed. Clearly, his last meal had been an easy feast. She brushed the seeds off the table and into the trash and set about opening up the breast. She whistled softly to herself.

Marla came in from work at two a.m. "It's disgusting, this bunch of bird parts you've got here."

When Rebecca didn't immediately comment, Marla lifted the brown cotton on a Tupperware and looked at the bird bones teaming with dark flat beetles. "Good god, Rebecca! Birds in the freezer, bugs in the kitchen."

"Beetles, not bugs," Rebecca said. "Sarcophagus."

"Sarcophagus." Marla repeated. "What's that mean? That I'm living in an Egyptian bird morgue?"

"They're completely harmless. They just clean the bones."

Marla peered once more into the container before snapping the lid shut again. "I'm trying to figure out what happened to you in that laboratory." She pulled out a chair and plopped down in frustration. "He's not coming back."

"I don't want him to."

Marla was wrong. It wasn't only Anton. Or the laboratory. Or David. It was all of those things. Only Rebecca hadn't tried to explain any of it because she realized the importance of everything she was leaving out. She had never told Marla about Chicago.

"Did you know," she said, "that sound is a wave that gets caught, or depending on how you want to look at it, trapped in your ear?"

She made another snip, and using the tweezers, lifted out a piece of reddish flesh and dipped it in a bowl of alcohol. On the outside it was nothing more than a small Y of cartilage. Inside were tiny flaps, valves that vibrated when air was pushed past, making sound. She held the syrinx up for Marla to see. "This is it. The syrinx. The organ of sound and song. Without this, a bird can't sing."

Marla eyed the flesh.

Rebecca continued. "But even with this, most birds can't sing unless they hear themselves. There must be auditory feedback."

"You're better off without him, Beca," Marla said.

"For people too," Rebecca said. "We have to hear ourselves. Otherwise we lose our ability to talk." She dropped the quail's syrinx into a vial with alcohol and screwed the cap on tightly. She printed in small clear letters: syrinx, male, *Callipepla californica*.

"You know," Marla said. "I've been thinking that we become inhabited by the people we know. They get inside us and influence what we do and don't do. Either we're following in their good footsteps or rejecting anything that reminds us of them. Maybe by the time we're old, we're not even us anymore, just jumbles of the people we once knew."

The photographer. His drunkenness, his hands around her throat, being locked in the dark room, the abortion. The idea that he was still inside, influencing her was not something Rebecca was willing to consider.

"Rebecca, are you listening to me?"

"Of course."

"Well I think you should let this go. You need to stop dissecting dead birds. You need to get back to doing what you do best."

"I happen to be very good at this."

"You're not good at it. Anyone can cut out a bird's throat. You're good at photography." When Rebecca didn't respond, Marla said, "I'm going to bed."

Rebecca heard the sound of water running in the bathroom and then the click of Marla's bedroom door closing. The kitchen was quiet again. Tomorrow she would mail the vial to a laboratory in Pennsylvania. Those syringeal specialists, the few souls in the world who studied the shape of this organ, would never know who sent the syringes. She liked to imagine their excitement each time another brown envelope arrived, how they would tear it open with happy curiosity wanting to discover which new syrinx, perfectly dissected and preserved, had been sent to them this time.

Rebecca didn't know why, but she always stitched the birds back together again. Tonight while she sewed up the quail she was vaguely aware that this continual opening of dead birds, this dissection and preservation of tissues and organs, was a reckoning. She cut and sliced, labeled and shipped. With time she would learn that what felt like contrition could also be a salve.

Outside his office window, a mixed group of birds landed in the recently flushed oak. David wanted to get out into the evening, but he needed to finish writing a keynote address he'd been asked to deliver about the importance of the silent partner: the female bird that didn't sing. Silence as a presence. Silence as a collaborator.

Some months after the sabotage, David had found a three-ring binder in the conference room library, which he hadn't even known existed. The saboteurs had erased the computers and broken the CDs with the data, but here in this binder, he saw that Rebecca had been keeping track of the birds, recording which ones she'd bred, which ones had been involved with which experiments, which ones sang, which ones didn't. She hadn't only recorded information about the males, but she'd recorded which females had been used as well. As he paged through the sheets, he began to notice a pattern. Whenever the female "Blue 15" was used, the males sang a lot. He flipped through a few more, stopping to read the notes in the margins. On one page she'd written: *"Blue 27" doesn't stutter when "Blue 15" is put in front of him.*

Unbelievable, to be sure, but here it was. Could stuttering be controlled by the receiver? Everyone studied male birds because they sang. Did this mean that for all these years, when they'd been ignoring the females, they'd been missing half the song?

He went back to his yellow notebooks, smiling when he saw Sarah's handwriting alongside his own. He wanted to talk with her about this new idea. They'd begun to correspond again. Surely there were parallels in her work. Why did one therapist, listening and giving bits of feedback, work for a patient, but another therapist did not? He would write to her tonight.

He picked up the phone and called the distributors. Whereas before he'd been dabbling with any species that sang, trying to understand the mechanics behind song, now he wanted to focus. He ordered two new flocks of the scarlet-beaked zebra finches. One group he put in the aviary at the institute and began to breed them, keeping track of the mothers, the fathers, the number of offspring and their songs. The second flock went to the aviary by his house, where he did the same. Instead of breeding males and females in small cages, as he'd always done, he let them live together and choose their own mates, and then he spent hours recording their songs and behaviors to learn which males were attracted to which females and which ones produced the most clutches. The work didn't require a large grant, and he wasn't in a hurry.

After Sarah left, he thought that the rest of his life would be a slow process of loss—Ed, Munin, his research, but he had been wrong. Ironically, the act of sabotage had changed everything. From one day to the next, he was given a new life, a clean slate, an open door.

He returned to writing his keynote. His work was showing that the female listener had a great deal to do with a male bird's song. Perception was as important as signal. Males sang to some females more than others. Some females could make a stuttering male fluent.

Sarah. David realized that grief had pushed them apart. Their communication, which could be seamless and synergistic, had become syncopated and out of time after Ed's death. Destructive interference. Wavelengths cancelling each other out. Amplitude zero.

David imagined Ed's smile if he were alive to learn that birdsong had helped to foster a revolution in brain science. And he thought of Anton, who had finally devised the technique to watch neurons connect when new behaviors were being memorized and then, when those memories were silenced with drugs, watch them disappear over time. In a very real way, the elusive engram had been found and Anton had found it. Everyone now knew that nerves were built and laid down not just once during development, but all throughout life. The brain was plastic, malleable, forgetting and remembering, again and again. Ed's secret. *I forget myself.*

David finished his talk, left his office, and went into the foothills behind the institute. Lazuli buntings, towhees, and chickadees were singing in the clear, cool evening. He leaned into the hillside, lowered his head and began the climb. An hour later, he arrived at the top of the ridge, warm and exhilarated. The valley would change in the coming months, going from the fleeting green of spring to the drought of summer, and he hoped that this year, they would get the powerful thunderstorms in August. Sarah had written that she was coming home and he was counting the days. Their life together was inextricably bonded by time and memories, arguments and collaborations. Looking out over the valley, listening to the birds surrounding him, he thought, *how could you ever know what it really cost any animal to sing?*

Halfway down the mountain a large magpie landed in the clearing between the conifers, paused, turned its head left and then right, studying the corpse before it. Iridescent wings flashed purple, black and white in the sunlight. With a lowered beak, the magpie took a step in and prodded the limp bird, another magpie, this one with a shriveled leg. When there was no response, the magpie let out a loud, dissonant caw. A short moment later, a nearby bird answered the call, and soon, other magpies began to arrive, in groups of two and three, their white breasts and wing patches flashing in the sunlight as they swept down. Before long, twenty squawking, flapping birds had congregated around the dead magpie. One by one, they turned toward the dead bird, pushing at the limp body with their beaks and then letting out baying caws. They flicked their wings. They spread their tail feathers. They cawed and squawked and chattered as they moved around the bird, and then they abruptly stopped. They stood and waited together in the silence, listening perhaps to the hum of the city below, or to the sound of the rattling squirrel nearby. Then, almost simultaneously, they lifted up and without another sound, save the swoosh of their wings, dispersed towards the shimmering valley below.

When the moon's reflection began to blink on the water, Rebecca looked up and saw that the birds were passing now, groups of twenty or thirty, mostly grebes, avocets, a few willets, migrating north. As they flew in front of the full moon, their dark silhouettes tapped out a sort of visual Morse code, dots and dashes made up of short and long flashes of moonlight. She stood, shaking out a cramp in one leg as she scanned the mangroves to her left and then peered out at the Gulf of Mexico, the water broad, and from this vantage point on its Mexican edge, seemingly endless. But it did end. Depending on the winds and weather, twenty or thirty hours from now these birds, thin and panting with tattered feathers, would touch down on the southern coast of Texas.

Without needing a flashlight, she walked over to her bag, took out her camera and set it gently on the ground. She slid open the legs of the tripod and fixed them into the sandy soil. Her watch read 4:00 a.m. Behind her she could hear sounds she couldn't name, the groans and exhalations of a forest at night. Owls probably. Bats likely. The buzzes and calls of count-less insects, monstrous and resilient, scurrying across the wet leaves. The creaking of tree trunks, the fall of a branch. The gulf before her gleamed like a mirror. The birds above, those migrating in intermittent waves, made no sound at all.

The naturalist from the lodge who dropped her off after midnight had offered to pick her up again at daybreak, but she'd refused and pointed at the pamphlet with the map. "It doesn't look too far. I'll walk. Morning is a good time for pictures."

She stood now looking out at the Gulf. Moonlight and shadow. Black wings on a deep purple sky, which would lighten just enough in the next hour to get the pictures she wanted. To think that in this same spot, some sixty-five million years before, an asteroid, six miles wide, had slammed into the earth like a bomb, the atomic fallout bringing layers of dust and iridium, the death of the dinosaurs, the opening of the way for mammals. And now birds, small feathered relics of those dinosaurs, migrated over this watered crater twice a year. Two billion birds a year. North in the spring to eat and breed. South in the fall to eat and wait out the cold.

She bent and looked into the camera. For the next two hours, she studied the sky, focused and clicked as the birds above beat their wings in steady repetitive flaps, propelling themselves through the cool air over the Gulf, always north toward their final summer destination. As she watched them, intermittently pressing the button, hearing the sound of the shutter opening and closing, she felt she was the sole witness to a marvelous secret.

Just after first light, she put the equipment away. She hoisted the pack over her shoulders, snapped the waist belt and turned toward the path that would take her back to the lodge. A while later, just before the forest opened up to the place where she expected to find a trail to the left, she was stopped short by a series of sounds, songs she recognized, but that made no sense. Even before she considered the improbability of the species in the region, her binoculars were pressed to her eyes. Sure enough, she saw them. Zebra finches. Perhaps twenty of the gray frenetic, red-beaked birds fluttering and calling under a wire screening next to a small wooden house. Outside the house, on the other side of the enclosure, an old woman was hunkered over a reed mat, using the light of the morning to sort through rice grains. Rebecca saw a large black bird, a great-tailed grackle, swoop in behind the enclosure. It landed on the ground near the woman, its tail giving a broad upward bob before it inched its way toward the rice grains. The woman picked up a pebble and lobbed it at the bird. The grackle hopped to the left, easily sidestepping her toss. The woman made a shushing sound, felt into a pocket in her apron and threw a small handful of seeds off to her right, this time with more force. The bird ran quickly toward the seeds and pecked. The woman grunted softly, glanced up at Rebecca and nodded. Rebecca tried for a smile, but she was overcome with emotion—first the zebra finches and now this grackle, reminding her of Munin.

Instinctively, she counted the males. There were eight. The rest were gray females. She stepped closer and the birds set off in a fast flapping and lined themselves up along a swaying wooden perch. They took turns flitting off the perch to the wire walls of the enclosure. They hung sideways, grasping onto the mesh with their small red claws for a moment before returning to the perch. Their heads twitched nervously, left, right. Their black eyes, wary and expectant, stared at her. Unconsciously, she touched the tips of her fingers to her palms knowing the softness of feathers, missing the feeling of having a tiny, warm body in her hand, a heart pounding quickly under her thumb.

She heard Anton's voice, the repetition, almost stuttering of her name. She heard the talking and laughing through dinner, the background of birdsong during the day, the hum of their whispers at night. His hand lifting her chin to kiss. His arms firmly around her from behind. The rough texture of his closely cropped hair. The baby-like softness of his skin in the places she most liked to touch. Their bodies meeting and separating and meeting again. She turned quickly away from the finches and continued on toward the lodge, no longer with an appetite for breakfast, wanting only the solitude of her room, the cocoon-like protection of a canvas hammock folded around her, and hopefully, the unconscious dumbness of sleep.

She woke a few hours later thinking of the laboratory, and lay in the hammock remembering. For some time, she had regretted her role in the lab, the work there, and what came at the end, but not anymore. Nor the time in Chicago. It had made her what she was now, a photographer recording the grainy stillness of birds without borders, birds heading north just as they had done for millennium, completely oblivious to her or anything else below. She thought of Anton, David, the birds, how their memories had woven threads into the fabric of her consciousness. She was connected to them all, and could never be free.

Anton rubbed his eyes, reached for his glasses on the table, but didn't put them on. He felt a cool draft of air and instinctively ran his hand over his head. Disoriented by silence and cold, he realized that while he had been dozing mid-morning, dreaming in a half-sleep, noon had passed. Outside the light was dim, the winter sun low and weak. The silence took a moment longer to understand. It had snowed. A quality of silence he hadn't heard in quite a while. The predicted afternoon storm must have arrived and must have been bigger than expected.

Snow was not a given any more in the mountains of Südtirol. Increased temperatures, shifting weather patterns; global change, which the Americans had tried so hard to avoid by denial, had come anyway. The village children who came to his house for breads and cookies in the afternoons had no memory of great snows, and more than likely, if he told them about past winters, how the layers of snow built up between October and March, they would chalk it up to the faulty, nostalgic memory of an old man. One of these days he would take out his mother's photographs and they would gasp to see how snow used to drift above the slate roofed houses, how cars were buried six months a year. He would tell them how all that snow reflected light, like a mirror, back into your face. It could make you think twice. It could burn you on a cold winter day.

The scent of lemon and yeast wafted from his kitchen and he realized that while he was dozing, he had been thinking about David's laboratory. The birds. The laboratory. Rebecca. Their first lunch together. The muted bird. It was strange how memories of her came back like this, with emotional force when he was half-asleep. When he was awake he rarely thought of her; her existence erased from his daily consciousness.

Earlier that morning he heard a radio program about monarchs on their breeding grounds in Mexico. The program started with a loud, fluttering, flapping susurration, and he understood that he'd been mistaken in assuming that their wing beats were silent. Butterflies made noise. People just didn't hear it. What was it the Greeks had said? *Eyes and ears are bad witnesses for man.* And Gianetti always said: *Sensory systems are hypothesis generators.* But if eyes and ears were not to generate those hypotheses, then what would? Eyes and ears were all anyone had.

Despite all the advances they had made in understanding memory, the excitement he had felt as he saw a nerve connection disappearing when the cells were turned off, the papers published in *Science*, his promotion to laboratory head when Gianetti retired, the engram having been "found," he realized that he had learned little about his own memory. He still could not say how the experiences with Rebecca in the laboratory had become memories that hibernated and emerged, seemingly at their own will and with unpredictable emotional pull. And what erased a memory? Sadness, anger, or sheer will? Despite everything he had learned studying memory, he still could not answer that simple question. He could describe how a memory was formed, but not exactly how one was forgotten.

Early on, people thought that memories might be recorded once and then set forever. If the wiring was right, they could be reviewed and revisited, but it wasn't so. Memories, he had proven, were created anew each time they were called forth. They were imperfect, undependable, changeable, subject to twists and turns of neurons, brain chemistry, environment, time. Every rendition was a variation that came from, and was created out of, the present moment. Memory was less like a book that you could put on a shelf and take down from time to time, and more like a story you had to rewrite over and over—only as soon as one draft was written, the previous draft disappeared. Memories were as much about today as yesterday. And how many memories needed to be jettisoned at any one moment so that new information and thoughts could come in? You could never be sure.

There was still a sadness when he remembered her, a nostalgia for something lost. He couldn't put words to it, but when he thought of her, he felt a kind of dissonance. It made him think of Pythagoras, who spent twenty years plucking and measuring sounds on his instrument, figuring out harmony. Pythagoras who believed there was a planetary harmony, a sound so sweet and constant that it couldn't be heard until it was gone.

He saw the snow through the window, the dark day outside. It still bothered him sometimes. Was it David's intentness, the mass euthanasia, or the uncertainty that had occupied his mind? Did she do it?

"The birds," she said as she peered into the microscope, "it seems like they're trying so hard to be heard."

Anton put on his glasses and got up to make the breads. In the kitchen he mixed wheat flour with rye flour, yeast, warm water, oil and anise seed. He began kneading. What he sometimes liked to remember was the Sunday afternoon when they were at his apartment and she approached him from behind, slipping a blindfold over his eyes.

"Shh," she said. She led him to the bedroom. "This is an experiment."

He felt her undress him, heard the zip of his jeans and then the ruffle of them being pulled off. There was the click of his belt buckle as she folded the clothes and set them aside. Without his eyes, he listened, hearing one car after another moving down the street. There was the ring of a bicycle's bell, a child perhaps. Behind that, the incessant chirps of house sparrows and then suddenly, the fast tick tick tick, cluck cluck cluck of a family of quail hurrying across the front lawn. He did not hear her undress but felt her body and then there was no sound at all. Just touch and kiss and breath. He neither saw nor spoke, but felt the sensation of her skin cool on his skin, her citrus scent.

It was as if they had gone to some far off place, lush and magical, their bodies writing words on the white sheet. Rebecca had known how to move past the barrier of language, his accent and awful mispronunciations, past the difficulty, or triviality, of words. Afterward, they held one another. Outside the humid space of their bodies was the American desert, the dry, cracked soil, withered leaves, the inevitability of fire. Between them was quiet, a world apart from the laboratory, far-away from the sounds of song.

Anton kneaded the dough, pushing and pushing, and then he stopped. The thought that came to him was that he had created his suspicion of her out of a motivation to leave. He had been afraid to stay, fearing it would mean he would be trapped like Francesco, or like the white-crowned sparrows, who upon escape, often turned and flew straight back through the open door of their cages.

He knew she had gone back to photography because he had seen her photographs in magazines. He could imagine her somewhere in a rainforest. She would be there taking pictures, her red hair grown long again. He began kneading the dough again. He measured out the figs, raisins, candied orange and lemon, walnuts and spices and doused the mixture with a bit of wine and rum. Now that he had begun remembering, he wanted her to remember too. He believed that she might also remember back to a time in her life when they had spent entire days together with the small manic birds, positioning cages of female finches in front of males, tempting them to sing, living day after day in a world of tiny birds and their whining songs. She had loved him. He knew that.

Anton passed the afternoon this way, letting his mind imagine new memories, while his hands formed breads for the children in the village. The children. They came in the afternoons. They smiled and laughed and handed him the coins their mothers had sent along. More often than not, he closed their fingers around the coins, nodded toward their pockets and watched as they slipped them away for safe keeping.

He mixed the dough with the fruit and kneaded some more. He thought about David and his stuttering work, about the little device that delayed auditory feedback so that people could communicate better and his finding that a silent female bird could determine the quality of a male's song. He rolled out the pieces of dough, one-inch thick, and then carved them into bird shapes. He sensed now that it was fear that kept him from loving deeply, but he could not say what he had been afraid of. Just as birds needed to hear in order to sing, perhaps humans had to be loved in order to learn to love. Practice. He never had much of a chance to practice. With his mother, who was so often gone, nostalgia had become the most dependable emotion. Nostalgia a proxy for love.

He used pieces of candied cherries for the eyes, almonds for the beaks, candied orange for feathers. He slipped them into the oven. When they were done, he would coat them with honey syrup. He went to the cupboard and took down the birds he made the day before. He wrapped each in a separate way, tying blue, purple and red ribbons around the packages.

He realized how far away he was. He had spent most of his life missing his mother, and now, with her death in the war, he could never stop missing her. All those years he had resented her for being too quiet, though he realized now that she'd really been talking in her own way, in the only way she could. The photographs. The images. He hadn't had the maturity to understand the silence between words, what could not be said.

And he missed Rebecca. You miss what is left incomplete, what you never totally understand, the people and relationships that die without revealing their purpose. Finding the memory traces, which he'd thought would be extraordinary and gratifying, had helped nothing in his life.

He looked out the window at the winter day and waited for the children. The snow that had fallen mid-morning, quieting the village, had begun to glisten in the afternoon sun. He remembered the feeling of ice spray pinging his face when he was young as they darted down the steep mountain on sleds. There was the long trudge up again, and the seconds of exhilaration coming down. The thought that today's children didn't experience snow as he once did, saddened him. He looked forward to their visits, shiny eyes, flushed cheeks, skittish energy. Their minds soft like dough, thoughts and memories forming for the first time. Memories laid down to be massaged and reformed through the years of life and new experiences. He wondered about sound. Was it really the last sense to go at death? He closed his eyes and listened. He thought he could hear them coming. Their voices, chimes in the wind.

ACKNOWLEDGMENTS

This book is the product of a decade-long conversation with Franz Goller, who gave me space in his birdsong laboratory, and shared with me the mysteries, discoveries and troubles around communication. The sketches in the book are his.

For Joie Smith, who talked with me for over twenty years, and with whom I continue talking every day. I also thank Don Feener, always. To Lynn Kilpatrick, who originally pushed me to do more with a short story about birds, and to the readers who commented on multiple drafts: Frances Torti, Debra Baldwin, Cass McNally, Ellen Wilson, Lynn Cohne, Deborah Threedy, Julia Corbett, Franz Goller, Krista Caballero, Trudi Smith and Calvin Jolley.

Tim Schaffner, editor and publisher extraordinaire, saw the book's potential and prodded it on to something much better. Thank you, as well, to: Sean Murphy, Jordan Wannemacher, Scott Manning, and Abigail Welhouse.

For support, I thank Centre d'Art i Natura, Farrera, Spain, and Mapping Meaning. Finally, gratitude and love to Calvin for his raw, naked and ardent attention to detail on and off the page.

SOURCES

The novel is a work of fiction. While the science of birdsong and memory is generally accurate, I have chosen to emphasize certain aspects for dramatic effect. The following books and papers were useful in the research.

The Conference of the Birds, Farid un-Din Attar, Penguin Classics 1984 Afkham Darbandi (Translator).

David's quote: "Speech is a river of breath, bent into hisses and hums by the soft flesh of the mouth and throat." comes from *The Language Instinct: How the Mind Creates Language,* Steven Pinker. Harper Perennial Modern Classics. 2007.

In Search of Memory: The Emergence of the New Science of Mind. Erik R. Kandel. W.W. Norton & Company. 2006.

"The flourishing of one is never independent of the other." *When Species Meet,* Donna Haraway University of Minnesota Press. 2007.

"Continuing the search for engrams: examining the mechanisms of fear memories." Sheena A. Josselyn. *Journal Psychiatry Neuroscience* 2010, 35(4):221-8.

Origins in Acoustics: The Science of Sound from Antiquity to the Age of Newton, Frederick Vinton Hunt. 1978. Yale University Press.

"Searching for Engrams." Mark Hübener and Tobias Bonhoeffer. *Neuron* 2010, 67: 363-371.

"What is memory? The present state of the engram." Poo et al. 2016. *BMC Biology:* 1-18.

Some of David's comments about the importance of stuttering were based on those of Dr. David Rosenfield of Baylor College of Medicine in Houston, Texas as recorded in "Flutter Stutter" by Matt Walker. *New Scientist* Issue 2209, published 23 October 1999.

"Hugin and Munin" poem. Rasmus B. Anderson's translation at the Northvegr Foundation.

Hugin and Munin
Fly every day
Over the great earth.
I fear for Hugin
That he may not return,
Yet more am I anxious for Munin.

The character of Ed Matheson III was inspired by Theodore A. Parker III (1953-1993).